RUST.

MW00782197

SOLAR PLEXUS

A BAKU SAGA IN FOUR PARTS

Glagoslav Publications

SOLAR PLEXUS
A Baku Saga In Four Parts

by Rustam Ibragimbekov

Translated from the Russian by Andrew Bromfield

© 1996, Rustam Ibragimbekov

Represented by SUSANNA LEA ASSOCIATES
www.susannalea.com

© 2014, Glagoslav Publications, United Kingdom

Glagoslav Publications Ltd
88-90 Hatton Garden
EC1N 8PN London
United Kingdom

www.glagoslav.com

ISBN: 978-1-78267-116-9

A catalogue record for this book is available from the British Library.

CONTENTS

List of Characters

Alik (Alexander Krokin)
Nata — Alik's wife
Georgy — Alik's son
Alik's sister
Nadir — Alik's brother-in-law
Lucky — Alik's nephew (Alik's sister & Nadir's son)

Eldar
Fariz — Eldar's father (The Rector)
Khalida — Eldar's mother
Vika — Eldar's wife (formerly in love with Marat)
Izik — Eldar's younger brorther
Tamila — Izik's wife

Marat
Marat's grandfather (The Doctor)
Sultan — Marat's father
Marat's mother (the typist)
Gena — a relative of Marat's mother
Gena's mother

Seidzade (The Writer)

Other neighbours & friends:
Old Khanmana (a neighbour from the courtyard)

Alexandra Sergeevna (a neighbour from the courtyard; friends with Alik's sister)
Titch — Marat's friend
Rafik — a friend
Frida — Rafik's first wife
Aida — Rafik's second wife
Seimur — Fariz's neighbour
Nuriev — a newspaper correspondent for *The Baku Worker*
Gudiev — an investigator in a case against the Doctor

Press House Drama Group:
Maya — Alik's love interest
Comrade Emil — the drama group leader
John Agaev — a fellow actor
Valya Guryanov — a fellow actor

Institute:
Ramazanov — Provost for science
Gumbatov — Provost for academic matters
Gasanov — an institute worker
Gasanova — Gasanov's wife
Sofa Imanova — Gasanov's mistress
Amanulla — Fariz's driver

27 Shemakhinka street

The Agakhanovs
MARAT and his mother (the typist)
after they moved

Aliki's sister and her husband Nadir

LUCKY

SEIDZADE

Chair where
sick Eldar sat

Fariz Rzaev and Wife ⎱ Izik
⎰ ELDAR
(The Agakhanovs' old apartment
where The Doctor lived)

ALIK (and his sheep)

Old Kharmana

"The solar plexus is an aggregation of nerve ganglions in the human abdominal cavity.

Azerbaijan is a sovereign state. Baku is the capital of Azerbaijan.

A powerful blow to the solar plexus is fatal."

> — *From an unpublished textbook of the Azerbaijani language*

ONE

Alik

Of course, my sister could have exaggerated some things, or not told me everything, she is a woman after all; but even if she is more at fault than she believes, she has a husband and a brother, and it's up to them to decide how she should be punished, since the necessity has arisen. The man who does not understand such simple things and has allowed himself to raise his hand against a woman must pay for what he did. He must certainly pay, no matter how important a position he may hold...

Alik carried on slicing the water melon rind into the bowl and shoved it with his foot, moving it closer to the lamb that was tied to the bed. The little bell on the slim leather collar jingled quietly, and three nickel-plated spheres on the headboard of the bed began jangling too. There had been a lot of them once (two big ones and eight small ones on each headboard), but they were easy to unscrew and they had all gradually disappeared, a few at a time — Alik and his sister had loved to play with them when they were still children.

The lamb squinted approvingly when Alik threw a few pieces of watermelon flesh into the bowl from his own plate, and forgot about the strips of rind. Alik smiled — as soon as the first white bread had appeared in the shops in forty-five or forty-six (he didn't remember exactly when, it was almost eight years ago already) — long queues formed for it immediately. Only shortly before that people had waited all night for the black bread that had now become plentiful. But before even a month had passed, people simply couldn't manage without white bread any more.

Alik stroked the lamb and went behind the partition to wash his hands. After filling the washbasin with water from the bucket, he splashed the remainder over his boots — there was clay stuck to them because they were laying a gas pipe into the yard of the house. The gas had to be delivered from somewhere far away, and they had collected money from the residents, but Alik had been excluded from the listings because of the fire safety regulations — either his living space was too small, or there was too much wood in the flat. The wall of the corridor that faced the yard was made entirely of wood, and the partition dividing the washbasin and the kitchen table from the passage into the room was plywood. The floor on both sides of the partition wasn't combustible, though, it was hard asphalt, but the engineer and the fireman with the moustache hadn't taken that into account.

The difficulties over the gas hadn't really bothered Alik: there was no way that he would be left without gas when they were piping it in for everyone else. And indeed, two days ago the gasmen who had begun digging the trench in the yard for the pipe promised to put in a gas stove for him without permission from the engineer and the fireman, on condition that he took down the plywood partition. He agreed, of course, he didn't really need the partition, his mother had put it up when his sister still lived with them, but now it was more of a nuisance than anything else.

After washing his hands, Alik changed his clothes and went out into the yard. The gasmen had littered it with pipes, and there was a work table heaped high with their tools standing in the arbour under the grape vine. That was why all the neighbours were sitting in their flats. Usually on such a windless September evening the yard was full of people, but now he couldn't see anybody, even in the windows. There was only old Khanmana kneading dough, as she always did on Saturdays, under the first-floor balcony; the *tandoor* stove in the corner of the yard, between the stairs and the arbour, had been smoking when Alik got home from work.

Khanmana had made the *tandoor* two years ago, immediately after she moved into their yard from Bilgyo. And a month later, when the clay was completely dry and rang like metal if you tapped it, how the neighbours had gasped when the old woman lit a fire and then waited for just the right amount of time before slapping the first flat cake of dough on to the red hot wall and then, a few minutes later, the fire-breathing opening of the *tandoor* had yielded up a yellowish-brown *churek* with slightly burned edges. None of them had ever seen how bread was made, all their lives they had simply bought it in the shop.

But Khanmana herself was even more astounded when Alik rolled out some dough and stuck his head into the *tandoor* in order to slap his own flat cake on to the wall. The old woman could scarcely believe her eyes when she saw his cake there beside all of hers. The neighbours were surprised too at first, but then they remembered that he used to study in the bakers' school at the bread factory, in forty-four, after seventh class at school. His sister had a child, her husband, Nadir, was still away at war, they hadn't received their father's "killed in action" notice yet, and Alik had to do something to help the family. One of their father's comrades who, like their father, used to drive a bread van before the war, came back from the front with one leg missing and offered to get him a place in the bakers' school where he'd been working as a mechanic for a year. Food and a grant were provided, and, after graduating, you got half a loaf of black bread in addition to your pay, if you could sneak it out without the guards noticing. Everyone else managed it, but that half-loaf was the reason Alik never became a baker — he couldn't bring himself to steal it, not even for the sake of his little nephew. So he had been forced to graduate from the driving school instead.

Khanmana was kneading her dough on a large copper tray with serrated edges, a home-made sieve lying on the small bench beside her; the old woman could turn her hand to anything: she mended her own shoes, made trunks and stools and even gradually extended her basement by taking advantage of hollows in the foundations of the building. In two years she had shifted the wall about ten metres and an entire new room had appeared.

Alik walked closer and looked at the dough disapprovingly.

"What don't you like about it?" the old woman asked with a frown.

"Have you put enough salt in it this time?"

Even though Khanmana was fifty years older than Alik, she didn't take offence at his jokes, and she never missed a chance to answer back.

"Teach your wife to make it to your taste, if you ever find one! How's your lamb?"

"Alive and well, thanks to your prayers…"

"Half-starved, no doubt."

"Yes, half-starved, because you never feed him!"

"Why should I feed your sheep?"

"You brought him here, you should feed him."

"I thought you were going to eat him, not make friends with him! Were there many guests at the circumcision feast last night?"

"Yes."

"So why did you go to bed so early?"

"You saw me?"

"I see everything."

"Don't you ever sleep? I need to find you a good husband, one of the watchmen, then you'll sleep like a sixteen-year-old girl."

"Promises, promises..."

"There's one who's been waiting to get married since Tsar Nicholas's reign, but he's too fond of playing his own whistle. He grabs hold of it at the slightest excuse..."

The old woman laughed, and adjusted her hair where she

thought it had come out from under the faded silk headscarf which she tied with its ends in a tight knot so that they stuck up like ears.

At Alik's request, Khanmana had brought him a lamb from Bilgyo in early August, for his nephew's planned circumcision. For years his sister had not been able to bring herself to do what had been done to all the neighbours' boys ages ago, and then everything had come together very conveniently: her husband, Nadir, went away on a work trip, and Alik decided to make yet another attempt to get it done. His sister fluttered her hands in fright, then tried to put off the final decision until her husband came back, but eventually she gave in when Alik explained that after the operation the boy would not be able to go to school for a week or two, and the summer holidays were already nearly over. As for Nadir, he didn't really care whether his son was circumcised or not, so it was a good thing that he wasn't there, he'd be spared unnecessary bother.

They brought the lamb from Bilgyo ready for the feast, but the Lezghin who earned his living from circumcisions and regularly made the rounds of the yards offering his services, had disappeared. While they were waiting for him to reappear, the boy became very attached to the lamb, and Alik had grown used to the animal too. So when the Lezghin finally did put in an appearance, the *shashlik* for the guests invited to the family festival was made from meat that Alik obtained at short notice from a butcher he knew. The meat was fresh, fatty and, to judge from the sheep's ribs, young, but Alik reminded the butcher that he had had a bad experience with meat bought there two months earlier that looked just as good, but had been lacking in fragrance and flavour. The butcher exchanged glances with his puny fourteen-year-old nephew, who was helping to joint a carcass hanging in the doorway, and asked Alik what sort of taste he thought a sheep which lived in a flat with electric light, ate white bread, listened to the radio and watched the television with the rest of the family would have?

Fortunately, the *shashlik* turned out very tasty, Alik's nephew barely even cried when the red-haired Lezghin deftly stretched out the pink flesh and sliced its end off with the narrow, well-honed blade of a cut-throat razor. There were quite a lot of guests, mostly relatives and neighbours, and there were plenty of presents at the head of the bed on which Alik's nephew lay, pale and frightened, but happy at having passed this severe test with dignity.

Alik walked across the yard towards his sister's place. The conversation with Khanmana had annoyed him. Exactly what he had feared had happened: Nadir got back on the day of the circumcision after all and kicked up a big fuss, and his stupid and insulting behaviour towards Alik was apparent to everyone in the yard, otherwise Khanmana would not have asked why he went home so early that evening, when the festivities at his sister's apartment were still in full swing.

Of course, Nadir had good reason not to like him: no doubt it was hard to forget when a sixteen-year-old boy had almost stabbed you with a kitchen knife in the passage to your own courtyard. All the rest of it — the photographs in the arms of various Hungarian, Polish and Czech women, or whoever they were, and the brazen drunken stories told in his sister's presence about the jovial European life, and the buxom lover Tosya, who lived in the post office yard, and the many other things that had almost resulted in Alik's sister being left alone with a child on her hands — all of that, naturally, was forgotten, but the hatred, the humiliation and the fear remained forever. What other explanation could there be for Nadir's attitude to him in all the years since then?

Forced back against the wall between the rubbish bins and the water metre, the erstwhile liberator of Europe had not even contemplated offering any resistance, his military experience told him immediately that there was only one likely outcome, and he gave his word that he would thenceforth remain an exemplary husband and a caring father. Otherwise he would have been left lying in the dark gateway, all punctured — Alik had no other option, although he had no desire to cause anyone any harm, least of all his sister's husband.

The rubbish bins by the gate had been doused with some dark, stinking liquid that had driven all of the yard's cats back up to the first floor; on the narrow balcony running round the yard two of the women were beating out the stuffing of a mattress that had clumped together during the winter, and he had to wait a moment for them to stop brandishing their long, flexible sticks before he could go up the stairs.

For several days now his nephew had been walking round the flat in a red loincloth, occasionally pulling it away with his left hand, so that it wouldn't touch the wound that hadn't healed yet. Nadir couldn't possibly be in at this time in the afternoon, but when he heard voices in the room, Alik nonetheless pricked up his ears in alarm — he didn't want to run into his sister's husband and his friends. As he walked into the kitchen, where his sister spent most of the day, Alik listened more closely to the conversation in the room and realised that it was his nephew who had visitors.

His sister wasn't in the kitchen, although there was something boiling in a large copper pan on the flame of the noisy primus stove.

"Who's there?" his nephew shouted from the other room.

He and his four best friends, who had passed through the ordeal of circumcision several years earlier, were looking at something in a photo album that suspiciously resembled the one in which Nadir kept photographs of his girlfriends at the front. But once he was seated at the table, Alik relaxed — the album contained cards from sweet packets, most of which he had given to his nephew himself (including two rare ones, with portraits of the famous American movie stars, Mary Pickford and Douglas Fairbanks).

At the age of thirteen, his nephew, who Alik's sister claimed had been born under a lucky star, acquired the firm reputation of being someone very fortunate, and he bore the entirely justified nickname of Lucky. As far as his friends were concerned, his greatest stroke of luck was his uncle, Alik, and they took every opportunity to show their admiration for him. Now, for instance, when they saw him, they all got up off their chairs (apart from his nephew, Lucky, who always had an excuse for everything, this time it was the operation he had so recently endured).

"Sit down, sit down," said Alik, lowering himself on to a chair pulled up by one of his nephew's friends, Eldar, and surveyed the young lads with pleasure. The next generation had turned out worthy successors to their elders, certainly no worse than their parents. Perhaps even better.

Alik knew them well, he had known them since he was as old as they were now, twelve or thirteen, when they had been abandoned to his care by their mothers, who worked all the hours of daylight. Back then a thirteen-year-old boy had to be able to earn his own keep, so while he was telling his nephew and his friends fairytales that he vaguely remembered from his own childhood, he had to crochet women's stockings out of the threads that his mother brought home from the factory. In the afternoon, when he came home from school, the hooks were free and it was a sin not to make use of them.

The lad he liked most of all was Marat, whose mother spent nights on end hammering away on an ancient typewriter. He liked Eldar too — for his loyalty to his own friends. Even today, after everything that had happened between his sister and Eldar's parents, he was still here. Alik wondered if Fariz knew where his son was.

Alik's nephew and his friends were waiting respectfully for him to begin the conversation. He knew this, but he didn't know where to start: there was no point in asking his nephew if he was well, it was obvious from his face that the mild blood-letting had done him no harm. And he didn't want to ask trite questions like "How are things?" or "How's life treating you?" Of course, he could inquire about what was happening in their drama group at the Press House, but this very question, the only one that really interested him, was hard to ask. Naturally, the lads had no idea about anything, even John Agaev only knew part of what had happened; Maya was hardly likely to have told him all the details, but even so he couldn't bring himself to mention it.

And yet he had to say something.

"Where's your mum?" he asked his nephew.

"With Alexandra Sergeevna."

Whenever she had a free minute, Alik's sister went running to her solitary old neighbour on the ground floor, who worked in the doll factory.

"We're starting work on a production of the play Snowball," Eldar announced.

Last winter there had been a lot of talk concerning this play about a little black boy when, yielding to pressure from his nephew and his friends, Alik had attended the drama group at the Press House for several months. Now he knew that those winter months had been the very best of his life. But at the time it had seemed just the opposite. They were rehearsing Sergei Mikhalkov's play Special Assignment. There weren't enough actors for the adult roles, and so the leader of the circle, comrade Emil, a short, swarthy-faced Mountain Jew, had agreed that Alik could play Captain Gorkusha. That was the name of one of the officers. The other, called Streltsov, was played by John Agaev, a student at the industrial institute. Alik remembered him from school, before he had left after the seventh class. Even in those early years John had shown great promise, and at the school parties (to which Alik was dragged along by his former classmates), he was always a great success, performing the aria "Life in this World is Impossible Without Women" from the operetta Silva on an Italian accordion, a trophy brought back from the war. He was taken very seriously in the drama group. Comrade Emil even allowed John to skip rehearsals because of his heavy work load at the institute and his previous services to the group. And John proved that he deserved this trust: what took Alik more than three months to learn (the text was the hardest thing for him), John, wearing his dark-blue jacket (it was *Boston wool*, as one of the girls in the circle explained), was able to master in just two rehearsals.

Every time, as Alik strained his taut nerves, desperate to make sure that he wouldn't, God forbid, blurt out the wrong words, he forgot the instructions that comrade Emil had drummed into his head during rehearsals. It was especially difficult in the scene where he had to invite Maya (her name in the part was Vera) to dance — at that point he became so confused that not only was he unable to smile with condescending confidence, as comrade Emil demanded, but he actually blushed, stammered and started dancing with the wrong foot. A vein as thick as a piece of macaroni inflated on comrade Emil's forehead, his usually kind eyes bulged out of his head and his thick eyebrows that looked like Turkish swords knitted together above the bridge of his nose; he began breathing noisily, flaring his nostrils and hammering his right fist into his left palm, with the fingers spread out wide. Afterwards, it's true, he would apologise, but at those moments he was quite unable to control himself and he seemed on the point of having a stroke.

Once John started turning up for rehearsals, everything went more smoothly, more cheerfully. He quickly placated comrade Emil and, leading Alik aside, tried to impress on him that he should on no account feel bad, he had acting ability in abundance, there was nothing for him to worry about. Emil's neurotic outbursts were so unjust that it was simply stupid to take any notice of them. Alik knew perfectly well that John was lying, but even so his words had a calming effect. He felt particularly ashamed that Emil had shouted at him in front of his nephew and his nephew's friends. But in any case Alik would never have left the drama group, if not for that terrible idea of John's. It really had been terrible, there was no other word for it.

Without having mentioned anything about the drama group, that is, about what had been bothering him more than anything else in the world ever since the twentieth of February, Alik got up off his chair, told his nephew to follow him and went out into the corridor.

Before he was even asked, Lucky immediately began telling him what had happened to Alik's sister that morning. She had been shoved hard by Eldar's father, Fariz, so hard that she had fallen against the banisters and scraped her entire side raw. And Fariz just got into his Willis automobile and drove off to Divichi where, to judge from the car and his grey, military-style jacket, he held a position of some considerable importance.

Fariz's younger son, five-year-old Izik, had peed into the yard from the first floor balcony yet again, and Alik's sister slapped him on the bum for it. They had explained more than once to Izik, who was not so little that he couldn't understand, and to his mother as well, that it was not right to go peeing on people's heads, but she had only laughed and hadn't even told her son off. And then the boys, with Eldar's permission, decided to punish Izik themselves — they caught him in the yard and were going to pee all over him from head to foot, to make him realise how unpleasant it was, but at that point Alik's sister intervened to save the boy, and had given him a gentle slap on his rear end. He started bawling, Fariz immediately came dashing out of the house and, without bothering to ask about anything, pushed Alik's sister. No one knew what would happen now: Fariz had gone off to Divichi, Alik's sister had been crying all day long, and Nadir, her husband, had been on duty in the hospital since yesterday and wouldn't be back until late in the evening.

Alik calmed his nephew down and explained that their neighbour had made a mistake — no one had the right to raise his hand to a woman. And people had to take responsibility for their mistakes, no matter what position they might hold. The neighbours' gossip about nobody being able to do anything to this Fariz was just nonsense, no one could commit injustice with impunity. The boy just had to wait until his father came back from his shift, after all he had been right through the war, in which bigger men than Fariz had been taught the error of their ways.

Lucky was completely satisfied with this explanation and even became quite cheerful. Alik stroked his curly hair and went out into the yard.

Despite the heat, Fariz's door was closed: neither the child who was so fond of watering the heads of people living on the floor below from his own little tap, nor his parents, were anywhere to be seen. There were small particles of wool flying up into the air, glinting in the rays of the setting sun. For a moment the female neighbours stopped brandishing their sticks and gazed at Alik with undisguised curiosity.

Walking down the steep staircase into the dark front entrance and from there out into Shemakhinka Street, he cast a glance to his right: as usual at this time of day, several people had already gathered on the corner there, under the acacia. And so Alik turned to the left and walked up along the steep street. There was no doubt that everybody knew about Fariz's attack on his sister — she wouldn't have been able to avoid talking about it. When he reached the end of the block, Alik turned a corner, and then turned another one and walked in the opposite direction along the parallel street, towards the centre of town.

The big round clock at the New Square showed a quarter to seven when he took up his usual position by the grocery store — it was hard to spot him there, among all the people darting backwards and forwards — and began observing. In about ten minutes, Maya ought to come out of the entrance. At five minutes to seven she appeared on the upper step of the short stairway and looked towards the shop. He might have believed she could see him, if he had not been certain that she couldn't. He involuntarily turned his eyes away and took a step backwards.

Maya walked down on to the pavement and then, swaying her broad shoulders slightly, set off in the direction of the Press House. He waited for a little while and followed her, hanging just far enough back that he wouldn't lose sight of her.

At the water kiosk she drank a glass of water, glanced round in his direction again, or so, at least, it seemed to him, and walked on. One block further on, she stopped for a moment in front of the window of a jewellery shop. What could she be interested in there? He ought to walk up and ask, smiling the way comrade Emil had taught him to do. And why not? He was about five years older than her, after all, which was quite a lot considering that she was only eighteen. And he would find the money somehow. No matter what he had to do.

She walked on more quickly, and he lengthened his stride accordingly. The best thing, of course, would be if the need suddenly arose to protect her from something. Then he wouldn't have to smile and ask questions, it would be clear straight away what kind of man he was and how he felt about her. And then perhaps the bashfulness that prevented him from speaking to her would finally disappear.

He stopped at the last column in the row and watched Maya's sturdy, broad-shouldered figure walk on as far as the revolving glass doors of the Press House. Once again he noticed the way her shoulders swayed. He didn't see anything else, because his gaze never moved down below her back.

Now he was free until nine o'clock. The rehearsals never lasted less than two hours, he knew that from his own experience. The memory of those lovely winter evenings in the cool hall of the Press House, with its smell of floor polish, made his heart ache — how could he have failed to appreciate that first chance in his entire life to sit beside intelligent people? Comrade Emil alone was a real treasure! People went to the Sailors' Club especially to watch the way he galloped along on a donkey in the film *Nasreddin in Bukhara*, with his head wrapped in a turban — his face in close up, filling the entire screen. And their rehearsals were so interesting! Emil's shouting made him feel ashamed, but it was interesting. And the way he invited Maya to dance the waltz — Alik turned cold inside, as if he was jumping from the top platform of the parachute tower. There would never be anything like it again! Ah, John, John spoiled it all. He spoiled everything. But it was partly Alik's fault too — how could he possibly have agreed? What an idiot. How could he have listened to what John said?

The whole business had only taken John a few days. First he had arranged things with the girls, then with his uncle: since his mother died, he had lived with him and he had a flat by the Chernogorodsky bridge where no one had lived for several years.

At first Alik thought it was all idle talk, he simply couldn't believe that the girls (especially the taciturn tenth-class pupil Valya Guryanova) would agree to go to meet them. But John had absolutely no doubt he would be successful.

When they had bought the wine and snacks and were waiting for the girls by the pharmacy on Telefonnaya Street, John inquired with a businesslike air which of them Alik preferred.

"Choose whichever you like."

"We'll get to that later," Alik had said, trying to break off the conversation.

"Oh no," John had protested. "There mustn't be any confusion. Personally, it's all the same to me — but I'm for clarity. Who do you like most?"

He had been forced to confess.

"Excellent," John said merrily. "The right choice. Maya's a cert!"

Of course, he ought to have made sure just what John meant by the word "cert", but at that moment the two girls, so very unlike each other, had got out of the trolleybus — first the tall, austere Valya, with her long hair, and then the sturdy Maya, with her constant smile and short crop — both of them looking spruce and smart and rather festive.

"Well done," John said approvingly and smiled in exactly the way that Alik had been unable to manage all winter, despite comrade Emil's very best efforts. "You look first-rate. And you're not even late."

It took them a long time to open the door of the cold flat, which hadn't been heated for a long time. Once inside, John hastily laid the table with wine, salami and bread and told everyone not to take off their coats.

"Not until we get warmed up," he said with a cunning smile.

As well as the table the room contained a cupboard, a sofa and a small locker with a gramophone on it. There were enough chairs at the table, but for some reason John suggested that they ought to drag it over to the sofa. Alik was forced to drag it; if he hadn't, then the girls would have helped John — both of them obediently rushed over to help.

"Valechka, sit here close to me," John ordered, slapping his hand down on the sofa beside himself, as if he were calling a dog. But the austere Valya Guryanovaa didn't take offence, she obediently occupied the place he had been pointed out. Maya and Alik sat on chairs.

"It's a bit chilly in here," said Maya.

Alik agreed.

John poured the wine and they drank from glasses that they had found in the cupboard.

"A nice flat," said Maya, looking round the room. "This is the dining room, and that must be the bedroom?"

"That's right, Mayechka," John said with a smile. "Why don't you and Alik take a look?"

Maya shrugged and glanced sideways at Alik who lowered his eyes. Who could have imagined that John would be so forward?

"Right then, let's have one before you leave us," said John, raising his glass. "And don't forget to take some wine with you, it'll be more fun that way."

If one of the girls had given the impudent rogue a slap across the face right then, it wouldn't have surprised Alik. But they didn't even comment; although they didn't touch their wine either.

"Why don't we put some music on?" Maya suggested.

"What music?" said John, stopping Alik as he reached out for gramophone. "That hasn't worked in ages. Well, are you going in there or not?"

"Where?" Alik asked stupidly, understanding perfectly well that John was talking about him and Maya withdrawing into the bedroom.

John gave him a pitying glance and turned to Valya.

"Valyusha," he said, putting his hand on her shoulder, "friends have to be given the first chance, that's true. But if they won't, we must. Shall we go?"

And instead of throwing his hand off her shoulder, the proud Valya Guyanova followed John into the bedroom without saying a word.

That was the turning point. Quite clearly, there were many things in life that Alik did not understand. And now there could be no doubt about the meaning of the word "cert" that John had used at the trolleybus stop. Well then, a "cert" was a "cert". When in Rome… At least, he would do everything you were supposed to do in a situation like this, in order not to provoke any sneering comments. And he wanted to try it anyway: was he a man or wasn't he? Just feel the way his heart started pounding!

After that he had acted as if he were following someone else's orders. He asked Maya just one question: "Don't you feel cold?" and then, without waiting for an answer, he walked up and put his arms round her. Taking no notice of her look of surprise, he kept hold of her and pulled her towards the sofa; perhaps some resistance was offered, but he didn't even notice it; one jerk — and there she was beside him on the sofa.

He squeezed Maya's soft round shoulder under the woollen jacket with his left hand and stroked her knee with his right. With his side pressed tight against her, he could feel how tense her entire body was.

"So what now?" she asked when their eyes met.

"Nothing."

"What do you want?"

"Don't you know?" He finally gave the smile that he hadn't managed to produce for her all winter (if only comrade Emil were there now!) — the smile of a man certain that he will get what he is after.

She replied to his smile with a look that almost made his hands withdraw of their own accord. From the next room they could hear Valya Guryanova's muffled giggling and the squeaking of the bed.

"Let me go," said Maya.

He tried to kiss her, making several attempts one after another, but failed: she turned her head away with short, sharp movements, and his lips landed on her cheek or her chin.

"Let go!"

He threw her down on her back; now they were lying beside each other, his left hand was still under her head, but his right was free. He turned on to his side, looked into her eyes and found he was breathing heavily.

"Well, what next?" she asked.

"You'll see."

She laughed calmly and suddenly gave a wide yawn.

"All right, get on with it."

The tension he had felt in her body was instantly dissipated, the hand with which she had been holding down the hem of her skirt fell limply to one side, her eyes closed apathetically.

It wasn't quite true that he didn't know what you're supposed to do in a situation like this, after all, he was twenty-three, and he had heard plenty of talk on the subject, so he immediately stuck his hand up her skirt. His open palm touched the silky surface of a stocking, so unlike the ones that he, his mother and sister used to crochet during the war, moved up along her leg and reached the edge of the stocking, beyond which there was a narrow strip of skin; this contact threw him into a fever, and she cried out quietly, his hand was so cold. His palm twitched as if from an electric shock and jumped up higher, skipping over some knitted garment that clung close to the body, after which there was another stretch of soft, smooth skin. "Her stomach," he thought, then he grabbed hold of a narrow band that felt like the elastic of her knickers and jerked it down hard.

She carried on lying quite still, with her eyes closed. Her short, dark-brown, slightly wavy hair made the boyish face that was so out of keeping with her plump woman's body look even rounder.

His hand carried on pulling down on something that was strangely unyielding. Later it was explained to him that that was the stocking suspender belt and it was absolutely pointless to pull it on it. After a little while he worked that out for himself and was suddenly aware of something he had stopped noticing much earlier — how deadly cold it was in this flat that hadn't been heated for several years.

She lay there as if everything that was happening to her had nothing to do with her at all. Not even the cold.

It was quiet in the next room now.

With one final tug on the belt that encircled her stomach so tightly, he pulled his hand away and fell back to one side.

For some reason she didn't take the chance to get up, but carried on lying there with her dress pulled up on to her stomach. She didn't even straighten her hem. He did that himself. He sat down and realised that he was trembling, as if there was a hard frost. But it wasn't the cold that was to blame. He had stopped feeling the cold again. On the contrary, he was consumed by a fever — he suddenly saw what had happened from afar, and a burning sense of shame wrung his heart and set his body shaking.

Of course, if he had had his way that evening, everything would be different now — John Agaev wasn't hiding from anyone, was he? But even if nothing had happened, why had he run away? That was the shameful part! At least he'd had the wits to pretend he was angry. At least he'd slammed the door behind him. And telling John to go to hell, that had been the right thing too; it was a pity of course, but it had been right. After all, he had never liked him, and Alik could easily have punched him in the face for the shameless way he had behaved that evening. "What's wrong? Where are you going? Wait!" Only a cheeky swine like John could have run out into the courtyard in nothing but his underpants, and then grabbed him by the arm and shouted at him. Alik ought to have given him a real earful, but instead he had just fallen quiet. But then, it was a good thing after all that he had managed to control himself and not punch him. He had really wanted to! For everything: for that Boston wool jacket, and that Italian accordion, Valya Guryanov's submissiveness that evening, and his own failure.

Although, of course, you couldn't call John a total rat. All those times he came round afterwards, trying to persuade Alik to come back to the drama group. Alik's nephew and his friends begged him to go back too. The poor kids just couldn't understand. It was only when Maya asked them to say hello to him from her — he didn't understand why she'd done that — that they started to get an inkling. But even so, they were upset. He had quit rehearsals so unexpectedly, just before the opening night. And after all that torment, too. Poor comrade Emil.

By nine o'clock Alik was standing at the tram stop opposite the Press House. From there he had a good view of the main doors, and at any moment he could either get into a tram or retreat inconspicuously into the covered market. But she didn't usually come across to this side of the street. Instead, as she came out of the doors, she turned in the direction of the Nizami Museum, in order to go home along Vorontsovskaya Street, past the "Fantasy" bath house. She never took a tram, even in winter.

Once again it seemed to Alik that she looked in his direction when she appeared in the doorway and only turned the corner after she had spotted him among the people at the stop. He was almost certain of it. But when he crossed street and saw her figure hurrying away, he relaxed and increased his pace, while maintaining his distance, of course, in case she suddenly turned round. The last thing he needed was for her to see him running after her. It would be a different matter if they just happened to meet somewhere by chance. And not on the run — hello-goodbye — but so that he had a chance to do something for her, some way to show how he felt.

Vorontsovskaya Street wasn't crowded in the evening, but there were groups of people at the entrance to almost every courtyard — chatting, chewing sunflower seeds, playing lotto or dominos. The men were less numerous than the women, they could hardly be heard as they made their quiet, serious conversations. The public here was mixed — Azerbaijanis, Russians, Armenians — and, in general, not too respectable: at the slightest sign of trouble someone would go running to the militia. They might start the trouble themselves, but if they were answered back they raised a terrible uproar. Nothing like the street where Alik lived, no one would go running to the militia there. Everyman stood up for himself. And if he couldn't, he put up with things. Well, not everyone of course, every family has its black sheep, as the saying goes.

And then Alik thought of his sister. What on earth had made her get into a fight with that Fariz? He had never been particularly honourable, and nowadays he was out of control, he was capable of anything.

Maya reached her entrance. Just to be on the safe side, he slowed down a bit — she might glance round. But she didn't, and Alik immediately sped up in order to catch up with her on the stairway.

He barely caught a glimpse of her in the gloom of the entrance: two quick strides up two steps at a time, and she disappeared completely round the bend in the staircase. He was no longer afraid of being noticed, he wanted to get another look at her, before listening to her rapid steps that were almost running, the knock on the door on the third floor and the click of the lock. After that the door would slam loudly and everything would go quiet. And he could go home.

Alik strode straight up the three short steps leading to the entrance door and came face to face with Maya. She smiled.

There was no way out — he couldn't run away a second time, he had to move forward: say hello, looking off to one side, walk round her and stride decisively towards the stairs. What else could he do? He couldn't just stop.

"Were you coming to see me?" He felt the question stab him in the back with a shame as sharp as any knife-blade: he was forced to slow down.

What he ought to have done was say 'Yes, I'm on my way to see you' and just go from there, no matter what, but he said 'No'"without even turning his head to look at her — God forbid that their glances should meet.

But she didn't give up, she overtook him and stared at him point-blank with a smile in her eyes.

"Who are you going to see, then?"

"No one in particular," he said, amazed at the stupidity of his own answer.

"I see," she said, still looking him straight in the eye. "How long are you going to keep following me?" And she brushed something off her upper lip, something light, it could have been a cobweb or maybe a speck of dust. "What are you following me for?"

"I'm not following you." This answer was even more stupid than the one before. And his eyes automatically began staring down at the floor, the way they used to in school when he was caught out not knowing the lesson.

"All right then," Maya said in a voice just like the first-to-fourth-class teacher whose name Alik had forgotten: she used to pronounce those words in exactly the same way when he stared down at the desk and didn't answer her questions. After that came the welcome instruction "sit down", and he would be left in peace for a long time. But there was nowhere to sit here in the hallway.

"We need to talk," said Maya.

Could she really have seen him following her? The thought was another stab with a sharp knife, but this time from the other side, in his chest, and the burning sensation that began there moved up to his neck and face. It was a good thing that the hallway was dark.

"Did you hear what I said?" Maya's voice asked from somewhere off in the distance. "We need to talk."

"What about?" It would have been impossible to imagine a more stupid answer. The burning sensation grew stronger.

"Don't you think we have anything to talk about?"

"No, why? We can have a talk."

"Thank you," she said and even curtseyed slightly, like Dina Durbin in the film *His Butler's Sister*. "Come on."

She turned gracefully and stepped out into the street. Now he had to take his blazing face out into the light — the damned summer day still wasn't over, although it was half past nine already.

"What's wrong?" Maya asked and burst out laughing. Then she suddenly stopped laughing and even frowned, trying to make herself seem more serious.

That short laugh splashed into his burning face, hissed like water in the steam room at the baths and the sweat began streaming down his neck and his back, between his shoulder-blades.

"What are you laughing at?" Alik asked morosely, even though she had stopped.

"How red you are!" Maya said with a smile and suddenly reached out her hand to touch his face.

He actually flinched in surprise. Something white touched his forehead and he closed his eyes, then realised it was a handkerchief.

She wiped his face and neck, and was about to reach under his shirt collar, but he moved away.

"Well, where shall we go?" she asked, putting the handkerchief away in the pocket of her frock. "Why not the boulevard?"

"All right," he forced out with great effort, and they set off back along Vorontsovskaya Street, past all the groups of chatting, seed-chewing, domino-playing people.

"Just look at them stare," Maya said, twitching her shoulders irritably, "lousy gossips."

"Do they know you then?" Alik asked, surprised to hear his own voice.

"Sure they do! They've got nothing to do but spy on me. Who did she go with? Where did she go? They want to know everything. At first I used to get angry and then I decided, to hell with them, let them wag their tongues if they want. Granny gets upset, though."

She had come from Vitebsk and she lived with her grandmother. Alik knew that, but simply in order to make conversation he asked:

"What granny?"

"My granny."

Her father had been killed at the front. Her mother had married again. And Maya didn't get on with her stepfather — Alik knew about that too.

"What do you think, will I make an actress?" she asked, and as his glance met hers, Alik was amazed once again at what beautiful eyes she had, as big as any sheep's, and they said sheep's eyes were the biggest. But, of course, Maya's eyes were of a much better colour — a light greyish-blue, like the sky. A colour he loved.

"Of course you will. Comrade Emil praised you very highly."

"What does he know?" Maya asked with a laugh. "He only has the education. He's never acted on the stage."

"What about the film?"

"Only as an extra," Maya said with a dismissive wave of her hand. "Even I've been asked to play in those. Anyone can get into a crowd scene as an extra."

"But you did everything he said, and now you start criticising him!"

"I'm not criticising him, he's a nice man. But he's no authority. And I need a man who will give me direction. Lezhnev has a drama group in the Twenty-Six Club. From the Young People's Theatre. Do you know him? He's a different kettle of fish altogether. A real actor."

"So why didn't you go to him?"

"I work in a print shop. So I went to the Press House. And then when I found out all about things, it was awkward to leave. And I got used to the boys and girls there. And to Emil as well. He makes such an effort."

"Yes," Alik agreed gladly: he would have given away a hundred Lezhnevs for comrade Emil, even if he wasn't an authority.

Chatting about this and that, they eventually reached the boulevard. It had finally got dark. Most of the people there were strolling couples.

"Why don't we go to Studencheskaya Street?" Maya asked.

Alik didn't understand where she meant, but he didn't show it. Maya was obviously talking about a side street, because she turned off into a spot where it was a bit darker under the trees, then sat down on an empty bench.

"It's more convenient," she said, "and there aren't so many yobs here."

Alik didn't say anything. Studencheskaya was fine with him, although this side street was no different from the others — the same benches under the trees, the same asphalt under your feet and lots of couples standing, sitting or walking.

"Did they tell you I said hello?"

"Yes."

"Then why didn't you answer?"

"My sheep must be thirsty by now." Alik suddenly remembered.

"What?"

"He has to be given water at ten o'clock. He's used to it."

"What sheep?"

"Mine."

"You have a sheep?"

"Yes."

"And where do you keep it?"

"In the corridor."

"At home?"

"Yes."

She laughed loudly. Several couples glanced round in annoyance.

"Is it big?"

"Not very. Six months."

"And what are you going to do with it?"

He was forced to tell her the whole story of the lamb and his nephew's circumcision, but she couldn't understand that part of the story.

"Why did you go to all that effort?"

"What do you mean? All his friends had been circumcised, he was the only one left."

"Well, so what?"

"It's embarrassing."

"Who makes you feel embarrassed?"

"The neighbours."

"Why should you feel embarrassed? You're Russian, aren't you?"

"Yes."

"Are you sure of that?"

"What do you mean?

"There's no way to tell by looking at you! Your eyes are light-coloured, but your skin's dusky."

"That's a tan."

"And your hair's dark."

"If someone's Russian, does he have to be blond?"

She laughed again.

"And your sister married an Azerbaijani, then?"

"Yes."

"And how is it?"

"Fine."

"And is it true that you reach for your knife at the slightest thing?"

"Me?"

"Yes, you! You even jumped off a roof with your knife once — didn't you?"

She could easily have heard that story from his nephew or one of his friends — there was no point in trying to deny it.

"Yes, I did."

"There, you see," she said with a satisfied smile. "I know all about you. You're a wild man, you'd kill someone without even turning a hair."

He couldn't help smiling at that. So he was a wild man? He wouldn't hurt a fly unless he was forced to. In fact, he told her, he crossed to the other side of the street every time he saw a drunk or some young thug walking towards him.

"Why?"

"In order not to get involved. If they said something out of order, I'd have to respond."

"My, my, how very careful you are." She was looking at him with a slightly mocking smile now. "So why did you jump off the roof?"

"I warned them not to swear. But they took no notice."

"Who? And you jumped down on them with a knife?"

"They had knives too."

"There were two of them?"

"Three. They started getting rowdy in the middle of the night. Swearing and cursing, waving knives about. And my sister and I were sleeping on the roof. I told them: be quiet, there are women and children all around here. But they told me to go to hell, so I had no choice but to jump."

"Was it a high roof?"

"Yes. I broke my leg."

"And what did they do?"

"It turned out they knew me. They apologised."

"And what if they hadn't apologised?"

"I don't know. I didn't think about that, I just jumped, that's all."

"I've been told about your heroics."

"Who told you?"

"Everybody. As soon as you turned up, the talk started. And Emil warned us to be polite with you, just to be on the safe side."

"Emil? That's impossible!"

"He told me so himself."

"Then why did he yell at me?"

"He's the nervous kind. Aren't you the nervous kind too?"

"Yes, I suppose so."

"I was really furious with you."

"When?"

"That time… When you attacked me. I'm sick of it: no matter who you meet, they come on to you, attacking like wild animals. This one's just the same, I thought. Doesn't even know how to kiss, and he's pawing at me. Haven't you ever kissed anyone? Well, why don't you answer? I can tell you haven't."

Neither of them said anything for a while. They sat there quietly without moving, listening to the branches rustling and the couples whispering.

"All right then," she said, "let's go and give water to your sheep."

He stood up straight away, but she carried on sitting there. Then she got up slowly: there was something strange about the way she looked at him, in the darkness her glance seemed somehow hazy.

"Kiss me," she said, putting her arms round his neck.

When he pressed his dry, tightly closed lips against her mouth, Alik just felt clumsy and awkward. But she didn't let go of his head, in fact she only pressed it all the harder against her own. So hard that it hurt. And suddenly something happened to his lips and they softened with a strangely sweet, melting sensation.

On the way to his house they carried on kissing, stopping in every dark spot. But she couldn't hold out for long, she started choking, as if she were underwater. And when he let go of her, she gasped greedily for air. They were hardly talking at all now. One thing was strange, though: if she had seen him following her, why had she only told him today? Why had she left it for so long? But he was too embarrassed to ask.

The entire yard was asleep when they finally reached his house. There was no light even in Khanmana's basement, and the old woman went to bed late.

The lamb was sleeping too. At the sound of footsteps he lifted up his head and scrambled hastily to his feet, with his hooves slipping on the asphalt floor. The little round bells on the bed started jingling.

"How lovely," Maya gasped, and dashed to put her arms round him.

The aluminium bowl that Alik, had filled with water as he was leaving was empty.

While the lamb was drinking greedily, Maya kept one arm round him and whispered sweet nothings in his ear.

"But what's going to happen later, when he grows up?" she asked, looking at Alik in alarm.

Here in the bright light, it was impossible even to imagine that only recently he and this girl had been kissing, she seemed so beautiful and inaccessible to him now.

"I don't know. He'll carry on living the way he does now."

"But that's impossible."

"Why? He's not bothering anyone."

"What about your mother?"

"She's hardly ever here."

"Yes, I heard." It was clear that Maya knew just as much about him as he did about her. Alik liked that. It was good that she knew everything about him and it didn't frighten her or put her off. Not even the fact that he had only finished seven classes of school, or his crazy mother, or the sheep in the house, or the asphalt floor.

Still squatting down beside the sheep, Maya straightened her hair and glanced around.

"This place needs tidying up."

"The room's clean. Let's go in there."

They walked through into the room. The sun hardly ever shone in there through the only window because the wall of the next house blocked it, so the air was always cool and slightly damp. He had made the bed neatly in the morning. The sideboard was old, pre-war, but it looked respectable. On the table there was a cut glass ashtray, a gift from the professor's wife many years ago.

"Sit down."

They sat facing each other, on opposite sides of the table.

"So you saw me following you?" Alik asked, surprised at his own boldness in starting just like that, asking questions to get things clear!

"Yes."

"A long time ago?"

"In winter."

"I sensed it."

"Why didn't you come up to me?"

"I felt ashamed."

"I kept waiting and waiting. I just couldn't wait any longer."

"You have plenty of patience," he said with a smile. "What if I'd stopped following you?"

"Then it wouldn't have been you. Doesn't your mother ever come here?"

"Rarely."

"She sighed and looked at him in commiseration. Then she leaned across the table and ruffled his hair.

"What are you doing?" he asked, embarrassed.

"I like you a lot," she explained seriously. "I can sense strength and gentleness in you at the same time. A rare combination. If only you don't get spoiled, of course."

"How would I?" said Alik, still feeling embarrassed. "It's too late to change now."

"At twenty-three? You could still change ten times over." They both said nothing for a while. "What year was your father killed?"

"Forty-two."

"Mine was killed in forty-five. Near Prague. Your mother's a good woman. Mine got married straight away."

"Mine was already old. She was forty-five when the notification came."

"Age is no hindrance to a woman. Old women get married too."

He remembered Khanmana: if a suitable bridegroom turned up, she would get marriage like a shot. There must be some reason why she kept on extending her living space.

"Well, shall we go?" Maya asked.

"Maybe I could put the kettle on for tea?"

"It's late. My granny will tell me off… I'm really sick of it."

"How old is she?"

"Sixty?"

"Is your mother young?"

"Not yet forty."

"Is she beautiful?"

"Very. When my dad was killed, she was thirty," Maya said and got up.

And just then his sister came into the room, without any knock or warning, as usual.

When she saw Maya there, she was embarrassed and turned away from them, and then asked, without raising her tear-stained eyes.

"Where have you been?"

"Say hello first."

"Hello," Maya said politely.

Alik's sister nodded her head in greeting, without looking at her. She could hardly hold back the tears that were already in her eyes.

"Has Nadir come home?" Alik asked as gently as possible.

"Ages ago."

"Isn't he asleep yet?"

"He's waiting for you."

"I'll drop in later."

"When?"

"Soon."

"He has to get up early," said his sister, hiding her face from Maya as she edged towards the door.

"Has something happened?" Maya asked.

"Yes."

He didn't want to tell her about what had happened between his sister and Fariz. Maya realised this and didn't ask any more questions.

They went out into the yard.

"They're putting in gas," Alik told her as they walked past the arbour with the gasmen's table in it.

Maya didn't say anything.

"She had an argument with her neighbour," Alik said to give at least some explanation of his sister's strange behaviour.

"She doesn't look at all like you," Maya said thoughtfully, putting her arm through Alik's. He felt much calmer immediately, her touch set his heart at ease.

"I take after my father," he said, "and my sister's like our mother. My father was dark-skinned too."

"Are you seeing me home?"

"Of course."

"But they're waiting for you."

"Never mind. I've got time."

They set off at a brisk walk towards the city centre, down the steep slope of his street. It was the first in his life that Alik had walked here arm in arm with a girl. His girl.

They walked past one block in silence. Then they stopped by the former mosque and their teeth clashed as they started kissing. The salty taste of blood on her bitten lip alarmed him, but she just took a breath and pressed herself against him again. And he couldn't remember how long it lasted, maybe ten minutes, maybe an hour…

Outside her house they put their arms round each other again.

"Will you come tomorrow?" she asked between kisses.

"Of course."

"Come straight there, to the Press House."

"All right."

"And don't forget to bring the lamb with you."

They laughed.

"Okay now, run. They're waiting for you."

"It doesn't matter…"

He wanted to say something important to her, something about their relationship, about how serious it all was for him. So that she would know that.

"Well, why are you just standing there?" she asked, putting her arms round him.

"You mustn't think…" he forced himself to say. "I'm not just… Don't worry."

"What are you talking about?" her surprise was so sincere that he felt embarrassed.

"About you and me…"

"But why should I be worried?" she asked, throwing her head back so that the light of the street lamp was reflected in her eyes.

He didn't know how to explain to her. It seemed obvious enough: girls were always afraid that their boys wouldn't marry them; that they would toy with them, have a good time and drop them. That was how it had been with his sister, she'd been worn out with worrying whether Nadir would marry her or not.

He tried to explain all this to her and she finally understood.

"My dear darling," she said, running her hand through his hair again, "are you trying to propose to me?"

"Not right now, but in general. When you want. Just so that you know..."

"Are you serious?" she asked with a smile, still stroking his hair.

"Yes."

"Have you forgotten that I'm planning to be an actress?"

"So what?"

"You don't object?"

"Why?"

"Who knows what you might think? You're a real Asiatic type. You might make me stay at home all the time." She put her hand on his shoulder. "To be quite honest, I am fed up of my granny..."

"But won't your mother object?"

She shook her head very slightly, and something flickered through her eyes, a kind of shadow: he realised it would be better not to remind her about her mother.

"My place is a bit damp," he said, trying to change the subject, but they'll put gas in soon."

"I'm not afraid of the damp," Maya said very seriously and stood up on tiptoe. "And anyway, I liked your place ."

They kissed again.

He could hear Nadir and his sister quarrelling when he was still on the stairs: they were yelling so loudly that neither of them even heard when Alik walked into the dark corridor and knocked his nephew's bicycle over with his foot.

"That's just it!" Nadir was shouting wildly: he had clearly had a drink since his shift finished. "You're always sticking your nose in everywhere. What business is it of yours what they were going to do to him? And now you want to drag me into it!"

"Nobody's dragging you into it."

"You poor idiot! What proof do you have that everything happened the way you say? Who saw him push you?"

There was no point in going into the room just then, while he was yelling like that, nothing good would come of it. But Alik didn't feel like waiting out in the corridor until it was all over. The only thing he could do was go away. He turned round, stepped over the bicycle and set off home. It was obviously the right thing to do, just go straight home.

But Nadir carried on shouting, and what he shouted out when Alik was already in the doorway made him stop dead.

"You people are always dumping everything on me. I've had enough! I'm sick of it! I suppose that little brother of yours cleared off straight away! He knows what's what, your defender of the family honour! He doesn't want to take the risk. So I have to do his dirty work!"

"There was a girl with him."

"What girl? Why hasn't she ever been to see him before?"

Alik kicked the bicycle out of the way and walked into the room. His sister was crying, leaning against the black upright piano, and her husband was shaving for the night, he kept inspecting his lathered face in the mirror while he yelled. There was some money, obviously his pay, lying on the table between the plates of bread and fried salami.

"Why are you bawling like that?" Alik asked in a calm, quiet voice.

The quick-witted Nadir immediately quietened down and started speaking normally.

"As if you didn't know."

"I know. But why shout? The whole yard can hear you."

His sister stopped crying and started hastily clearing the table.

"Don't make a fuss," said Alik. "I'm leaving."

"Where are you going?" — what a polite voice Nadir had when he made an effort! "We need to talk."

Without answering him, Alik asked his sister what time Fariz went to work.

"Early."

Nadir was outraged by her answer.

"You were asked what time, that means by the clock! And you just say 'early'," he said, twisting up his face as he mimicked his wife.

"How do I know when he leaves? I don't follow him around, do I? About six o'clock, probably."

Alik walked to the door. Nadir tried to stop him, but failed. Without even wiping the soapy lather off his face, he walked with Alik to the same passageway where seven years earlier he had almost been stabbed with a kitchen knife.

"You must understand," he explained to Alik in a hasty whisper, "she's been crying all day. But what can I do? I'm a doctor, you understand… She hasn't got any witnesses… Nobody saw anything, only the children. And who's going to believe them… Am I right or not?" he asked, catching hold of Alik's shirtsleeve. "There's nothing we can do officially, I know that for sure. But she refuses to understand. She just kept saying over and over again: 'He pushed me, he pushed me'. But now what can we do? Give him a beating, or what? I can't do that… I'm not…"

"Drop it," Alik interrupted him. "It's time to get some sleep."

Nadir was only too willing to stop talking; he stood by the door until Alik crossed the courtyard to his apartment.

No one knew what job Fariz did in Divichi. His wife Khalida had been close friends with Alik's sister right through the war, they had worked together at the garment factory. She used to leave her eldest son, Eldar, with them for the whole day — he was never parted from Alik's nephew. But somehow he had managed to pick up pulmonary tuberculosis. If Fariz had not been one of the first to be demobilised from the army, because he was an oilman with an education, then Eldar would certainly not have pulled through.

The first thing that Fariz did was to exchange apartments and move his family up to the first floor. And little Marat and his mother with the typewriter had move into their flat on the ground floor. For an additional payment, of course.

Khalida had remained friends with Alik's sister after the war, and Fariz had grown chummy with Nadir as well. Alik had no problems with Fariz then. He was a family man, respectable. They would light up the *mangal* in the yard and grill *shashlik* for the two families, eat together, and that was all, Fariz went home with his wife and son. But not Nadir, he always had to have a bit more fun. He couldn't stop. He used to stay out all night, that was why Alik had had to step in.

Yes, the two families had been very friendly. Then suddenly it had all ended: the family *shashlik* parties, the trips to the seaside together, the friends they had in common… He had even asked his sister if something had happened. Maybe Nadir had done something bad? But his sister couldn't understand it herself: the friendship had been broken off without any reason at all. Only Eldar had kept running across to see Alik's nephew, without asking permission from his parents.

Nadir couldn't give a damn about all this, but Alik's sister had been very upset. After all, she had been friends with Khalida for years. They had gone to school together. And the worst thing was that she couldn't understand the reason for the estrangement.

It was only years later that everything became clear. Khalida herself let it slip to someone that they had distanced themselves from their neighbours for no particular reason: Fariz had simply moved to a new job and decided to change his friends and acquaintances at the same time — that was all there was to it.

Ever since then he had done no more than say hello to the neighbours, looking off somewhere into the distance as he did it. He walked by with a quick nod, and not another word — as if none of them existed for him any more.

He had been moved to Divichi as some kind of big manager — that much was clear from the way Khalida bossed everyone in the yard about. And their little Izik made everyone's life a misery — he came up with some nasty new prank every day.

Perhaps Fariz didn't know about all this, he was a busy man. But in that case, why had he pushed Alik's sister? He loved his son, that was fair enough, who didn't love their own children? But how could he raise his hand against a grown woman because of the little boy? It was clear now that she hadn't been at fault in any way. In fact, she deserved to be thanked. What did he get up to over in Divichi, if he insulted perfectly innocent people like this here?

And what a fine fellow he used to be before! They used to eat linseed cake together in forty-two, when he was still at college. And how he had thanked them for helping Eldar when he came back from the front — everyone in the yard had helped to save the boy, trying to feed him up as much as they could — he had sworn then with tears in his eyes that he would never forget it. And just look how everything had turned out! He wasn't the same any more! He was like a completely different man! How strangely life changed people.

Did he really think he could act just as he liked? That he could get away with anything? He had insulted one person, then another, and another, but sooner or later someone would turn around and act with dignity. Nadir and his kind weren't the only people living in the world. Fariz was a clever fellow, surely he thought about things like that? All right, so he didn't have to bother about Nadir, but what Alik's sister? How could he have raised his hand against her? Even if Fariz had no conscience left at all, how could have forgotten what fear feels like? Conscience isn't tested every day of the week, but fear is different, you have to have it there somewhere inside you. So he'd divided people into two kinds — the kind to fear, and the kind he didn't have to — and he expected to live his whole life like that. He was deluded. It wouldn't work. Because sooner or later one of the people he didn't give a damn for wouldn't take any more, and they'd make Fariz pay for his insolence.

Alik didn't go home, but went straight to the hospital where his mother worked. It was perfectly possible that she had stayed there for the night; she had been doing that more and more often recently.

Of course, there was no watchman in the little hut at the gates, he'd gone off to sleep in the building again. You could shout as loud as you liked, but he wouldn't hear you. Alik was forced to climb over the fence.

The door of the new block was usually locked for the night but for some reason it was open today, even though it was so late. Everybody in the wards was already asleep. His mother could be in any one of them — depending on who she thought was in the greatest need of care and attention.

On the second floor there was a light in the duty doctor's room; obviously the night nurse must be sitting in there too. They would definitely know where he could find his mother. But he didn't feel like talking to anyone right now. Especially here, where his mother had worked these last few years since she went completely crazy.

He found her on the fourth floor, in the corridor. She was asleep, sitting on a small white wooden sofa; her head was nodding, and she looked as if she was going to topple over on to the floor at any moment.

When he got closer, he saw that she was holding on to the tall medical scales standing beside the sofa with one hand

"What are you doing sitting here?" Alik asked angrily when she opened her eyes at the sound of his footsteps.

"I'm on duty," his mother said, straightening up and assuming a wide-awake, businesslike air.

"Why? Are you a doctor, then? Or a nurse? Or an orderly? Once you've done your job — cleaned up and wiped the floors — you should come home."

His mother didn't even bother to answer, she just gave him a pitying look, as if he was unwell, flapped her hand at him and stood up.

"Where are you going?" he asked, changing his tone of voice.

"I've got a woman who's just had an operation. I have to check her condition," she said, and straightened the white coat thrown across her shoulders. He could see her own coarse grey calico coat underneath it.

"Why don't you come home?" Alik asked, speaking in a whisper now.

"I've no time."

"Just look at the state you're in. Don't you get any sleep at all?"

"What do you mean? I sleep..."

"I can see the way you sleep. Like a sparrow. Where's the duty doctor?" he asked, trying to frighten her a bit.

"You can't see him."

"Why not?"

"He's got visitors."

His mother turned round and set off rapidly, almost at a run, along the corridor.

He overtook her at the doors to the stairs and blocked the way.

"Wait, mum," he said, not annoyed any longer "All right, all right, don't get upset..."

There were tears trembling on the ends of her sparse, colourless eyelashes.

He suddenly felt so sorry for her that he almost burst into tears himself.

"Okay, okay, I'm sorry," he said, putting his arms round her and hugging her against his chest so that she couldn't see his face. "I won't do it again," — that was the way he used to talk to her when he was a child and she told him off for some prank or other. "But you're wrong too. It's good that you help people and look after them. That's a good thing. But you ought to come home too. Everybody works and does their shift, but they live at home. Please, I'm asking you. Do you hear me?"

His mother nodded guiltily, like a little child.

"When will you come?"

"Tomorrow."

"Definitely?"

"Yes… Are you going away, is that it?" she asked suddenly.

"I don't know." The question had taken him by surprise. "What made you think that?"

"I can feel it."

Alik shook his head in amazement.

"What can you feel?"

She didn't answer again and went back to her little sofa.

"You go now," she told him when he caught up with her, "or the doctor will see you."

As soon as she said that, there was the sound of footsteps on the stairs. His mother looked round anxiously.

"Don't worry, he's got visitors of his own."

A male figure in a dressing gown appeared at the end of the corridor. Even in the dim light Alik could see that it wasn't a doctor: he knew them all very well.

"Who's on duty today?"

"Samed Agaevich," said his mother, walking towards the man.

"Well, how is she? Has she asked for anything?" The man's voice sounded very familiar to Alik.

"The patient is sleeping, her temperature is normal, there are no grounds for concern," his mother said in a very serious and responsible voice.

"Thank you very much… I'm very grateful to you. And now the man turned towards the light and Alik recognised him — it was comrade Emil, the leader of the drama group at the Press House.

But something had happened to him during the last few months — he had changed a lot. His long hair had not been combed in a long time and hung down in clumps on both sides of his hawk-nosed face, his red, inflamed eyes were watering and blinked constantly.

He either didn't recognise Alik or didn't see him, although he gave him a bewildered look several times while he was talking to his mother.

Something had happened to comrade Emil, he couldn't have changed so much without a serious reason. But why hadn't Maya said anything today? Surely she must know?

"Comrade Emil, what's wrong with you? What's happened?" Alik asked, taking a step towards his former teacher.

"Who is this?" comrade Emil asked with a nervous twitch of his head, and he stared at Alik in bewilderment.

"This is my son," said Alik's mother.

"I'm Alik. Do you remember? I used to attend your drama group. In the winter."

"Alik? What Alik?" Emil asked himself helplessly.

"You used to shout at me all the time."

That helped — Emil began to remember.

"Alik, yes, of course… Hello…" And then, still gazing at Alik, he suddenly wrinkled up his face and burst into tears. "Milya… you remember Milya?" That was all he could say: he covered his mouth with a handkerchief and turned away to face the wall.

Of course Alik remembered Milya, comrade Emil's fat, dark-eyed wife. He was Emil, and she was Milya, who gave her husband his dinner before every rehearsal: after his main job somewhere outside the city, he didn't have time to eat at home. He used to shout at her too, but she never took offence, she was obviously used to it.

"Don't cry, comrade," said Alik's mother, "the patient's condition is satisfactory."

Emil shook his head in desperate disagreement.

"Metastases throughout her body," Alik's mother told him in a quiet voice, "they didn't even operate."

Emil swung sharply back round.

"Only, I beg you, Alik, don't say word to anyone. No one knows." He raised the handkerchief to his mouth again to stifle his sobs.

And only a few months ago, they had been a perfectly happy family. Emil and Milya. Who could have imagined that life would change everything so quickly? How precarious everything was! Only two hours ago Alik had thought he was the happiest man in the world. But now?

All night long he dreamed about something pleasant, but when he woke up in the morning, he couldn't remember what his dream had been about.

Of course, the dream had had something to do with Maya. He had no doubt about that. What else could he have dreamed about that would leave him smiling even after he woke up? Only Maya. There was nothing else in his life that could make him smile in his sleep. Nothing but her.

The lamb's hooves went clip-clop over the asphalt surface as it moved its little legs hastily, trying not to fall behind. Every now and then it stopped and lowered its head stubbornly, and then he had to pick it up. It already weighed about eight kilograms, but Alik only realised how heavy it was in Maya's entryway, after the steps had led him up to the dark-brown door with all those doorbells. Which one of them was hers? This one? This one? This one? And how could he ring the bell at such an early hour? If she lived alone, it would be a different matter.

He couldn't hear any sounds on the other side of the door. But even so he forced himself to ring — he had to say something to her before he went away.

"Who's there?" an alarmed woman's voice asked after he pressed the button several more times.

"Is Maya at home?"

"What?"

"Is Maya at home?" he repeated in a louder voice.

The woman behind the door muttered something unintelligible — he must obviously have chosen the wrong doorbell. Footsteps moved away from the door. He heard voices in the distance. Then again the same question was asked from behind the door.

"Who's there?" This was a woman's voice too, but old.

"Is Maya at home?"

"Yes. Who is this?"

"A friend of hers."

"What friend? Maya's sleeping …"

"Is that her grandmother?"

"Yes."

"I'm sorry for disturbing you. I've brought something for her."

"Who is it, granny?" he heard Maya's vice say.

His heart started pounding so hard that he could hardly breathe. "God only knows! At the crack of dawn …"

"Alik, is that you?" Maya asked in a quiet voice.

"Yes."

"What's happened?" The lock clicked, she slipped out through the crack of the half-open door and beamed when she saw the lamb. "Oh!" she exclaimed.

"It's for you," said Alik, thrusting the end of the string into her hand.

"You're crazy… What time is it now?" One of her cheeks was covered in stripes from her pillow.

"Six," her grandmother answered from behind the door.

Maya squatted down and put her arms round the lamb.

"Come to me, my darling, come on, don't be afraid."

Alik stepped back towards the stairs.

"You're mad," said Maya, pressing her face against the lamb's face, and now they were looking at him together — four eyes: two black and two blue. He had to say some kind of goodbye to them.

"He likes watermelon rind." That was the only thing Alik could think of on the spur of the moment. He set off quickly down the stairs, skipping every second step. What else could he have said to her?

He glanced at his watch and realised that he had to hurry.

Ten minutes later he walked into the courtyard. Whistling something that wasn't too sad to himself, he walked up to the first floor and sat on an old stool beside his sister's door. The yard was only just beginning to wake up, but two minutes later everybody already knew that he was there, and they realised immediately why.

On various pretexts, the neighbours appeared in the yard, one or two at a time, so that they could say hello to him. They were all wearing serious expressions appropriate to the moment.

Fariz still didn't come out.

There was the sound of the Willis driving up to the gates. Nadir was making some incomprehensible signs through the half-open door. Behind him Alik glimpsed the pale, anxious faces of his sister and nephew. The meaning of Nadir's signs became clear when the driver of the Willis walked up on to the balcony accompanied by another two men. They were dressed like Fariz, in grey uniform-style jackets buttoned right up to their chins.

When the three walked in through Fariz's door, which opened without a knock, Nadir started waving his arms about desperately again. Alik was forced to move closer in order to hear his whisper:

"The men were called out specially… You'll have to put it off."

Everything was already perfectly evident, there was no need for explanations.

"Do you hear me?" Nadir went on anxiously. "You'll have to put it off, it's too dangerous!"

Alik went back to his stool. He picked a thin stick up off the floor — a piece of the grape stalks that the woman had been using to fluff up the wool in the mattress the day before. He took a small penknife out of his pocket and, to pass the time, started carving the stick, trimming off its broken end. From the outside, he looked completely absorbed: in any case, he didn't look around.

Fariz was still procrastinating.

His sister came out on to the balcony and shed a single tear.

"Maybe you shouldn't, eh?" she asked uncertainly, on the point of really crying. "Please…"

"Go back inside," Alik told her.

Fariz was the third to come out of the door; the driver brought up the rear of the line. They walked in single file along the balcony towards the stairs.

Alik stood up. He called Fariz's name in a quiet voice, amazed at how calm he felt.

"What do you want?" Fariz asked nervously when Alik walked right up to him and moved the driver aside with his left hand.

"Hitting women is easy," Alik began, speaking the words he had prepared the evening before in a voice that his suppressed agitation rendered hollow. "But just you try hitting a man…"

On the final word Alik threw his body back as he did when he jumped off the tram and gave Fariz a resounding slap across the face. He knew he wouldn't be able to do any more than that — Fariz hadn't invited those two men just so that he would have witnesses. They had missed the slap, but they got everything else just right: one immediately grabbed Alik's right arm, and the other his left. The driver attacked him from behind and for some reason ripped his shirt open down to the waist.

Fariz didn't take his opportunity to answer back blow for blow: he was still too embarrassed to hit a man whose arms were twisted behind his back.

Out of the corner of his eye Alik saw his nephew in the red loincloth come darting out on to the balcony and his sister trying to tear herself out of Nadir's arms. At least he had been able to see his mother the day before.

"Where are they taking him? Let him go… Alik! Alik!" his sister shouted, straining her voice the way she had that night when he jumped off the roof at those three men with knives. Nadir had obviously explained to her what Fariz could do to a man who struck him in the face in front of witnesses.

They led Alik the same way he had walked with Maya the evening before, only seven hours ago.

He stopped at the former mosque, which had become a "Foodtrade" warehouse the year before. They had to pause too, after all they couldn't carry him. They didn't understand why he was looking at the old brickwork of the Muslim shrine. But he was saying goodbye to Maya. Going through in his mind what had happened beside this old wall the day before, kissing her on the lips, feeling the salty taste of blood in his mouth. Her blood...

When Alik returned home, Maya was already living in a different city. Fariz was working as a qualified specialist at the Surakhany oilfield, His mother had died and his nephew, Lucky, was about to graduate from school. And his sister was friends with Fariz's wife again.

TWO

Marat

It's a working day, but the quarry is silent; there's no repulsive screeching from the disc saws, the dust has settled overnight, the air tickles my nostrils pleasantly, my feet bounce against the firm ground, stirring up little swirling tornadoes of dust which, as they uncoil, merge into the white trail stretching round the quarry. My body has warmed up at last, as if everything inside it is bathed in a hot, viscous liquid that has splashed right up into my head — I feel a state of strange lightness, almost flight. There is more water than before on the bottom of the quarry. At least, that's how it looks from up here. It is dark-green from age and covered with rushes. If not for the three rather macabre-looking stonecutting machines frozen motionless right at the very edge of the quarry, this gigantic hole with its irregular corroded edges could be taken for a natural formation, like a hole in a rotten tooth, for something at least two hundred years old.

The only unbroken window in the house glints, reminding me that everything is not yet ready to receive my guest. The window is the only thing that distinguishes the house from the ones beside it, otherwise it looks just as desolate and deserted.

I reduce the length of my run to three circuits. A few things have been done already — the yard has been tidied up, the rug has been laid under the tree, the table has been covered with a white tablecloth — but I still have to carve the meat, which I left in the sun to thaw, and impale it on the skewers, so there'll be less fuss and bother later, when she arrives.

And iron my shirt. And there's the barbell too… Basically, I still have a lot to do. The meat in the refrigerator had frozen slightly, and I put it in the sun to thaw out.

My body, covered with drops of sweat, has begun to cool down. I need to warm up again before I use the barbell. Now that all the neighbours have moved out, I can do what I like, there's no one else to worry about.

I increase the load on the bar gradually, in order to reach the maximum load in exactly the right condition. Surely she can't arrive before eleven? But then, you never know with nineteen-year-olds nowadays.

The steel rod bends under the weight of the flat discs, my hands move smoothly up and down, the nap of the rug stops prickling my back, the patches of cloud dissolve into the sky and my body is flooded with the sensation of my own boundless strength…

My ear catches the distant sound of an engine, the slam of a car door, hurried footsteps, the creaking of a gate. Titch's face appears above the barbell. Titch must be very excited about something otherwise why wouldn't he sit down at one side, as usual, and wait, with an admiring expression on his face, for the weightlifting exercises to end?

"Marat! The bonuses are down the drain! Have you heard?"

What can I do with him? I try to teach him good manners, but it's all a waste of time. He only has to get worked up about something, like now for instance, and all his education just flakes away, like a dry husk. But then, it's not his fault. A man has to be educated from his childhood, and what could poor Titch ever learn from his father, who spent his entire life selling nine-kopeck meat pies for ten kopecks a time?

When Titch gets his answer, a disdainful movement of the head — quite enough to keep anyone with a bit of tact quiet for at least a few hours — he doesn't even blink. Leaning down over the barbell, with his eyes goggling in excitement, he jabbers away without a pause:

"Didn't you know… An order's come through…We have to dump half the plan… It's true… The quarterly bonus is down the drain…And the annual bonus too… I'm finished! Where can I get three thousand from? Do you hear?"

I have to stop him.

"Just calm down, Titch, why don't you sit down?"

That does the trick. Especially the tone in which it's said.

Now where will he sit down? At the table? No, he's guessed that the starched tablecloth wasn't taken out of granny's old chest of drawers for him. He's sitting down on the stool beside the tap. The sunniest spot in the yard.

Everyone in the yard who had tuberculosis used to warm themselves in the sun at that very spot, maybe even on the very same stool. But no, probably not: that stool must have rotted away a long time ago.

Eldar used to sit on it for hours at a time without moving, bundled up in shawls, he only had just enough strength to hawk up phlegm occasionally into a tin basin standing on the ground in front of him under the winter coats glittering with camphor flakes hanging on the branches.

We used to watch as his father, still wearing his army uniform, carried him out into the sun to get warm. And he would sit there resignedly, always staring at the same spot, a shrivelled little old man, aged just six, with sunken eyes.

There was a chalk line separating us from him, a fine line that we never crossed. It was strictly forbidden by our parents and we respected the ban, because something incomprehensible and dangerous began on the other side that line.

One day he dropped his apple. His face wrinkled up in pained annoyance and he watched with a feeble sidelong glance (for some reason he couldn't turn his head then, or perhaps he was bundled up too tightly) as it rolled across the ground, crossed the line and stopped just two steps away from us.

The apple lay there at our feet, but the terrible bacilli of tuberculosis were swarming in the air just beyond that line and, according to our parents, anyone who stepped across it was doomed to contract the fatal illness.

Eldar looked straight into my eyes and said "Give it to me". Those were the first words he had spoken in many days of sitting on the stool. Or perhaps I was hearing things. But when I gave him the apple, Eldar definitely said: "Thank you". He was a well brought-up boy, Eldar. And he's stayed that way that all his life. Not like Titch, who sits there sulking on that stool, without the slightest idea of the sad events took place in this yard all those long years ago, when people still lived here and they hadn't been squeezed out by the implacable advance of the quarry.

Right, now that the barbell has paused in the air for the last time in my outstretched hands and been put down behind my head in its place by the wall, I can ask just what it is that's got Titch so very worked up.

The terrycloth dressing gown is hanging under the stairs, I go to get it. Titch hurries after me.

"You promised to lend me the bonus money, didn't you? And the lads did too?"

"Well…"

"With the annual bonus, how much is that? Two thousand four hundred?"

"I don't know."

"Well, two thousand three hundred, at least. But now it's all down the drain."

"What's down the drain?"

"How am I going to pay for the car?"

"What's happened? Just calm down and explain"

"I told you… We've had an order to reduce output by half. But the old Plan is still in place. So the bonuses are down the drain."

"Who told you that?"

"The accounting office."

"When?"

"Today. I was registering my sick leave note."

"Another sick leave note?"

"It's the old one. You know the one I mean."

The meat has thawed and it yields easily to the knife.

"What's going to happen now?"

He waits for the answer like a judge's sentence that will decide if he carries on living or not. That damned Zhiguli has really landed the poor guy in a desperate spot. I do my best to reassure him.

Trust is a remarkable thing. The threat of being pursued by his creditors, the sad inevitability of having to part with his beloved car — all this is simply dismissed at a single word from me. And he instantly believes in the possibility of a miracle, simply because it has been promised by a man whom people are in the habit of trusting. He's still waiting anxiously for some concrete confirmation, though. But how can I say anything concrete until I've had a word with the management? Although it's clear that this rumour about the bonuses is absolute nonsense: they couldn't have sent us an order to work inefficiently.

"Everything's going to be all right…"

Titch brightens up and finally recovers the ability to think and talk about something else apart from his debts and his car. Running his eye over the table with the tablecloth and the pieces of meat he gives a crafty smile.

"Expecting guests?

"Yes."

"Someone new?"

"Yes."

He wags his head admiringly. He doesn't ask any questions, but that's not because curiosity has been satisfied.

The sound of a dull blow, muffled by distance, and the melodic tinkling of broken glass that follow it affect him like a hammer blow to a neurotic's knee cap: his entire body shudders convulsively and he goes dashing to the gate.

The car! He left it on the road — the waste plot beside the house is not really suitable for driving.

Where the windscreen ought to be there is a gaping hole and the hood and the ground round the car are sprinkled with tiny chips of glass. Titch is like a mother whose baby has been stolen while she was rummaging in her shopping bag: he swings his head this way and that in the desperate hope of spotting the person who broke the glass.

"What happened?" Titch stammered through trembling lips. "It didn't just fly out on its own, did it?"

"Someone smashed it…"

There is no other possible explanation.

"Who?"

I have to calm him down somehow.

"How much does that glass cost?"

"A hundred roubles."

"Don't worry about it. I just happen to have a spare hundred-rouble note lying around the place."

He's absolutely delighted, overwhelmed with joy, but he can't accept straight away: it's too awkward. And so he makes a feeble effort to protest

"Don't argue, Titch. I'm responsible for everything that happens on this lot," I reply.

He looks round the waste lot with hate in his eyes.

"I can't understand why you don't move out of here."

"Well, that's none of your business." A gentle grin.

"No, really… everybody else's moved out…"

I have to distract him somehow and get him to leave me in peace. I tell him about the park, about how first they're going to fill the quarry with water, and turn it into a pond, and then plant trees all round it — and it will be a park. Naturally, he listens dubiously. He finds it especially hard to believe that there will be an open-air summer restaurant and a boat-yard with rowing boats. But the broad descending steps of the stone hollow of the quarry really do look like the bottom of some gigantic pond that has been temporarily drained, and he finds that more convincing than my words.

"But how will trees grow here? It's solid rock."

"They'll truck in the soil. That's no problem."

"But they'll knock your house down anyway."

"Until they do, I'll stay here. And maybe they'll build new houses somewhere nearby."

He watches the expression on my face cautiously and fails to detect even the shadow of a smile. Then he gets into the car and looks out through the broken glass with a miserable air.

"Don't drive too fast, you'll catch cold."

He attempts to smile, but drives off without managing, it's a task that's beyond him right now.

As soon as he has gone, three long-haired youths in jeans appear from behind a pile of rocks. One of them, with a brightly coloured scarf dangling down to his knees, probably weighs in at about eighty kilograms, the other two are smaller and lighter. All three of them keep their hands in their pockets — either they're trying to frighten me or they really do have something prepared for the conversation to come. Their brazen faces seem familiar. But then, these long-haired types all look the same.

"Well, what are you staring at?" the tall one with the scarf says to get things started.

"Was it you who smashed the car's windscreen?"

"Who else?"

They're amused by the naivety of the question.

There is nothing more to be said. But they behave strangely, running behind the rocks and starting to make threats.

"That's just for starters," says the one with the bright scarf. "You talk to her again, and we'll smash your head in!"

So that's who they are: competing admirers, rivals, or something of the kind. If I chase them, I could catch one or even all of them (if they have any sense of comradeship, that is) and give them a thrashing. But to judge from their manners, these young guys are capable of any filthy trick, and then they'll take it out on her. What is this anyway — are all three of them after her?

"Why put it off till next time? Here's my head — try it."

They slowly back away, maintaining their distance.

"You've been told…" one of the "little" ones joins in nervously — he has a large, bulging forehead and a ginger moustache that curves down on to his chin. "You go near her again and you're for it."

"I definitely shall go near her."

"Then we'll see…"

"And what don't you like about it?"

"We've warned you. It'll be worse for you, and for her…"

"And who are you, her parents?"

"Friends." They laugh.

Maybe they really do have some kind of claim on her? They're certainly making a serious effort.

"Right, we've warned you, mate." That's the tall one with the scarf again. He's their leader. He jerks his head peremptorily, and they walk away rapidly, pleased with themselves.

Poor Titch. A victim of his boss's doomed love affair. And I feel sorry for the girl: if they watch over her this closely, her life can't be very easy.

Of course, apart from them, there's someone else I feel sorry for — this isn't the way I was planning on spending today, definitely not. A demeaning clash with young thugs instead of a date with a beautiful girl, strange rumours about bonuses, Titch's damaged car and a hundred roubles for a piece of glass… Things couldn't be much worse. The only thing to do now is drown my sorrows in a bottle of wine.

And if there isn't anyone to share the bottle with me, I'll have to drink it myself, I suppose. And while I'm sitting all alone at a table covered with a snow-white tablecloth and set with the last two plates from my granny's Kuznetzov dinner china set, I mustn't forget to take the meat off in time, so that it doesn't get too dry. And mop away the dripping fat with a slice of bread. And then, after smashing an onion with my fist — it's tastier like that — set to with God's blessing, for those who have lost interest in good food and wine are profoundly in error. And there's no need to hurry, simply because I'm dining alone and there's no one to chat to.

After satisfying my hunger and thirst, I distract myself from thoughts that are not exactly cheerful and sing something to improve the mood. Best of all would be some song from my young days. Even though I am only thirty-three years old, a bridge cast back into those recent, but already impossibly distant days of youth will lift my spirits, and that's exactly what I need right now. Why not "Come back to Sorrento" that I used to sing with my friends in sixth class at school, for example? Bawling it out at the top of my voice, I soon start to realise that being alone is not so bad after all. For there is no one in the yard apart from me, and the yard is on the edge of town, next to a stone quarry, and my voice disturbs no one as it drifts freely across the broad, rocky plateau with an immense hole at it's centre. And later on I can take down off the wall the rapier that won me the title of best fencer in the city for several years in a row, and enjoy fencing with an invisible opponent, from time to time thrusting the blade into the sack of sawdust intended just for that.

Normally brisk and self-confident, the director is hesitant and what he says isn't clear:

"You understand, it's not an order. It's more like a request from the minister, an experiment…"

"And for this experiment we have to work inefficiently?"

"That's not exactly right."

"That's exactly right, if we have to reduce the output of oil by forty per cent!"

"Less is not always worse," Eldar, the third man present, intervenes. He clearly feels he has kept silent for long enough after smiling joyfully and muttering the traditional: "How are you doing? I haven't seen you for ages".

I wonder what else he'll say? And where did he pop up from anyway? Has he really come back to stay? With his family, or on his own? He pontificates like a lecturer who's used to explaining obvious truths to the ignorant. He's sure that everyone should just listen open-mouthed while he tells them what to do. I'm not so convinced…

"And what's going to happen to the Plan?" My question is emphatically addressed to the manager.

The poor man is obliged to agree that problems do arise with the Plan, but only in my sector. As for the field in general there are hopes of overfulfilling the Plan.

"Beyond the slightest doubt."

What's he doing interfering in our business? Maybe he's some big boss in the ministry now? In any case, I can sense that this whole experiment nonsense is somehow directly connected with him.

*

"Understand this, my son," my mother said as firmly as always, aware of the correctness and necessity of what she was doing, but there were silvery tears glistening in her eyes, "there are only two of us, and five of them — an entire family… he's your friend and he's very ill. The damp could kill him. And one room is quite enough for you and me."

Meanwhile two porters and his father (he was still in his army uniform) were carrying things, their things, upstairs to the first floor, and carrying down to the ground floor everything that was still left of those times that my mother said had been so happy, when my father was still alive and we all lived a carefree, light-hearted life together.

My mother carried down the typewriter and the little round table at which she sat typing away for nights at a time. She was afraid of trusting anyone else with them: the Underwood typewriter and the table, which was cracked in several places, were both on their last legs already.

The Mülbach piano with the bronze candlesticks and ivory soft pedal stayed upstairs (for a certain payment, of course; the difference in square footage and the change of floor had probably been paid for too: his father was a decent man. And he was very decent too, was Eldar. About as decent as anyone could be…

*

"You see, it's what my research indicates," Eldar says confidentially, as if to emphasise that he's not afraid to admit his own interest in the matter. "I have demonstrated that when an oilfield is developed using the compressor method, the optimal approach, that is, the best way of doing things (he said that to make it clearer for me) is not to operate all the wells at full capacity, the way it's usually done, but instead to reduce the yield at some of them substantially… And then ultimately the total output of oil from all the wells will increase…"

Well, now he's really gone too far! And although I have absolutely no desire to discuss this subject with him — what does poor Titch care about his doctoral thesis! — I find it hard not to express my doubts.

The immediate response is assurances that afterwards, a little later on, they will somehow explain everything to me in detail, but that's not the most important thing right now. Now I have to decide if I am willing to help them or not.

I ask who "they" are.

"Well, me… science… the oil industry, however you like to put it. If we can prove my hypothesis, then we can obtain a significant increase in the output of oil across the country as a whole, together with quite a large saving of funds and energy."

"And your thesis will be approved too…"

That sounds rude, and he actually starts blinking resentfully. But he doesn't lose his self-control: yes, if his theoretical conclusion is confirmed in practice, his thesis will be approved. But what has that got to do with the crux of the matter?

There's no point in continuing the discussion (he realises that too) and I sum up on my way to the door: since I have no right to deprive people of their income, I am categorically opposed to any experiments until the Plan is amended by official decree and bonuses can be paid.

"Now don't go flying off the handle," the manager says, trying to calm me down. "It's just that the comrade said you were old friends. That's why we decided to put the suggestion to you. But no one's going to force you to do it. And nobody will allow us to cut back on the Plan… It all has to be done on a voluntary basis, so to speak."

The lads are waiting outside. They are warily silent. Titch, sitting off to one side, jumps up and hurries over to me. I smile, as if to say: Everything's fine, lads, what are you all so worried about? Your foreman's not the kind of guy to let some cock-eyed experimenters just gobble you up.

It's a long time before Titch can believe that the negotiations have really turned out well — information that originates from the accounting office is usually borne out.

There he is, Eldar from my childhood; searching for me with that offended glance. He's spotted me. And he's simmered down. So now he'll make one last attempt. Yes, he's called to me. He won't drop it so quickly this time…

He and the lads look each other over in a way that isn't very friendly. He looks at the lads, they look at him: they've instinctively sensed danger. He looks as dystrophic as ever. He has hardly changed at all. Still as skinny and rapid, only now he's just started going bald. But the old forelock, shifted two centimetres towards the top of his head, remains as spirited and rebellious as ever. And his Adam's apple is as sharp and agile as ever too.

Yes, you haven't changed much, Eldar. And above all, you're still as forthright and pushy.

"To be quite honest, I was really counting on you."

Why of course! The same as ever! What else could you say?

"How are you getting on?" Now we're in the train, after we've walked to the station in silence.

"Fine."

"Still living in the same place?"

He seems to feel that a sympathetic tone of voice is the appropriate thing just at the moment. I wonder how he'll take the news about the park.

"Yes. They're going to reconstruct the whole place soon."

"What about the quarry?"

"They're going to fill it in."

His eyebrows shoot up in surprise.

"Subsurface water... So they've decided to fill it up with water. It will be a sort of lake. With boats for rowing, and a park around it. They're even going to build a restaurant, to meet the demands of the workers."

"Why, that's great!"

"Yes, I think so too."

"Will they demolish the house?"

"They'll demolish everything there. It will be a small new neighbourhood. Literally just a few blocks."

"Is there any chance of getting a flat?"

"Yes."

"You're not... married?" It's difficult for him to get the question out, but he usually copes with such challenges sooner or later.

"No. And all's well with you, I hope?"

"Yes. Two children. Boys. Vika has graduated from the institute. Basically, everything's going as planned. Do you see much of the lads?"

"Not really ...

*

We were searched by some relative of Eldar's: a man with a hooked nose and shaggy eyebrows wearing a coarse grey shirt with a thin belt round the waist. Taking no notice of the cries of protest from Eldar, whom he usually obeyed respectfully, he turned our pockets inside out, made us put our hands up and felt all over our bodies from our armpits down to our feet — I could tell that it wasn't the first time he'd done it.

"Dad will throw you out!" The veins inflated on Eldar's skinny neck, he was shouting so hard. "Leave them alone! You stole them yourself!"

Once he finished his search, the relative went into the other room without saying a word: the face in the photograph hanging over the piano in there no longer belonged to my father, but to a well known figure of state (who also, as a matter of fact, soon disappeared). And everything had also changed in the former bedroom, where the search had taken place: standing in the corner instead of the old metal bedsteads with the nickel-plated backs (they had moved down to the ground floor with us) was a broad couch, covered with a carpet hanging down from the wall. The walls were covered with very tall bookcases that had round gilt handles, but were always closed. Everything in our flat had changed, even the old Dutch stove had been converted to a gas fire...

And later, when it got completely dark, Eldar admitted that he had stolen the gold watch with a gold bracelet and the six silver table knives himself. The wind swayed the flat metal shade of the lamp on its post and the pale spot of light darted to and fro across the waste lot.

He tried to persuade us that stealing the bracelet and the knives was not really theft, but the correction of an injustice: my mother spent nights tapping away on a typewriter to earn a tiny amount of money, but his family had plenty of everything: money and all sorts of junk, so there was no doubt that the knives and the bracelet could be sold off and the money used to buy me and our friend Rafik bicycles just like the one he had. Of course, it was insulting that they had searched us, but sooner or later the suspicions would be forgotten, and we would get the bicycles we had been dreaming about for so long.

That night, after he heard that his mother had informed the militia about the missing things, he dropped the watch and the knives into the crack between the dried-out boards of the kitchen windowsill. There was a space underneath them that had been discovered several years earlier, when a pre-war silver half-rouble had rolled into the crack …

*

"Why didn't you ever apply to go to college?"

"It's a long story…"

Now the attack's going to come. Not in order to justify himself or ask forgiveness. But in order to rid him of his doubts, if he has any. Eldar absolutely has to prove to himself and to me that he was right back then, and he has always been right, and it's not his fault if someone else has suffered because of their own laziness or unforeseen circumstances in their life.

I'm right, he's starting.

"I realise I was bit naïve back then. But when can you be naïve, if not when you're seventeen?" He smiles sadly and yet somehow sweetly as he is carried back to those days that are so long ago now, when the final school exam had been passed at last. "And I'm still convinced that we did the right thing by working before going on to study… It was good for all of us, don't you agree?"

"I agree."

"There's something you're not saying."

"Leave it…"

"No, honestly… And if you didn't go on to study afterwards, you've got no one to blame but yourself."

He's waiting for objections: a mocking smile instead of counterarguments adds to his fervour.

"After all, my motives were absolutely sincere."

"As always…"

"Yes, as always. Or don't you think so?"

"Can you believe it, I don't."

His eyelashes tremble resentfully, he's still as sensitive to mockery as ever.

"Can you justify your assertion?"

"I can… But I don't wish to."

"But you've insulted me."

"Yes."

Eldar's eyes are filled with moisture, tension, and a confusion that he tries in vain to conceal.

"Come on, at least try to explain why."

"You know perfectly well why."

The train has braked smoothly and come to a halt.

The station building is under reconstruction, so we walk around it, across the tracks. He walks beside me without speaking, sniffing resentfully, but he still won't leave me alone.

"And how are the lads doing? Do they come round to see you?"

"No."

"What, you don't see each other at all?"

"Not really."

Now here's a chance to reproach someone and, of course, he won't let it pass.

"But why? How can you live in the same city and not see each other?"

He watches every movement I make warily, but the expression on his face is as defiantly determined as ever. The desire to punch him in the face disappears as instantaneously as it arose. And immediately something like shame stirs in my heart. Shame for myself, still bearing a secret grudge (after all, almost ten years have gone by now), and for him, still as cowardly as ever, for all his assertive love of the truth.

The fear puts his nerves even more on edge, now nothing can stop the flood of denunciation…

"What's happening to you? What have you turned into? I live in the back of beyond, at the other end of the country, I don't have the chance. But how could you lose each other, living in the same city? What's to stop you at least taking an interest in how the others are getting on?"

He's sincere, as always. And for the most part what he's saying (or rather, shouting) is the truth. But the truth is always only one of many just truths. For him, the other versions simply don't exist. And he defends this single truth of his, foaming at the mouth, until the victory is won.

*

The idea of going to work after school came to Eldar suddenly, as we were climbing up the fire escape to the roof of School No. 134. Getting inside through the attic had been his suggestion too — at that time he was working hard on rooting out his own cowardice. The girls we had been counting on meeting at the entrance had failed to show up, or perhaps we hadn't noticed them. We stood there in the crowd thronging the school yard, and the desire to get into the graduation ball grew stronger and stronger as we watched the lucky ticket-holders walk through the cordon of monitors one by one. And so his suggestion of trying the attic was taken up immediately, although everyone realised that it was risky idea.

The first to start the ascent was Lucky, followed by Seidzade (who could ever have imagined in those years that he was capable of composing anything but sophisticated obscenities?), Eldar went third, moving slowly: he was a terrible coward, and he started to faint about halfway up the steps. Then me, and the last to go was Rafik — he was regarded as the most capable of all, he was keen on astronomy and was planning to go to Moscow University.

"But are you sure there's a way out of the attic?" Lucky asked when he had already gone up several steps.

"No, I'm not," said Eldar, still standing on the ground. "Why, are you frightened?"

Lucky didn't answer.

At about second-floor level he started moving more slowly. After another couple of steps my face ran up against his trembling calves.

I took another step, so that it was hard for him to fall. His limp body was braced on both sides by my arms and my hands were holding on to the steps; my head was pressed against his skinny shoulder blades.

Finally, mastering his fear, he went up another step.

"What are you doing there?" asked Rafik, coming on behind.

But this it was not the moment for explanations.

Lucky and Seidzade had already reached the roof.

"What happened?"

"He's falling…"

The general attention gave him strength. But it was impossible to press him against the steps and move upwards at the same time.

Seidzade and Lucky tried to persuade him to let go of the steps and grab hold of their hands. Eventually Eldar made himself do it, and they pulled him up.

Everyone was scared.

"What's wrong with you?"

"I don't know… I'm afraid of heights…"

"Then why did you climb up?"

"On purpose, to overcome my fear!"

"Idiot! What if you'd fallen?"

He was a strange kind of coward, Eldar — for some reason he used to exhort everyone to do the things that made him most afraid.

He got his breath back, but before climbing through the trap door into the attic, he thought he ought to make an announcement.

"I've decided to go get a job, lads … How long can you go on being a burden to your parents? I'll study in evening classes or by correspondence. And I suggest you do the same…"

It was strange to hear words like that coming from the mouth of someone whose father had spent several years in Party work in an agricultural region and had now become the rector of the biggest educational institution in the city. Everyone assumed that Eldar would continue his education in that very same college.

The sheet-metal covering of the roof rattled and rumbled under our feet, signalling every single step. We walked through the dark attic, full of old furniture and desks, and reached the doorway. There was a bright light coming through the crack between the two doors. We could hear an orchestra playing somewhere nearby and the murmur of cheerful voices. We threw ourselves against the door with all the strength we could muster, but the little lock, painted over with oil-bound paint refused to yield.

Eldar pestered everyone in turn to find out what they thought about his decision to go to work…

"Just wait, will you," someone hissed.

The hopelessness of the situation was clear to everyone apart from him, the chief culprit — he wouldn't be able to manage the steps a second time, and the lock wasn't yielding at all. There was only one thing left to do — ask the organisers of the ball for help. But we didn't know if they actually have a key to the lock of the attic door, and apart from that, it would have been annoying to have surmounted all those difficulties, only to find ourselves out on the street again.

Eventually he grasped the situation.

"Maybe you can go back over the roof, and I'll call for someone to open the door?" I could hear the pain of a man injured in unequal battle and abandoned by his comrades in his voice.

"What if they haven't got a key? Are you going to sit here until morning?"

Everybody was despondently silent. Lucky lit match after match, apparently hoping to find another door in the wall, one that wasn't locked …

After first explaining to everyone that the important thing was to scatter into the crowd of dancers as quickly as possible, I took a run. About three meters away from the door I leapt up off the ground and flew, with my right shoulder leading the way…

The lock and its fittings flew off and the door swung open with a terrible crash. A few couples strolling along the corridor recoiled in fright. We flitted past them and plunged into the crowd of dancers.

A minute later we were dancing away for all we were worth and have already forgotten how we got into the hall. All of us, that is, except Eldar. As I danced, I stumbled across his miserable gaze. Because he was so short, it took him a long time to pluck up the courage to approach a partner, and then when he was refused, he was incapable of repeating the attempt for a long time. Girls very *definitely did not like Eldar. And he suffered as a result. But he tried to make us believe that he couldn't stand them…*

In the winter of 1961 the lads and I had work practice in Moscow. We lived in the Oil Institute hostel on Lenin Prospect, although my mother had also given me the address of some relatives I could stay with. Relatives I had never even seen.

We switched the lights out in the hostel room as soon as the dancing started: the record player that had been rented out on the basis of a cash deposit three times what it was worth, kept wheezing to a halt, but no one was listening to it anyway — we just carried on holding each other tight, dancing in time to the music that was playing inside us.

My partner whispered sweet nothings to me with her moist lips pressed against my neck. We had met at the park near the Soviet Army club just three days earlier, and that had been long enough for her to fall in love. At least, that was what she was telling me. And it sounded entirely plausible unless, of course, she was an absolutely brilliant actress (but with talent like that, why would she be working as a lab technician?).

Eldar was sitting on the bed, with his hands propped on the bedside locker, his entire posture emphasising his lack of involvement in everything that was going on.

I tried to listen to what my lab technician was whispering to me, but could barley make out her words before she shrank away from me in fright the instant the knock at the door came. In addition to the ability to fall in love quickly, nature had also endowed her with powerful intuition: the knock was gentle and polite, it wasn't suggestive of even the slightest danger, but just to be on the safe side, she switched on the light and removed the bottle of wine from the table.

Four people came in. The old janitor, who was usually dozing behind his table at the entrance, a woman who looked like a hostel commandant and two young guys with red armbands.

"What are outsiders doing here after midnight?" the woman asked in a habitually severe tone of voice.

"We were just leaving," Lucky said with a charming smile.

"Who are the outsiders here?" one of the young guys asked menacingly as if he intended to throw anyone who confessed out of the window.

"I know these ones," said the woman, pointing by turn at Eldar, Seidzade and Lucky. "They're here on work experience. All the rest are aliens."

"We're not aliens," said Rafik, mirroring Lucky's smile and joining in the conversation, "we're Soviet people… Just visiting."

"Three minutes to collect your things," the second young guy interrupted him, "and then I want you out of here."

He was addressing our ladies above all.

"Couldn't you try being a bit more civil?"

Without deigning to answer me, he walked out of the room. The others followed him. The old janitor was strangely embarrassed by what was happening and he said a polite goodbye.

"It was his work!" my lab technician said suddenly, pointing angrily at Eldar, "I saw him talking to them downstairs."

From the way he howled, you'd have thought that she'd jabbed him with an electric cattle prod.

"Yes, I did it! I called them! To get you all out of here! You miserable cruds! And you!" he said, turning on us now. "All you're interested in is smooching in dark corners! It's disgusting to watch! Is that what we came here for?" having vented some of his outrage, he cooled off a little. "We have to stop these dance parties. How many days have we been in Moscow, and we haven't been anywhere, we haven't seen anything. Anybody would think there aren't any of them in Baku," he said, jerking his head towards the girls crowding in the doorway, but without actually looking at them.

In his own way, of course, he was right, our Eldar… But as a result I found myself out on the streets of a huge, unfamiliar city at night, in a temperature of minus thirty degrees. Rafik and the girls were better off, they went back to their homes and hostels. But I was obliged to take my father's old suitcase and set out in search of Bolshaya

Bronnaya Street and some relatives of my mother whom I had never even seen.

*

Eventually we come out on to the square in front of the station. Eldar is stubbornly striding along beside me.

"Where are you going in such a hurry?"

"Home."

"Maybe you could invite me along?" His tone is facetious, but at the same time distinctly mournful, as if to say: Just look how low we've sunk, begging each other for invitations!"

Without waiting for an answer, he goes on:

"Why don't we call in on Lucky?"

"He's in America."

"He's back already. I phoned him yesterday. Have you been to his new flat?"

"No."

"Give me two kopecks."

There's a tobacco kiosk beside the telephone booth. They have BT cigarettes, and that gives me something to do while he's making a call.

Lucky lives somewhere right in the centre of town now. Legends circulate about his flat, his car, his influential father-in-law, his beautiful wife, his passionate mistress, his friends with connections and his career successes. He is one of the most popular personalities in the entire city.

Eldar thrusts the receiver at me and the voice in the earpiece is as rakishly sincere as ever.

"Where did you disappear to? Remember what you promised me! You might at least have phoned, if you can't call round! I came to your place, but you work every second day, don't you?"

"Yes."

"That's why I missed you, then."

He's probably lying, but then, perhaps not. Why would he?

"How are you getting on? Are you the last one left there now? The yard's empty. There isn't even anyone to ask."

So he really did come round. A remarkable man, Lucky! Suddenly I want to see him very much.

"We'll come round now and I'll tell you everything."

"I'm waiting"

I hang up…

*

I am woken by low voices speaking outside the door, somehow sounding very cosy. The room in which I have been put to bed is narrow, only as wide as the window. The closed shutters make it quite dark in here, and the photographs on the walls are white patches. There are lots and lots of them, all different sizes. The broad, comfortable chest on which I am lying is covered with something very soft, evidently a feather mattress, or maybe even more than one. It really is very soft.

The conversation outside the door continues, calm and unhurried: it sounds as if the two people who have met for breakfast (I can hear spoons tinkling in glasses) have been talking to each other for a long time, for many years already, about the same long-standing subject. The husky bass male voice chafes familiarly:

"… No money, no friends, no happiness, no home, nothing — a total zero…"

An old-sounding woman's voice objects naively:

"What do you mean 'no home'? Isn't this a home?'

The bass voice is ironic and affectionate:

"Well, what kind of home is this? It's not a home, it's a saintly monk's cell. A shrine"

"I told you, you can bring anyone you like… I'd be glad."

"What about principles?"

"Whose principles?"

"Mine… How can we insult the memory of my ancestors who have dwelled within these walls? Only a highly moral woman is

worthy to step across the threshold of this house! And unfortunately I don't know any like that."

"Stop acting the buffoon. And not so loud, please, you'll wake the boy up. That voice of yours is like a trumpet…"

"The boy's our own blood all right, he likes his sleep."

"Quiet!"

"So exactly what relation is he of mine?"

"He's the nephew of your Aunt Nina's husband."

"That one who ran off with an Azerbaijani?"

"Yes."

"Why didn't you wake me up? I should have given my little relative a more festive reception. After all he's almost my own brother, even if he is a Muslim."

"Never mind, you'll have plenty of time to introduce yourself."

I hear the clatter of a chair being moved back and heavy footsteps. Apparently my "almost brother's" physical presence matches his voice.

"Where are you going?"

"To take a look at my little relative."

A massive shaggy head with small puffy eyes is thrust in through the door. My brother is at least thirty years old. His eyes are aglow with benevolent curiosity.

"Do we like art?" he enquires on discovering that I'm not asleep. "Would you like to view some Matisse?"

"What?"

"Not what, but whom. Matisse; the greatest impressionist of all!"

I nod uncertainly.

"Well done. Be ready this evening…" The head disappears.

I get dressed.

The mistress of the house, whom I am permitted to call granny, turns out to be the kindest and sweetest of creatures. While I drink tea, she asks after my mother.

Unfortunately, I don't have any happy news to give her. Thank you… Yes… It doesn't matter… No… She's still losing weight… She works a lot. She smokes a lot. She coughs at night. She can't sleep for shortness of breath. And she won't accept any treatment…

My poor mother…

My brother, despite his massive dimensions, is an energetic and impetuous fellow. He plunges into one more shop, comes running back out, flops into the front seat and we drive on.

Neon shop signs glimmer above the grey ramparts of snow at both sides of the road, but Gena — that's what my brother is called — pays no attention to them. He stops the taxi, following some strange reasoning of his own, at spots where there is no external indication of any commercial activity, asks me for money and flings himself out of the car.

The taxi driver looks around warily — after every exit like that the car carries on swaying for a long time.

"Nothing excessive," my brother explains. "Only what is absolutely essential. Artists love attention."

And he conscientiously runs through the contents of his bundles.

"Vodka… Beer… Olives… Fish… Salami… Pickled cucumbers (although for some reason the cucumbers are red in colour and officially called tomatoes).

"Let's go, old man!" my brother exclaims excitedly to the driver.

The car moves on.

The driver has been trying for a long time to discover where we are going.

"Just close by… Now turn the corner… As far as the traffic lights… And from there just keep straight on."

The back of his seat sags and creaks pitifully as he turns towards me with another sudden jerk.

"So that's what our life is all about, brother… the worship of art, and that's the whole story. Are you a student?"

"No, I work."

"But what about education?"

"I want to get in a correspondence course."

"That's not a bad idea, either. But it's still not as good… you ought to get a taste of the sweet student life. It's a wonderful time — the blossoming of the soul and the rampant desires…"

"So where is it we're going?" the driver interrupts.

My brother is offended.

"Why, how impatient you are, old man. Straight on as far as the tunnel, then we'll turn off and carry straight on again…"

"And is it far?"

"No… close by here."

"Where are we going, though?"

I'm interested in this question too — the meter is rapidly gobbling up the pitiful remnants of my money.

"To Bolshevo," *my brother mumbles in annoyance and turns towards me again.*

"To Bolshevo!" *the driver exclaims, and it's immediately clear to me that that's somewhere a long way away.* "Where in Bolshevo?"

"Past the station, over the Klyazma and to the right."

"But that's just a forest path!"

"We'll make it there fine," *my brother says, with a wink at me.* "Artists don't live on the main thoroughfares… Not yet… But, never mind, that's only temporary. I'm glad you're fond of art. How about reading? Do you read much?"

"It varies."

"But you like to?"

"Yes."

"Prepare a place in your suitcase."

"What for?"

"For a present; ten volumes of your own choice from the family library. On the word of a hereditary bibliophile. And how do you feel about music? Do you like Chopin?"

"Yes."

"Then today you're in for a treat."

Matisse proved to be a small woman with trousers that were stretched tightly over her sturdy legs. She was very glad to see my brother. They embraced exuberantly. We walked through a glass veranda to room where the heating was turned all the way up.

"Here, let me introduce you, I've brought my brother along," *he said, shoving me forward.* "And this is Tamara, a remarkable artist, a modern-day Matisse."

Matisse blushed intensely and started bustling about.

"Please, sit down. Oh, how much you've bought... And olives too... Well done, boys... Lusya will be really delighted, she simply adores them..."

"Her daughter," my brother whispered, and it became clear to me what he had in mind when he asked about Chopin. "Will you show us your works here, or later, after supper?"

"Later, later," Matisse said dismissively.

My brother accepted that, but let it be known that he was aggrieved by such a decision.

"That's the way we all are." He said sadly. "First we appease the hunger of the flesh, and then the hunger of the spirit..."

Both bottles of vodka are emptied in an instant, and then Chopin, looking remarkably like her mother, performs something like"Chopsticks" on the out-of-tune Soviet piano. And my profoundly content brother falls asleep right there at the table.

His final words are addressed to Matisse:

"Show the youth your works..."

Mother and daughter drag out a brightly painted wooden suitcase, throw open the lid, and I see rather likeable little plaster dogs with a neat parting midway between their ears.

"I feel a bit awkward," Matisse says as she shows me her works. "He really likes them..." — a tender glance at the sleeper sitting at the table — "they're all St. Bernards. He really likes that breed..."

An attempt to wake my brother ends in failure: he carries on sleeping even while she's answering my questions.

Matisse explains that it's impossible to get out of Bolshevo at this hour. The daughter maintains her silence: she's a taciturn individual in general, and she has had a dissatisfied expression on her face all evening long.

In addition to the table and the piano, there is a divan in the room (the wooden shelf above it is stacked with St. Bernards produced by Matisse) I can't see any other places to sleep.

"He always sleeps at the table," Matisse reassures me, catching my glance. "I'll just make up the bed — you can lie down and get some rest."

I am woken by a woman's muffled, monotonously repeated screams. Someone is screaming through tightly clenched teeth. Or there is a hand over her mouth. My brother carries on sleeping…

I dash to the door through which Matisse and Chopin withdrew after putting me to bed.

There's no one in the large dark room with two beds that haven't been touched. I pass through another doorway and run into some soft, yielding, but insurmountable barrier. There's a strip of light glimmering to my right: with a sudden dart towards it, I break through into the room, and realise that the door is curtained off with a carpet.

I am not the only person in that room. Matisse and Chopin are sitting on top of someone on the floor. Showing no sign of rage, Matisse is methodically and repeatedly striking at something soft (the blows sound like slaps). In time to the rhythm of the blows, a pair of legs is thrown up into the air and I hear someone's screams, muffled by Chopin's hand. (She is sitting on the shoulders of the creature who is being subjected to this flogging and preventing her, as far as possible, from making any noise.)

Matisse, who is sitting squatting on the creature's waist, has spotted me straight away, but she lands a few more blows before I can stop her

"What are you doing? How can you?" I exclaim in alarm, as I try to drag the mother and daughter off a third member of the fairer sex — a girl of about seventeen with a perfectly calm expression on her face who shows not the slightest surprise at my sudden appearance.

"The bitch knows whose meat she's eaten," Matisse says in a sombre voice as she walks towards the door curtained off with a carpet. Chopin maintains her silence, but she is harder to drag off the victim than her mother — clear testimony to her substantial inner resources.

She follows Matisse back to the room when my brother is still sleeping imperturbably at the table. When the kettle has boiled, the ladies make themselves a glass of tea each and drink it with gusto. I try not to ask any questions, but after the initial wave of excitement subsides, they give few points away.

"That'll teach her…" says Matisse.

"The lousy bitch," Chopin agrees.

"But who is she?" I ask.

"She knows what she's done" Chopin mutters, getting in ahead of her mother.

"She's sucking our blood…" Tears have sprung to Matisse's eyes — she's a more sensitive soul than her child, after all. "Well, you get some sleep, we won't disturb you anymore."

I manage to fall asleep quickly. The exact opposite ought to have been the case, owing to the abundance of new impressions, but obviously I really am tired…

*

And now Eldar definitely, absolutely, has to let his family know that he'll be home late, otherwise they'll be worried. I don't have another two-kopeck coin, so on the way to see Lucky we make a massive detour — Eldar's father lives right at the far end of the boulevard, in the House of Scholars.

I stop outside by the fountain pulsating out of the jaws of a long-tailed dragon and, after apologising yet again, he disappears into an entrance that is decorated with intricate carvings.

A knight with a sword is poised above the dragon in a pose that defies all the laws of anatomy. The knight and the dragon, and the building with its countless arches and columns, all appeared in the late nineteen-forties, but now they seem like monuments from ancient times. Especially the building.

How affectionate it seems they are with each other in their family, what mutual care and attention they demonstrate — if he doesn't say that's going to be late, his wife will be out of her mind with worry. Well, I suppose that's the way it ought to be, if they love each other.

I see a black Volga drive up to the entrance. The short man in a grey suit who gets out of it heads towards the fountain. It takes a while for me to recognise him, and then it's mostly from a certain sense of inner inhibition that increases as he gets closer. How small he has become, shrunk to half his size! Or was he always like that?

The clearly defined features of his face express nothing apart from the confidence that he has already experienced everything — both the very best and the very worst — that this world has to offer, and there is nothing that can possibly surprise him.

I wonder if he recognises me? It's unlikely. How many years is it since we've seen each other? At least ten. After they moved away, I still visited them, of course, but he rarely came out of his study. And after Eldar got married seeing them again was out of the question.

I say hello. It seems he has recognised me after all. Or perhaps he has simply taken me for one of his former students. He must have graduated so many of them in all this time! Probably tens of thousands.

He slows down and stops.

"How are you getting on?"

"Not too bad, thank you."

Why were we so afraid of him when we were children? After all, he never once even raised his voice to Eldar, or to any of us.

"Are you waiting for him?"

It seems he has recognised me after all.

"Yes."

"I'm glad to see you."

"Thank you."

"I suddenly feel that he really is glad to have met me. It doesn't show at all on the outside: well, perhaps the expression of his eyes is a little warmer. But I'm still not certain that he hasn't confused me with someone else."

"How are you doing?"

"Fine, thanks."

He looks hard at me, as if he's trying to remember something. He mechanically runs one hand through his hair, which has grown thin and colourless with the passage of time. For the first time in all the years I have known him I sense some kind of uncertainty in him: he wants to ask me something, but somehow he can't bring himself to do it. So I wait…

"Your mother… Is your mother gone already?" he asks uncertainly, in an apologetic voice.

"My mother passed away, you were at the funeral."

"Yes, yes… I remember. She was a remarkable woman. Are you on your way to see us? Ah, yes, you're waiting." He paused for a moment. "Listen, of course it's his business, I don't interfere, but perhaps you could talk to him, have a word… Tell him not to go away after his thesis is approved. You're friends, after all… Perhaps he'll listen to you… Will you have a word with him?"

There is so much naïve hope in this request that I promise to do it.

We say goodbye and he walks towards the entrance of the building.

*

I am woken by screaming again. I immediately recognise the mighty voice of Matisse. As I run (my brother carries on sleeping imperturbably) I catch a different, regular howling sound in the background — only Chopin could cry like that.

Matisse is lying in the same position as the first victim. Sitting on top of her is a hefty man with a crimson face, wearing a white sheepskin coat. The blows are being struck at the same soft spot —it seems this house has its own special traditions.

In floods of tears, Chopin keeps attempting to intervene, but at each attempt she is sent flying back against the wall like some piece of fluff.

My first impulse to help the artist ends in the same fashion — I come crashing down beside Chopin. The blow had caught me on the bridge of my nose: I had approached too close with my rhetorical question:

"What are you doing?"

I was about to add that it is unworthy of a man's dignity to beat a woman, but I didn't have time.

A second attempt… This time the blow catches me just as I am getting to my feet, but at least now that the man in the sheepskin coat has turned his attention to me, he has left Matisse alone. Now all I have to do is restrain him. And that wouldn't be too difficult, if only I could get up, but he is an experienced fighter and so he tries to build on his success: without allowing me to gather my wits, he forces me into the corner and kicks me hard three times. Three terrible blows — anybody not in such good condition would have spent the rest of his life living on an invalid's pension.

He dashes out through the door and then reappears in the doorway with a huge kitchen knife. Perhaps he has every reason to slaughter my brother Gena, but as far as I'm concerned, I know for certain that I want nothing to do with this whole business.

Fortunately, the door with the carpet is close at hand.

He chases me through all the rooms and the veranda and only abandons the pursuit out in the yard, when he evidently realises that in freezing conditions like this I won't get very far with bare feet and wearing nothing but my shirt.

My shirt, soaked in sweat and blood, instantly freezes solid. Sinking up to my knees in the snow, I get as far as the fence. Summoning up my final ounces of strength, I climb over it and find myself on the next lot. I don't know the exact time, but I realise that it is after midnight already.

There isn't a single light in the neighbours' house.

I am sitting on the doorstep, slumped against the door, when they finally hear my feeble knocking.

"Who's there?"

"Please open the door."

"What for?"

A light goes on over the porch: apparently they are looking me over.

My appearance arouses sympathy, but the door still doesn't open.

A pair of old felt boots and a padded jacket are pushed out though the opening of the small upper window.

"I'll bring them back."

My feet are frozen stiff and they've gone completely numb.

"Leave them by the porch."

"Thank you... Is the militia station far from here?"

"Once you're out in the street, turn right, then right again at the post office."

"Thank you."

My hands will no longer obey me either, but eventually I manage to pull on the felt boots.

I take ages closing the gate behind me. I just can't manage to shift the iron latch. Every touch is sheer agony.

I turn right and walk as far as the post office. Then turn right again. I finally see a brightly illuminated official-looking building. I walk closer. Yes, that's it — the militia station. There's another sign beside it — the fire brigade. Somehow that makes me feel more secure.

The door's open. At the end of the end of the corridor there's a dimly illuminated board with fire-fighting equipment hanging on it. Axes, and all the other stuff, painted a rusty red colour. It suits the situation absolutely perfectly. There's a cat sitting under the board: it runs off as I approach — something about me frightens it away.

I turn into a small vestibule in front of the duty room. A man sitting with his back to the door is talking on a phone which is hanging on the wall under a poster with word "Wanted" in large letters.

"Comrade!" *I call to him, feeling the bitter tears welling up in my eyes for all the violence that has been done to me.*

He hangs up. He is wearing a strange sort of uniform jacket — not militia uniform — and boots; and there's a white sheepskin coat hanging on the wall beside the telephone. He grins ominously and advances on me. An impulse of acute despair sends me dashing to the board and I tear one of the axes off it. He stops.

"Now, now..." *he says, reaching for his back pocket in a warning gesture.*

88

Why is he here? Where are the militia? Where am I?

"Why? Why did you beat me?" The tears are choking me, the words come bursting out in a jumbled torrent. "You animal, you brute! What have I done to you?"

He backs away.

"Why did you break into my house?"

"I didn't break in … I was invited."

"Who invited you?"

"My brother, Gena."

He's astonished.

"I know Gena, he promised to get my daughter a place in college. Put that axe down…"

"Where's the officer on duty?"

"I'm the officer on duty here."

He can tell from my face that I don't believe him.

"The militia's out on a call. I'm the fire brigade. Put the axe down."

So now what can I do? Split his skull open? And then what? Prison? And no way to explain anything to anyone? My poor mother.

"You're a bastard…" I say, trying to pour out at least some of my pain in words. "A brute, a monster…"

I raise the axe. He retreats, shielding himself with his arm.

"Why were you beating a woman?"

"She's my wife…"

I finally begin to fit the pieces together.

"And who's the other one?"

He doesn't want to answer. But he's backed up against the wall, and it would be hard to dodge a blow.

"She lives with me. I warned them not to touch her!"

The rude boar finally begins to assume human features.

I lower the axe.

"You old fool, I saved her. Didn't she tell you?"

"She didn't tell me anything. She phoned and said: They're beating me again. So I came running …"

His bestial face is completely transformed — there is so much pity and love in his voice and his eyes when he talks about that girl!"

I ask how to get out of there and back to Moscow. He explains.

"I ripped your coat," he says in a guilty voice when we reach the doorway.

"What do you mean, you ripped it?" I say, stopping dead. My mother bought that coat especially for the trip to Moscow.

"Along the seam, I think …"

And I find that my coat had been ripped in half from the hem right up to the collar, then clumsily repaired.

I see the girl standing at the gate from a distance: my coat and cap in one hand, my shoes and jacket in the other.

I try to go through into the house to get dressed.

"Don't go in there."

"Why not?"

Without waiting for an answer, I shrug and start getting changed out in the freezing cold. My toes are aching horribly. I put my jacket on and examine my coat.

"I sewed it up."

The crude hand stitching runs all the way along the seam from the top to the bottom.

She helps me put the coat on.

She has a round face with small, pretty features: small lips, small nose, small eyebrows, small eyes. The face of a little angel. The long hair flows out from under her rabbit-skin cap and down to her waist.

I mumble "Thank you" and set off along the route indicated by the fireman. When I eventually hear the footsteps behind me, I look round. She stops.

"What's wrong? Why are you following me?"

I'm not really interested in her answer, but even so, some kind of explanation for her behaviour seems only natural. Only she doesn't say anything, just stares down at the ground.

"Do you want to show me the way?"

"Yes."

"I'll get there somehow."

Again I hear footsteps behind me. I start walking a little more slowly. So does she. I start getting angry.

"Are you deaf, or what? Don't follow me."

Our glances finally meet. Her feelings are hurt, I see two huge tears well up out of her eyes.

"Now what's bothering you? What have I said to upset you? It's late. The middle of the night. You'll have to walk back alone… Don't you understand?"

"Without saying a word, she swings around and walks back towards the house. I feel a sudden urge to call out to her, I don't really want to be left on my own.

Without looking round again, she walks to the crossroads and disappears behind the snowdrifts.

I reach Bolshaya Bronnaya Street early in the morning on a snow-clearing machine.

*

Lucky meets us at the elevator. He lives in an old pre-revolutionary house, but he has installed an elevator in attempt to keep up with the times. Or rather, he has managed to have the state install it. Or rather, not managed to have them do it, but asked. Not even asked, really, simply expressed his desire. Or perhaps he didn't even do that, and it was some neighbour with connections who made it happen. But anyway, in the building where Lucky lives there are not only six-metre-high moulded ceilings, patterned parquet flooring and a tiled fireplace that's a museum piece, but also a modern high-speed elevator.

He embraces us, and leads us along a broad corridor with immense Venetian windows — it's no longer a corridor but more like a conservatory, with palm trees, cacti and other plants that I don't know. Then for some reason we go down a short spiral oak staircase with brass trimmings and find ourselves in a huge hall with that famous fireplace and old furniture encrusted with mother-of-pearl.

Naturally, the table is already set. The beautiful wife — a charming creature, genuinely delighted to see guests — appears for a few minutes to ask whether we would like anything else, although the table is already crammed with plates of food. The son runs in for a moment to say goodnight, and he is easily recognisable as a future genius, or at the very least a state dignitary.

Lucky takes pleasure in displaying his family in this museum setting, but there's nothing ostentatious about it. Then he squeezes each of us in his vice-like embrace.

"You can't imagine how glad I am to see your ugly mugs! Do you know what I dream about?"

No, we don't.

He leads us over to the table, mixes up some complicated cocktail for each of us from several different bottles and starts telling us about his dream, which is also the first toast.

"I dream of building a house," he says, raising his glass, "and gathering us all together in it. So that we could all live together and eat breakfast at the same table in the morning. If only you knew how much I miss you!"

His sincerity is infectious. He really does love all of us and we love him too, he's the only one who in all the years we have known each other has never done a single thing that we could reproach him for. We haven't seen each other very often in the last few years, but whenever he has a chance, he is tireless in demonstrating his devotion to his old ties of friendship.

The walls are hung with a huge number of paintings, masks and other evidence of his nomadic life style: he has been travelling round the world for years. He is a United Nations adviser and a member of some intergovernmental commission or other.

He pays no attention to the tension between Eldar and me, although everybody knows about it. We are both dear to him, so he avoids delving into the details.

"The others will be here soon." He makes up a second cocktail for everyone.

And indeed, soon Rafik and Seidzade arrive, and even Alik,

whom, for various reasons, none of us see for years at a time. It's easy to see how our friends are doing simply from their appearance. Rafik has finally begun to prosper. Seidzade's life is hard — either he writes badly or he isn't understood, but in any case the imprint of the loser has already distorted his face. Alik is still working as a driver; the difference in ages that was once so glaringly obvious is starting to blur. He doesn't look much older than his nephew Lucky.

"Let me announce the plan…" The glass is back in Lucky's hand again — he seems to have become rather fond of alcohol. "We have a table booked at the Intourist hotel restaurant; they say there's a new band there that's worth listening to, then we can come back here, or — he lowers his voice — go to a certain place where they'll be glad to see us. And at the same time you can take a look at my daughter. You haven't seen her yet, have you?" It's true, none of us have seen his daughter by the singer. "Well then, is the plan approved?"

Everyone has already succumbed to the sheer pressure of his energy and charm, and of course they agree with any suggestions he has.

"Great, then let's not waste time. Drink up, and we'll be on our way. To you, my friends! I feel as if we had never been parted for a single minute!"

Everyone clinks glasses. Even Eldar and I do it. Here at Lucky's place my intense dislike for this lover-of-truth doesn't seem quite so strong.

*

I wake up in the same narrow pencil-box of a room, on the same chest. (Much as I dislike the idea of seeing my brother's face, there's no way I can avoid it, and I don't want to offend granny — she isn't to blame for anything.)

I can hear spoons tinkling in glasses again, and leisurely conversation.

"You've debauched me, you have…" — my brother's deep bass voice complains playfully — "… taken away my innocence, undermined my principles."

"I'm very glad," granny says brightly. "How long can you go on living on your own?"

"Eh, granny, granny, what was wrong with me on my own?"

"You'll drink less"

"You think so?" A sudden flash of hope lends his bass voice a hint of baritone. "And which room are you going to put us in?"

"Live where you like."

"Oh no, you decide."

"Well, why not this one?"

She evidently means the room where I'm sleeping, because my brother remembers about me.

"But our little relative has turned out to be a bit of a hell-raiser. The tricks he pulled yesterday! A real rowdy."

"And where's she from? Your girl?"

"Just happened to pick her up. Right, shall we get moving, old girl? We'll be just in time for when they open …"

"And we have to buy some pillowcases."

"We'll get everything that's needed… A new life — in a clean bed! Such is our motto from henceforth."

"But is she going with us?"

"No point in it."

"Well, what's her name, at least?"

"Victoria… Vicky… Tory — whichever way you like… A royal name." He pushes his chair back noisily and stamps past the door. I close my eyes, just to make sure I don't have to make conversation if he gets the idea of looking in through the door.

After they leave I get up and collect my things. My money's almost all gone, just enough left for a ticket. I feel my face and discover a strange topographical rearrangement — the depressions have risen and the elevations have sunk, levelling everything out. And everything hurts, even my eyes.

I pick up my suitcase. And although I know there's no one at *home, I tiptoe out of the room. Then I realise what I'm doing and start moving more confidently.*

I sit down at the table to write a goodbye note with an apology for leaving at such short notice. What reason can I invent? Nothing appropriate comes to mind, so I go to get washed. And then, outside the toilet beside the washbasin, I run into her. Her hair is woven into a plait and she is wearing my brother Gena's shoes on her bare feet.

Taken aback, I greet her as if we have been living in the same house for years, and go into the toilet, although I was on my way to get washed. I hang about in the toilet for a while, and then find her still in the same spot. I start getting washed. Then I surprise myself by breaking the silence.

"How did you end up here?" I ask and immediately understand how stupid the question is. "Have you known him for a long time?"

"No."

"Well, how long? A year, two, a week, a day?"

She says nothing, staring into empty space.

"What's wrong, can't you hear me?"

"I can hear you."

"Then why don't you answer? Did you just meet him yesterday, then?"

"Yes."

"And so you just went with him straight away?"

I don't expect an answer. The question is rhetorical, so to speak.

"And if I'd taken you, you'd have gone with me? What are you, some kind of object? Anyone who wants you just takes you?"

There are tears in her eyes.

"What are you crying for? I'm just telling you the truth. How did you get to know that fireman? Where did you meet? At a fire?"

"No."

"Where then?"

"At an artist's place ..."

"What artist?"

"Sergei."

"And how did you get to know him?"

"I was living there."

"How do you mean?"

"In the attic."

"Was he painting you, or what?"

"Sometimes he painted me."

"In the nude? And how did you end up with him? Haven't you got any parents?"

"No."

"What do you mean, no?"

"I'm from an orphanage. My parents were Hungarian."

"How do you know?"

"My granny told me?"

"What granny? Your genuine granny?"

"No… I was just living with her."

"And how does she know?"

"Someone told her."

"I see."

Although, of course, I don't see a thing.

Her face is suddenly transformed for an instant.

"Are you going away?"

"Yes. Why?"

The spark fades again and she subsides into silence, as if she has used up her entire vocabulary on the question.

"Why did you ask? All right, have it your own way! If you don't want to talk, then don't!"

I walk back into the room and sit down to write my note. Eventually I manage to squeeze out a few lines: "Dear granny, I have to go away urgently. Thank you for everything. I'm sorry I haven't said goodbye, but that's just the way things have worked out".

I realise that I ought to add a few warm words of gratitude, but thanks to my brother Gena, I find I can't.

I go out into the hallway with my suitcase. She's still standing there between the toilet and the washbasin. I take no notice of her. I put my coat on.

"Take me with you," I hear her say when I already have my hand on the door handle.

Well, how do you like that?! How simple everything really is — just take her and carry her away!

"Do you know where I'm going?"

"No."

"Then why do you want to go with me?"

She has to be able to give some explanation! I'm starting to get angry. There's something disgusting about this indiscriminate complacency.

"You mean you'll go anywhere, just as long as someone takes you with him?"

Two large tears rapidly well up in her eyes and roll down her cheeks.

"But you went with this Gena, even though you don't know him at all?"

"I can't stay there any longer."

I haven't thought about that.

"And if I don't take you with me, will you stay here? Don't you have anywhere to live?"

"No…"

"But why don't you work? Or study? You could live in a hostel."

"I was working."

"Where?"

"On a building site."

"Why did you leave?"

Anyone would think she was incapable of explaining a single thing she's done.

"Of course, being an artist's kept woman is a lot more convenient…"

"I got ill."

Two more tears well up.

"What was it?"

"I don't know. I kept feeling dizzy. Take me with you."

"What kind of nonsense is this? How can I take you? I live with

my mother. What can I tell her? Who are you? We only have one room… Do you still have dizzy spells?"

"No."

"Why don't you get a job? Doesn't it disgust you to live like this? You're beautiful but you sleep with anyone who comes along. Isn't there anyone you really like?"

Silence.

"I asked you a question. Is it all the same to you who you sleep with?"

Silence. And another two tears.

"All right. I'm going. Cheers."

The tears rolled down to her chin, dropped on to her dark wool blouse and disappeared. But they left two damp tracks on her cheeks.

Before I left my relatives' house for ever, I stroked her shoulder…

In the restaurant we are met by the head waiter, Yasha: a perfect parting in his hair, the bearing and manners of an English lord. He knows all of us and bows to Lucky.

"This way please. Always glad… Your table is waiting for you… This way…"

He seats us where we have a good view of the orchestra and the oval dance floor, but at the same time far enough away for the music not to interfere with conversation.

"Well, it is a perfectly decent band!" Lucky exclaims in surprise.

He carries on enjoying the music, and that is yet another proof of his faithfulness to old attachments and enthusiasms. All right, in that case, he'll like what we have to say.

"They have quite a good singer here."

He gives me a curious look.

"Do you come here?"

"Sometimes … I drop in with the lads — after work."

"So you haven't lost the taste for life, then?" He gives me an approving slap on the shoulder. "And what about women? You used to be a great expert."

Everybody waits eagerly for my answer. I'm the only bachelor there:

"I do all right …"

"No one had any doubts about that. But you're not planning on getting married?"

"Not just yet …"

She arrives a month after my mother's funeral, in the summer of nineteen sixty-three. The neighbour's boy, who has shown her to the door, doesn't go away — he's curious to see what's going to happen next.

I don't recognise her at first. Long hair hanging outside a light-coloured raincoat, eyeliner, high-heeled shoes. A brand-new suitcase in her hand.

The guys carry on sitting at the table. As I walk to the door I hear Eldar's voice: "Now who is it?"

The neighbour's boy winks at me. I give him a slap round the ear.

It's not just on the outside that she has changed. She holds out her hand to me in a truly regal gesture, stares me straight in the eye and declares in a loud voice, like a radio announcement:

"Hello!"

She has evidently been preparing for this meeting for a long time. I take the suitcase and put it by the wall beside the door. I can hear whispering and animated movement behind me. The lads know about her, because I've told them. I offer her a seat.

She trots out some kind of nonsense in that same radio-announcement voice.

"I've come from Krasnovodsk. Passing through. I've been escorting a delegation from a Hungarian trading house…"

I interrupt her:

"Let me introduce you. These are the lads. And this is Vika."

We sit down at the table. She casts a stealthy glance that everyone notices around my room, the room that is unfortunately now mine alone…

"Please accept my profound condolences," she declaims solemnly.

I thank her with a nod. I'm afraid of bursting into tears. Her appearance suddenly sharpens the sense of loss: it somehow seems very wrong that there is a woman here in this room so soon after my mother's death, and this woman came here precisely because mother has died...

"And what were you doing with this delegation?"

"Escorting them."

"Why, do you know Hungarian?"

"A little."

Everyone smiles. I find it necessary to intervene.

"Vika's parents were Hungarian."

"Ah, so that's it!"

Alik, of course, takes everything on trust; the other naïve member of our group, Rafik, isn't there — he's in Moscow, because the semester hasn't finished yet; but none of the others — Eldar, Seidzade and Lucky — believe in her Hungarian origins.

"Right, what were we talking about?" Eldar asks, making it clear that the guest has been paid enough attention and it's time to get back to serious men's talk.

Lucky carries on with his story about our adventures in Moscow, and the rest of us introduce corrections and amendments. The only listener is Alik.

"And then he..." — this story is about me — "... goes dashing over to her and at the very last moment, literally at exactly the same time as the other guy, he invites her... And this is the last dance... Get the picture?"

Alik nods impatiently. He's completely absorbed in the story. Anything to do with our action in the field is fascinating to him. Since we were kids he has been our mentor in such matters.

"...The girl doesn't know what to do. She looks at the other guy — they all know each other there — and she looks at Marat. And the other guy smiles confidently, really arrogant, 'Come on, Galka,' he says, 'how long are you going to keep me waiting?' And he grabs hold of her hand. But she..." — at this point Lucky laughs, and every one else does the same — "...jerks her hand away and goes with Marat. Can't you just see it? Well, then it really kicked off!"

"What did she die of?" Vika, still examining the room, asked in a low voice (at least she managed to get that bit right).

"Her lungs… But how did you know?"

"Granny told me."

"Are you still living there?"

"No… but I do go to see granny sometimes."

"…So, there are five of us," Lucky continues, "but there are about ten of them."

"More."

"Fifteen."

"At least twenty, for sure."

"Well then, this other guy says to him: 'Do you know what manners are?' and Marat says: 'I know all right, and if you did, you wouldn't go grabbing a girl's hand like that'. And he says: 'Maybe she's my sister…' — 'All right, cut the crap, what's your problem?' And it's pitch black, with bushes all around, the most remote alley in the place. And they've surrounded us on all sides. And then this guy laughs and says: "My, my, what a hot temper, you can see straight off that's he's from the south!' Then Marat …" — Lucky points to me again for greater emphasis — "…says to him: 'Listen, there aren't many of us, but bear in mind that we'll take five of you for every one of us and leave your wives widows'. The other guy laughed again, but you could see he believed it. He thinks about it, thinks again and then says: 'All right, go'. But Marat says to him: 'You go, we've still got business to finish here — he's hinting at the girl. The other guy turns white as chalk and can't say another word. Well, they left… And at the exit, I see some guys saying hello to the other guy. And they seem very polite, somehow. That makes me curious, so I ask: 'Hey guys, who was that?' and they say: 'He's a boxer, middleweight champion of Moscow. Loginov's his name'. Can you imagine?!"

"Well, so what?" says Alik, his pride offended for us. "You'd still have had them. You know Marat would have dealt with him!"

He looks at us hopefully, he really wants me to back up his point of view. I smile.

"But he's a boxer."

"You'd have gobbled him up, giblets and all."

I don't object.

"Will you be in these parts for long?" Lucky asks with emphatic politeness.

Which makes the reply sound particularly rude.

"None of your business."

Lucky looks around at us in puzzlement, as if asking why he is being insulted.

"Have I said something to offend you?" He enquires politely.

"It's not important." For some reason she's in an aggressive mood

"How do you mean, not important?" Lucky is calm, only the corners of his mouth are curled up in a slight grin, but he once threw his sister's fiancé off a first-floor balcony with an expression like that on his face. The fiancé had also taken the liberty of being impolite. "You're insulting me. Or did you have someone else in mind?" Still smiling, he looks round as if to check whether there is anyone else her words could have applied to. But there isn't anyone behind his back. So he waits for an explanation, which is not long in coming:

"No, it was meant for you."

"What for?"

"Nothing really. I just felt like it …"

Lucky looks at me as if he is inviting me to find a way out of this impossible situation.

"Stop it," I tell her strictly.

She's about to say something else, but when she hears my voice she obediently shuts up.

The first one to get up is Alik. Then all the others do the same. I see them out into the yard. They can barely contain their laughter, but they restrain themselves because of the neighbours.

"Why has she suddenly turned up?" Eldar asks.

"Damned if I know."

"And what are you going to do?"

"Tell her to go to hell." Alik says, taking his usual uncompromising approach in such matters.

"How can he throw her out at night?" Lucky protests nobly. That would be too awkward!"

"Never mind awkward! She's loopy. No doubt about it."

"Yes, she's a strange girl," Seidzade agrees, but I can tell that he's not condemning her out of hand like all the others.

"Do you want me to throw her out?" Alik suggests.

"No, that really would be awkward."

"Do you want her to stay with you?"

"No."

"Then we have to find her a place until tomorrow. And then she can clear off."

"But where can we put her?"

"Can't your aunt take her?"

Eldar has an aunt who lives alone in a two-room flat. He can't deny that, but he doesn't feel like taking some strange girl (it would be the same if she wasn't so strange) round there to spend the night.

"There's no other option," Lucky puts in before Eldar can say anything.

So now he can't object. He's always on the side of justice and truth, and there's no way he can use them as an excuse this time.

"We could try to get her into a hotel," Seidzade suggests.

"They won't take her without an official travel warrant."

"Go on, go on," Lucky urges me. "He agrees."

Eldar doesn't say anything, which means he doesn't really object. I go…

When the door opens, she jerks her head up in alarm. I move closer.

"It's already late," I say in a very gentle, concerned voice. "You need to get some sleep. And we can talk in the morning.

She doesn't say anything, just waits for me to go on. But I don't really have anything else to say.

I repeat:

"It's after eleven… Any later, and it will be too rude to wake the aunt up. She goes to bed early…"

"What aunt?"

"The woman you're going to stay with tonight."

"I'm not going to any woman's place."

"But why not?"

"I don't want to."

"Then what do you suggest? You have to understand that I can't keep you here."

"Why not?"

"In the first place, it's too awkward, with the neighbours. And, well, in the second place, there's no point anyway…"

She gets up and walks towards the suitcase.

"Where are you going?" I ask, stopping her in the very doorway. "Wait. What's wrong?"

The dark fury pulsing in her narrowed eyes stings me like an electric shock.

"I'm not going anywhere with anyone! That's not going to happen! Do you understand?"

So that's how she's taken the suggestion of spending the night somewhere else.

"What do you mean? Are you crazy? Don't talk nonsense. There'll be no one else there except you and this woman, just the two of you… What's wrong, don't you believe me?"

She peers into my face. Then she calms down a bit and her voice softens:

"I believe you."

"It really would be difficult, you know, with the neighbours…"

"I'll leave early, no one will see. I'll just sit here."

The eyes that were so furious only a moment ago are so full of entreaty now that I give way immediately.

I go back out into the yard.

I explain to the lads that I really have no choice but to let her stay. I can see from their faces how they take the news, each in his own way, but all of them are surprised.

"Just throw her out!" says Alik, clenching his teeth and glaring at me — demonstrating the way you have to talk to people like this.

At that moment his face is truly frightening. Enough to convince anyone.

They all leave, having decided that I must have changed my ideas. All of them, that is, except for Seidzade. He believed me, I can tell from the way he shakes my hand.

When I get back she has already changed into a housecoat.

"Do you have any tea?"

She's brisk and businesslike, as if she has done nothing else her whole life except make tea for me.

There's almost no tea left, just a few leaves at the very bottom of the packet, but that doesn't put her off. For some reason she's very cheerful. She hums a little tune to herself.

"I've completely changed now," she assures me over tea.

"So I see."

"No, really. Do you know why?"

"No."

"Because of you. Yes, yes... I've changed completely. Don't you believe me?"

I shrug.

"I used to do what everybody told me."

"And now?"

"Now only what you say."

"Me?"

"Yes..."

"Why's that?"

"Because I love you."

"She blushes, but she doesn't look away. Her expression was defiant: Do what you like with me, but I'll still say what I think anyway.

"And what made you decide that?"

"I think about you all the time."

"And why were you rude to my friend?"

"Who was that girl?"

"What girl?"

"The one you asked to dance. Was there something between you?"

"Well, what if there was…"

"That's why I was rude."

The mention of the girl from the park near Soviet Army club upsets her so badly again, that she's on the point of breaking into tears.

"What's wrong, are you jealous? That was before I met you… And anyway, you don't have any cause. It's ridiculous…

She interrupts me: I get the feeling that she hasn't even heard what I said. The important thing for her now is to say what's on her mind. The words sound like an oath, her voice is a clear as a bell.

"No one is ever going to touch me again. Never… For the rest of my life."

I grin. I just can't believe that. But I'm curious about why she's made a decision like that.

"You don't believe me? I swear! Only you!"

"What do you mean, only me?"

"Only you can do whatever you like with me. Even kill me."

She really is a bit crazy. Or maybe more than a bit, totally and completely crazy.

"Really, it's true, do you want to kill me?"

"What sort of drivel is this you're talking? Why would I want to kill you?"

Then comes something I'm absolutely unprepared for. She bursts into tears, with loud sobs that seem to erupt from somewhere deep inside her, and she comes dashing towards me:

"I don't want to live. Kill me, kill me… I'm a wretched filthy creature…"

She keeps trying to go down on her knees. When I try to stop her, I can feel her shaking all over, as if she has a fever.

"Come on, calm down. That's enough. Stop it, I tell you."

But she still manages to get down to my feet and thrust her face against them. I lean down and stroke her hair.

"I'll go away, I will. I'll stay here for two days and then go away. Honestly."

"All right, all right, just don't cry …"

She keeps pressing herself harder against my legs and weeping *floods of bitter tears that soak through the cloth of my trousers and reach my skin.*

That night she doesn't sleep a single minute. Through my sleep I can feel her gently stroking me and kissing me, and whispering something that I can barely hear, as if she is praying: "Dearest, dearest, my handsome, strong love… My sweet hands … Sweet neck… Sweet eye …"

The only person who ever caressed me like that, with such tender devotion, was my mother, when I very little. My poor mother…

At dawn, just before daybreak, I notice her start behaving strangely — she shrinks away from me and huddles in the corner. Her face is frozen in a mask of fear, as if someone is pointing a pistol at her.

"What's wrong?"

"Do you hear it?"

"What?"

"The cutting."

Yes, I can hear a whining, rasping sound.

"That's the quarry…"

"What?"

"The quarry. They're cutting stone for building."

"Is it far away?"

"Yes… don't take any notice."

But she can't settle down for a long time.

It bothers me badly for a while too — it makes a vile sound when metal bites into stone. A sickening squealing, with absolutely no respite. Like throats being cut one after another…

*

"Look at the way she's looking at you!" Seidzade says with a smile. It's his first smile of the evening (literary workers are slow to recover from the troubles of the day).

"Who?"

"That enchanting creature … over there by the doors."

I glance round, but I'm too late to see the face of the girl walking out of the door in the company of two young guys.

"And she waved to you as well! You're still as much of a hit with the women!" he exclaims in frank surprise.

"Yes," I say. "So what?"

He registers the slight note of defiance in my voice and puts his arm round my shoulders — assuring me that he didn't mean anything bad by it.

"Are you simply surprised that women can like a man without higher education?"

"Don't talk nonsense... I'm amazed that women can still like us at all. Especially ones as young as that."

He pulls me against himself.

"You've had a bit too much."

"Just a little bit."

"A little bit more than just a little bit, you're starting to get stroppy. I know you. What's that you call it?"

"A heightened sense of justice."

"You're in great shape, Marat." He looks me over approvingly. "Pumping iron?"

"You bet I am."

"Good for you... I'm a disgusting sight when I get undressed — like a sack of shit."

"But there's gold in here," I say, knocking on his forehead. "Why don't you give me something of yours to read?"

"You wouldn't like it.

"Why not?"

"You're a traditionalist."

"If someone loves Dumas, does that make him a traditionalist?"

"If Dumas is all he loves, then yes."

"Well, what's to be done about it? Write better, and then we'll love you too!"

Eventually the waiter brings some kind of huge package — Lucky's order. We take it and walk down to the cloakroom on the ground floor. The others are already down there. Warming the motor and grabbing a breath of air.

With his usual forethought, Lucky has parked the car on the other side of the street, in order not to attract the attention of the state automobile inspection service.

Seidzade keeps his arms round me. The package is heavy. I wonder what Lucky has bought so much of. We reach the central line of the street. A car appears from the right and comes hurtling straight at us.

"What's he doing?" Seidzade whispers in panic and pushes me back, while he stays where he is. I try not to drop the bundle and it's only when the car comes to a halt just a few centimetres away from us that I finally realise I'm drunk. I'm more interested in the bundle that I almost dropped than the car with its bumper right up against our legs. The sight of the gleaming metal that has somehow miraculously failed to cripple us is the only thing that brings home to me what has just happened. At that very moment the car — a yellow Zhiguli — reverses with a squeal of brakes and goes rushing past us.

I catch a glimpse of the long-haired driver's face in the window. He seems vaguely familiar.

"That's her," says Seidzade.

"Who?"

"On the back seat. The girl who was looking at you."

Now I understand which girl it was who was looking at me in the restaurant!

Alik comes running up, holding a crowbar. He shouts something insulting after the yellow car.

"It's a joke," I say to calm him down. "They were just joking…"

"You know them?"

"Yes, I know them."

He looks at me doubtfully.

She certainly does have strange friends. Where have I seen that yellow car before? The intense effort sets my temples throbbing, but I carry on rifling through my memory... Yes, of course, it was on the day we met.

Down on the bottom of the quarry they were crowded round some instrument or other on a tripod — from a distance it looked like a still camera or a movie camera, and the yellow Zhiguli was standing right at the edge, as if it was keeping them under observation from up there.

It wasn't the first group of students to make a geodesic survey of the quarry, and there was nothing strange about her coming into the yard and asking for something to drink: it was so hot that the tar on the roof was melting and dripping off.

After emptying the mug with slow, deliberate sips, she confirmed that they were doing their geodesic practice, and then left. No more than a few words were spoken, but I was left with a feeling of more to come. There had been some kind of promise in her calm, attentive gaze and slow, leisurely movements. The sense of anticipation remained with me all those days when they were doing their practical work; and it was still there when the students gathered up their instruments and left the quarry.

Her second appearance on the final day, on the pretext of saying goodbye, and my invitation to visit next Sunday or Tuesday, whichever was best, an invitation made spontaneously, without any premeditation (such haste was explained in part by the fact that her friends were waiting for her at the gate), aroused a strange feeling in me — some weary hope trembled and stirred, as it can in a game of cards when, after a long period of bad luck you're suddenly dealt a major card, but although you're delighted, you realise that this very card could mean that you will lose once and for all.

The yellow Zhiguli confirmed the apprehension I felt at the first clash with the long-haired trio — one of those youths with moustaches had claims on her, serious claims. They were pushing too hard altogether.

Lucky is on top form, he's always at his best when he meets us. It's impossible to stop him. He carries a little girl grimacing against the light in from the other room and lifts her above his head to show her off to us.

"Have you ever seen anything like that? Isn't she beautiful!"

He kisses her gently and hands her to her mother, who watches all this with a tender smile. I can tell that every time Lucky appears in this house is a celebration. Here he is loved and indulged.

When she comes back out of the bedroom, our hostess asks us the same question that Lucky's wife did three hours earlier — would the guests like anything else that isn't already on the table? She has Czech beer and prawns for instance.

We exclaim aloud in delight.

Lucky has already filled the glasses. He puts his arm round our hostess's shoulders and proposes a toast to her. (I remember having seen her a few times on television when she won an international competition of some sort; despite being famous, she gives the impression of being a likeable and modest person.)

"I'm very glad that you're here, lads," Lucky says, and she listens reverently to every word he says. "We really had to come here today. Here in this house I am genuinely happy. I want you to know that. And let's drink to the person who gives me that happiness."

He kisses her on the forehead before clinking glasses with us. And I swear that I have never in my life seen a happier face than hers at that moment …

*

My neighbour seems to be deliberately waiting for me at the gate. For appearances' sake he's messing about with his pigeons, but the moment he sees me, he leaves them alone.

He says hello. Asks how are things going, how's the job? Then, with an apology, he moves on to the real topic of conversation. Asks me not to take this amiss. Cautions me that he's speaking on behalf of all the neighbours, who love me like a son.

The moment he stopped me, I already knew what the conversation would be about. But I can't tell him to go to hell: he's sincerely concerned about my behaviour. I used to sit on his knees when I was child and just at the moment he's absolutely sober, although he's fond of taking a drop.

And I don't feel like playing the fool, either. Of course, I could act as if I don't know what he's talking about. But I won't be able to keep it up for long.

"Of course, friends and acquaintances come in all shapes and sizes," he continues, "but she really isn't the kind of bride your late mother used to dream about for you."

I reassure him as best as I can that Vika is not my bride, just someone I happen to know, she'll stay for a few days and then go away…

"Be careful — she'll drag it out… You'll get used to her, and then it'll be too late. I know how it is — I came unstuck like that myself once…"

The whole yard knows how he came unstuck. And that's precisely why he shouldn't be trying to teach me how to behave: nobody could ever possibly get used to his wife. Twenty years they've been living together, and all that time she's been telling the neighbours that he poisons her at night with some kind of gas. Well, what can I tell him? I gave him a vague sort of answer, indicating that I've taken note of his cautions, and go home…

Vika serves supper and sits down facing me, propping her chin on her hands (her fingers are short and stubby, and the nails are bitten down) and then she watches me eat with genuine devotion in her eyes.

I tell her that after training I have to meet the lads. Her face is instantly transformed — now it is full of hostility. I start making excuses: I can't keep on offending them like this, we haven't seen each other at all lately, I never leave the house; and after all, it's her own fault — she fouled things up with them… And in general, everything's a lot more complicated than she thinks.

She listens intently to every word with her eyes fixed on me, waiting for what will come next.

"You know, I'm glad that you came. But I have interests of my own, my work, my friends…"

"What friends?"

Everything else has been ignored, this is the only word in which she has sensed danger, the only one she's interested in.

"All sorts…"the reaction is instantaneous:

"Have you got a girlfriend?"

Well, what can I tell her? I'm not really all that keen on the girl, but she does exist. And she's very keen to see me.

"Of course I do," I say, as if I'm talking about something absolutely unimportant. "I see her sometimes."

"Have you been together long?"

"I don't remember exactly… About six months, I suppose."

"Is she beautiful?"

"Not bad."

"Have you got a photograph?"

"I had one somewhere… A group photo. We saw in the New Year together."

"Show me."

I go and get the photograph.

"This one?" Staring at the people sitting round the festive New Year table she spots her rival immediately.

"Yes."

"She's beautiful,but stupid." She tosses the photo aside in disgust and turns away from me, offended.

I take the rapier out from behind the cupboard and sling my bag across my shoulder.

What words of comfort can I offer her? I can't think of anything, and I suggest that she could read to pass the time whilst I'm gone.

I pull a pile of slim books about film stars out of the cupboard: Mozzhukhin, Pat and Patashon, Nata Vachnadze, Douglas Fairbanks… My mother's favourites.

It's even harder to explain to the other girl.

She meets me after training as usual. A pale, confident face, with slightly raised cheekbones. You couldn't exactly call her brainy, but she is beautiful.

"Where did you get to?"

"Didn't the lads tell you? We had a lot of work on…"

She carries on standing there at the entrance to the "Storm Bird" club.

"Where shall we go?"

"I don't know." Somehow I don't feel like going anywhere with her…

"What's wrong?"

"Nothing, I'm a bit tired."

She's wearing an odd, straight dress with no waist and ruffles on the hem. It makes her look pregnant. It's new fashion, I suppose.

"What are you looking at?"

"The dress?"

"Ah–ah …" She smiles. "Do you like it?"

"Not much. Listen, let's get together in a few days. I'm not feeling too great."

She's surprised and offended, but she doesn't doubt me in the least — she really is very beautiful, and we have an unclouded history of six months together. I do fancy her and I hope that in a few days everything between us will be fine again.

"I'll explain everything to you then. All right?"

She agrees: what else can the poor girl do?"

I see her to the stop and put her on the trolleybus. After I wave goodbye, I see Vika standing just half a metre away from me — with a triumphant, accusatory expression, a bitter smile, on her face. The betrayed Motherland in the person of a border guard who has caught a villainous defector on the state boundary would be less outraged than she is now. I try to smile.

"What are you doing here?"

"I saw everything."

She swings round rapidly and walks away. I catch up with her.

"What did you see?"

"The way you looked at her."

"What way?"

"Like someone in love."

"Nonsense. Have you been following me?"

Then the sobbing starts.

"I'm going to die, I'm going to die…"

Passers-by turn to look at us. I'm so furious at her unfair reproaches that I start to shout, and immediately there are ten times more of them.

"Shut up! You're hysterical! Stop it immediately!"

I walk away, pushing aside some over-curious man in a hat. After I've gone a few steps, I hear the clatter of footsteps behind me. When she reaches me, she hangs on my arm. Her eyes are full of submissive entreaty…

Alik's truck is rushing us along to the beach. The wind blows in our faces, drowning out our words, the truck jolts over the uneven asphalt surface and we can hardly stay on our feet. We have to shout in order to hear each other.

"Who will you bring?" Lucky sways as the truck jerks, and his lips touch my ear.

"I don't know…

I turn towards Eldar.

"What if I bring her, Vika?"

"Bring anyone you like."

The lads exchange glances. It will be the first time the two of us have been out together.

When I get back from the beach I find her reading. She's already read everything about the film stars. Now she's working her way through The Count of Monte Cristo. *I tell her about Eldar's birthday. She doesn't take her eyes off the book.*

"I won't go." The reply is categorical.

I sit down beside her and put my arm round her shoulders.

After a long pause, she says:

"I haven't got anything to wear."

She really doesn't have anything apart from the skirt and blouse that she wears all the time.

"No problem. We'll think of something."

"Better take that beauty of yours instead. She'll be more suitable." *Her tone of voice is caustic and bantering, but she can't conceal the hurt in it.*

I kiss her several times on her ear, her nose, her eyes …

"There is no more beauty, I promise you."

"They'll laugh at me."

"Who?"

"Your… Lucky and the others."

"Never… But you're right about the outfit. We'll have to think of something."

"And who are his parents, this friend of yours?"

"His father's the rector of a big college."

"Rector — is that like the director?"

"Yes. They used to live here, in this room. And we were on the first floor. Then we swapped: they went up there, and we came down here."

"And where do they live now?"

"Right in the centre, in the House of Scholars with the fountain in front, where the 'Artistic' cinema is. Remember? We've been there."

She goes over to her suitcase and rummages in it. From somewhere its darkest depths, almost under the lining, she extracts a thirty-rouble note.

"Do you have a thrift shop here?"

"Of course we do. Do you want to buy something?"

"A dress. Will you help?"

Of course.

She beams and gives me a grateful kiss.

Apart from us, there are several of Eldar's relatives, also young people, at the table. Seidzade and I have identical cheap jackets of yellowish speckled ratine wool, and this is glaringly obvious against the background of smart dark suits.

Vika's wearing a blue knitted dress, bought for eighty roubles in the thrift shop. Her manner is quite self-assured. She manages her knife and fork adroitly. Occasionally she asks in a whisper for something to be added to her plate. The whisper is so quiet that I can't catch it straight away. But that's not because she is feeling shy, it's to emphasise our togetherness.

When the dancing starts, one of the relatives immediately invites her. I dance with a neighbour who lives on the floor below. She's already slightly drunk, and her powdered face is as white the wall.

"A new love?"

I reply with an ambiguous smile.

"From out of town?"

"Yes."

"So the local personnel aren't good enough any more?"

I laugh and suggest a drink (to avoid having to dance). We go to the table.

Vika is dancing rather strangely, wiggling her hips.

"You know, she's not bad at all," Lucky says in surprise.

I take the opportunity to ask him to make up with her.

"I should," he agrees. "We never see you anymore."

Eldar listens to the conversation with great interest.

"She isn't going away then?"

"Not just yet…"

Eldar straightens his tightly knotted tie.

"What if she doesn't go away at all?"

It's the first question he's asked about Vika, he hasn't joined in the conversation about her before.

"What do you mean, of course she will!" I say, completely rejecting the possibility. It's absurd. The idea could never even enter my head.

"Maybe she just won't go," Eldar carries on pressing me. "You said yourself that she wouldn't be staying for more than two or three days."

"Yes."

"And how long is it now?"

"A month… A bit longer. I couldn't just throw her out."

"But you will be able to later?

"She'll go away herself."

"Do you want her to go away?"

The question is unexpected. Do I want that? Not very long ago I wanted it very much.

"It's all the same to me."

The conversation breaks off, but I can tell that Eldar still has something to say...

After we get back home that night and are getting undressed, she shares her impressions with me:

"Why have they got so much of everything?"

"So much of what?"

"Crystal, china, pictures, furniture... And such a big flat."

"How should I know? His father's had a good job all his life, with good pay, gifts... Why are you suddenly so interested in that?"

"It's interesting; I've never seen anything like that before."

I turn out the light.

*

By three o'clock the prawns have all been eaten and the beer drunk. It's time to be going home. But Lucky's grip on us is like a stranglehold. He seems completely sober, just more talkative than usual, and he rejects any attempt to get up from the table.

"I know you..." The long curly hairy shot through with grey makes him look like a gypsy. "You'll go crawling off into your corners. Then just try to get you all together again!"

"No at all," Seidzade tries to reassure him, "tomorrow, the day after, whenever you say, we'll set a time and get together."

"No tomorrows. We have to greet the dawn together ..."

"But we're causing a nuisance. Making noise. Stopping people from sleeping."

"They're delighted that we're here! How about you?" he asks, turning to me for support. "Are you tired?"

I'm not tired. I'm very content here with the lads, but for decency's sake I also say that I don't want to abuse our hostess's hospitality.

"Stop jabbering such nonsense!" he says, genuinely angry. "Who is it a nuisance for? I told you: they'd be delighted if we sat here for the rest of our lives." He glances round at our sleepy faces — Alik has already closed his eyes and is snuffling hesitantly. "All right, if that's the way it is, let's go and eat some hash. You need livening up a bit."

"Where are you going to find it at this time of night?" Alik asks keenly, without even opening his eyes.

"Where there's a will... We'll find it. Well then, are we off?"

We tumble out into the street, stop a battered old bus and ride it up the hill, to the park where Lucky assures us that the hash is being cooked for us.

Eldar is sitting directly behind me. He hasn't said a word to me all evening. But I know him — he's just lulling me into a false sense of security. Sooner or later he'll launch another assault, using his most just and cogent arguments

*

It's obvious straight away that he's come on important and urgent business. It's always that way with Eldar. Nothing but emergencies! A total mobilisation of all forces! Absolute commitment! And always in the name of some very just cause. In the name of the truth!

He's flexing his jaw muscles. His collar is turned up, his voice is low and hollow, the unfiltered cigarette is tossed aside like a revolver that has been discharged and is useless now.

"I need to talk!"

It's spitting with rain. The appearance of the sky suggests that it is bound to get worse. There's no shelter anywhere nearby. We could go into the office, the working day's over. But there are still people there, and that probably won't suit him.

I point up at the sky:

"What are we going to do?"

He doesn't hear my question.

"Was it true what you said yesterday?"

"What did I say yesterday?"

"You know, about Vika."

Oho! How naturally he pronounces that name! As if he's been talking about her all his life.

"And what exactly are you interested in?"

He drops back a step and declares solemnly, like a judge who has just learned of the sudden emergence of facts that demonstrate the criminal's guilt beyond all doubt:

"You said that it's all the same to you if she goes away or not, didn't you?"

"Well, maybe so," I agree. "But what are you so worked up about?"

"It's not all the same to me."

"What's not all the same?" I still don't get what he's driving at.

"If Vika goes away or not."

"You want her to go away?"

"No, I want her to stay."

"What for?"

"I'm going to marry her!" he informs me as proudly as if he's joining the Resistance on the eve of some terrible threat to the Motherland. "You don't love her," he continues. "You said so yourself. And sooner or later you'll dump her anyway. But she deserves to be treated better than that."

"When did you realise that?"

"It doesn't matter. You'll never marry her, will you? She'll be better off with me. You must agree…"

Anyone would think he was trying to persuade me to give him a piece of property for safekeeping.

"Why are you asking me to agree? Maybe we should ask her?"

He gets a bit embarrassed then, and squints sideways at a piece of rusty piping. He seems to find it very interesting.

"I have asked," he admits after his detailed examination of the pipe. "She agreed."

"What? You've already spoken to her?"

He raises his honest eyes to look at me and withstands my gaze as a matter of principle.

"Yes. I told her I want to marry her, and she agreed." It all sounds quite incredible, like some stupid kind of joke — the idea of him suddenly deciding to get married, and her accepting his proposal. But anyway, I ask:

"In that case, what has it got to do with me? Get married, if you've already agreed to."

"But you're my friend!"

This is getting ludicrous.

"Then why did you talk to her about it, if I'm your friend?"

"For her sake. She'll be better off with me. You can't deny that! I'll do everything for her!"

"I have to talk to her."

"No!" he exclaims, with a decisive gesture of his hand.

"What do you mean, no?"

"Please, don't torment her."

I walk round him and set off home.

But he finds a way to stop me.

"She doesn't want to talk to you!" he shouts after me, and I slow down. "She said so." I can sense that he's telling the truth. "Honestly. That's why I came, she's afraid."

"Afraid of what?"

"Of you…" He frowns reproachfully. "And I'm against it too. She needs to rest now."

"Is she at home?"

"No," he says, putting in the full stop. "She's at our place. I've explained everything to my mother…"

Everything in the room has been tidied away. The Count of Monte Cristo *has been put back in its place on the bookshelf, beside* The Three Musketeers. *There's a piece of paper sticking out from under the ashtray on the table. But it's not a note, it's the receipt from the thrift shop, for the eighty roubles paid for the dress. Why hasn't she just thrown it away, instead of folding it carefully and leaving it in an obvious spot?*

The receipt is lying on the same table where my mother's coffin stood two months earlier. And the grief I feel as I look at it is as sharp and bitter as on the day of the funeral.

*

Lucky leads us through the alleys of the park to a huge glass-walled beer pavilion.

Gazing in through the glass walls, as if it were an aquarium, we can see the entire interior space, crowded with tables and chairs that have been set upside down on them. On one of the tables there's a pot, with a man dozing on a chair beside it.

"He's a friend of mine," Lucky warns us. "No money, or you'll offend the man."

The door swings open. A very old, very polite man shows us to the centre of the hall and seats us at a table, apologising for the fact that we will have to wait about half an hour as the hash is not quite ready yet.

I glance into the pot. The hash looks ready to me, but the old man obviously wants the meat to separate completely from the bones. Beside the pot there's a pile of soup plates and some spoons wrapped in a newspaper. A half-kilogram tin wrapped in gauze contains vinegar with grated garlic. Everything has been brought from home, just as the pot has. The old man looks like the night watchman: he has a metal whistle on a chain dangling from the button of his fur waistcoat.

The thick, transparent liquid with its amber-yellow surface film glugs calmly and regularly. The smell of the steam swirling above the boiling hot upper layer discourages sleep very effectively.

"Is the hash good?" Eldar doesn't even try to hide the fact that the hash is only interesting to him as a pretext. "We haven't had a proper talk yet."

"About what?"

He doesn't notice my frankly derisive tone. Or he pretends not to.

"Tell me honestly, is it that you don't believe in my idea? Or…" — he pauses suggestively — "…do you simply not want to help me?"

How can you ever explain even a part of what you're feeling? I don't even attempt to do it. Of, course, I'm not being entirely fair now, he's not the kind of man to be trying so hard simply for the sake of his dissertation. But he'll get it approved eventually anyway. And so I talk to him about that, in order to get him off my back.

He looks at me with a sad, thoughtful expression.

"You've changed a lot."

"But you haven't. Only please, don't try to explain to me that it's better to produce more oil than less. I know that without you."

"Then what's the problem?"

He's desperate for an explanation, he's demanding one. And he's convinced that he's in the right. In every single instance he is always right, and he always appeals to the most exalted feelings.

"If the experiment is successful, then across the country as a whole we'll be able to extract thousands more tonnes of oil…"

What a bastard a man must be when he refuses to do everything he can to help a project which — according to him — is of such great importance for the people and the country!

"…It's been proved theoretically — the effect is produced by the non-linear form of the stratum. But practical confirmation is still required …"

"And for that there has to be a small sacrifice. The annual bonus for twenty employees. A mere trifle, isn't it?"

"I didn't say that…"

"But that's what you mean. Why shouldn't you sacrifice something yourself."

"If it depended on me, I'd make the sacrifice."

"Strange but the way it always happens is when you have an idea, someone else makes the sacrifices."

"Give me one example…"

He can't remember anything himself: I see how hard he's struggling, wrinkling up his forehead, but nothing, literally nothing with which he could reproach himself surfaces out of the depths of his memory.

"If you mean that business …"

Aha, so we do remember a few things… But I particularly don't want to talk about that. And I can't really be bothered trying to convince him of anything: I'd have to shovel my way through too much garbage. And there's no point anyway. There's no way he can be changed.

Now there'll be more arguments, each one more convincing than the last, jab after jab, only the flesh these needles are being thrust into has already lost all feeling. And in the final analysis, a man has the right, at least once in his life, to act in the way that suits him, and not someone else, or others, even if they are right a thousand times over! He can get so tired that it justifies his not responding just once to an appeal for sacrifice in the name of the common good.

I leave him by the pot with the boiling hash (he can't stand it and has never eaten it) and go over to the lads.

Alik is asleep, Seidzade is enveloped in mournful reverie. Lucky and the old man are reminiscing about some wild boar hunt they went on together a long time ago. They have known each other for years and years. Strange that he didn't tell the lads anything about his big thesis idea. He doesn't usually miss a chance to get public opinion on his own side. He must have felt that this time support wouldn't be forthcoming.

Wouldn't they be surprised at my behaviour — they wouldn't believe their ears! Well, never mind, sooner or later it was bound to happen. As it turns out that each of us is living his own life, it's only fair for the same rights to be extended to everyone.

I get home after six in the morning. It's completely light already. The quarry is working away with a vengeance — dump trucks loaded with stone drive off one after another. Judging from the chorus of howling, all three stonecutting machines are at work.

This time Titch has driven his car right up to the gate. The windscreen has already been replaced, the business with the bonuses has been settled, so what's brought him here so early?

He jumps out of the car — he looks very agitated again. I walk over and ask him why he isn't getting some rest before the night shift.

"Is it true?"

"What?"

"They say that guy — the one who wrote the thesis — is a friend of yours …"

"Well, so what?"

He looks away.

"And his father's some big wheel."

"Well."

"The lads are saying they can pressure you. They'll come at you from all sides — and that'll be it!"

He follows me into the yard, but stays beside the gate. As he talks, he watches the car out of the corner of his eye. The mysterious attack on his vehicle has finally undermined his faith in people: up to his ears in debt, he's spent so much time pulling the wool over the eyes of his numerous relatives and friends that there aren't many people he still trusts.

I barely manage to control a sudden feeling of irritation. I don't understand the reason for it, but I'm certain it's not just because of Titch.

"Some sort of experiment, isn't it?" he asks, still squinting sideways at the car.

"Yes."

"Some sort of stupid nonsense?"

"No."

My tone of voice starts to worry him so much that he forgets about the car.

"So what's it all about?"

"A way of extracting more oil for the same cost."

His face, which is far from handsome anyway, crumples into a grimace of misery.

"Then why are they cutting our output? That's the wrong way round — that's less, not more."

I want to sleep very badly, I can't keep my eyes open, but something makes me carry on with this basically pointless conversation — I know there isn't going to be any experiment.

"Less in our sector, but more in the others. And more in the field overall."

He is genuinely offended.

"Why more for everyone else, and less for us? Some method that is! So we go broke, and everyone else is just fine?"

"Yes, that's the way it looks."

"But why us?"

"And why anybody else?" I enquire dispassionately, and he is finally convinced that we won't get the bonus that he has been counting on so much. And straightaway he starts the usual claptrap.

"So where's the guarantee that this experiment is going to work?"

"There isn't any guarantee."

I can't understand the reason for the constantly increasing irritation that I feel. Titch senses it: he stops arguing, glances to one side and mutters something in an uncertain voice.

"What?"

"I said, so there's no guarantee, but we have to go broke," he complains to someone invisible.

And at that point for some reason I explode:

"You're not going to go broke! You're not! You'd let all the others go to hell. Just as long as we're all right. You can ride around in your car without bothering about a thing. You'll get your bonus. Don't worry about it."

He drives away, pretending to feel reassured.

I stretch out on the divan without getting undressed. The cushion under my head was embroidered by my mother. Cross-stitching was her final hobby.

*

It had to happen sooner or later. I'd say it wasn't exactly a chance encounter, quite the opposite (although for a long time I wouldn't admit it to myself) — if I spent all my free time strolling around near Eldar's house, I was simply bound to run into her.

To judge from the little briefcase in her hand and the stern, businesslike expression on her face, Vika was already studying somewhere.

"Well, how's life?" I ask in a perfectly friendly fashion, emphasising that I have no grudges or old scores to settle.

"Fine, thank you." her tone of voice is restrained and dignified.

"Why didn't you bother to say goodbye?"

I'm still speaking lightly and ironically: well, perhaps still just a little sadly, just the tiniest little bit, like some benevolent old teacher who has long ago grown accustomed to his pupils' pranks — he isn't even really upset when one of them copies during a test. Since she doesn't answer, I continue:

"After all, it wouldn't have taken much. Elementary politeness. Just a note: 'Goodbye, forgive me, I love someone else.' That's all. There wouldn't have been any sobbing and hysterics, I assure you. Or violence."

"I know…"

"Well, then. And why did you have to say you were afraid of me?"

"Who did I say that to?"

"You know who."

A short pause:

"I wasn't afraid of anything. I didn't want to see you."

"Why?"

"I don't know."

"But maybe you could explain the way you behaved?"

"What for?"

"What for?" Even an experienced old teacher can lose his bearings in a situation when the experience accumulated over the years is no longer any use.

"We had a relationship, after all…"

"We didn't have anything." Her tone is openly hostile.

"What do you mean? Remember the things you said to me!"

"I never said anything." She looks away.

"You!" Teachers are not supposed to lay a hand on their pupils, even if they really want to. "Do you have any conscience at all?"

"No."

"Why are you talking to me like that?"

"Like what?"

"Like that. As if I'm your enemy."

"I have to go." She steps to one side.

"Wait." Sometimes a teacher is obliged to set his dignity aside and resort to pleading.

"I'm late."

"We need to talk!"

"What for?"

"So you don't think we have anything to talk about?"

"No."

"Okay, if that's the way it is, then go."

When a pupil's behaviour, which at first seemed seriously wrong, but not deliberate, turns out to be base villainy, the teacher has no choice but to part company with him, or her. Reconciliation might still be possible, for the benevolence of the teacher's heart knows no bounds… But if the pupil walks away without looking round even once — then a complete break is inevitable. It's the only thing left to do …

But even so I run after her and catch up with her.

"*What a viper you are, after all! So you were lying to me all the time!*"

"*Yes!*"

"*Why?*"

"*I just felt like it…*"

"*Are you saying all these things to me on purpose?*"

"*Yes.*"

"*Don't you understand that you're humiliating me?*"

"*And when you humiliated me…*"

"*I humiliated you?*"

"*All the time!*"

"*Don't talk rubbish!*"

"*A fine, noble individual you are. Just waiting for me to go away.*"

"*That's not true. That was only at the beginning.*"

"*You kept me hidden away from everyone. You were ashamed. You were even ashamed in front of the neighbours. Not good enough for him, is she. Too ill-mannered, too coarse, she hasn't read much…*"

"*I never said that to you…*"

"*Do you think I didn't feel it? It was you who taught me, I wouldn't have noticed it before. You just pitied me, that's all, I could see. Just pitied me, like some beggar. I can't bear the sight of you. And leave me alone, do you hear? I hate you.*" She tries to leave again.

"*Vika, wait, please. That was only earlier… I really like you. Honestly, I can't stop thinking about you. I'm sorry if I offended you. But I didn't mean to. We ought to live together. I don't have anyone either. You told me you loved me.*"

"*I said all sorts of things…*"

The ungrateful pupil pushes aside the teacher's hand that attempts in vain to detain her and with a wave of her little briefcase, she walks off to her new Master.

She walks away, forgetting all the good things that were done for her and remembering only her grudges.

And what grudges they are! Is it really my fault that I know too much about her? And that it required time to shrug off that heavy burden? Time that I wasn't allowed…

*

A woman's voice shouts for help, drowning out the noise of the quarry. The voice sounds very familiar. And I also know the name of the person the voice is calling. I've heard it often enough .

"Marat! Marat!"

Where do I know that name from? And that voice, that voice, I used to hear it often, before, a long time ago… a very long time ago…

"Marat! Marat!"

I struggle painfully to remember. But I can't. The voice has come very close. The breath touches me, burns me…

I see a face above me. A clear forehead, a severe, smooth hairstyle, early wrinkles round the eyes and in the corners of the mouth. A sad smile, freckles, a lightly powdered nose, a single colourless hair on the chin.

"I'm sorry," The voice is low and throaty, it doesn't fit (even now, after all these years) with the childlike prettiness of the round face. "I knocked… But you didn't hear."

"I did hear. But I thought it was a dream, I was asleep."

"I realised you were. So you painted the town red?"

"Yes."

"Eldar's asleep too. Are you surprised?"

"What about?"

"That I've come."

"No."

"No? I am …"

Vika strides round the room. But not because she's nervous. Or if she is nervous, she's controlling herself magnificently. The most conspicuous thing about this woman is a certain calm, sad assurance.

"Did you ever think of me?"

"I thought of you… sometimes."

The man leaning against the back of the divan is calm too. Even indifferent. The sleepy dullness of his voice intensifies this impression. And he likes that. What has he got to feel nervous about, anyway? It was all a long time ago and it doesn't mean anything any more. Like an accidental glimpse of the marks in the third class at school — although once they used to make him very nervous.

"He told me everything." (How lovely this woman smells!) "I never thought you were so vindictive."

Her keen glance searches for some reaction. But there isn't one. Let's see what's coming next.

She sits down on the chair beside the divan.

"How are you getting on?" she asks, looking round the room.

"Okay, thanks. Everything's just fine."

"You look well. You've hardly changed at all." She casts another glance round the room. "Amazing! Exactly the same as it used to be... What about the quarry? Remember how frightened I was?"

"Yes?"

"Is it getting closer? It was a lot further away then."

"Yes."

"And what's going to happen?" her voice is full of sympathy.

"They're going to close it."

"Close it?"

"There's going to be a park here."

When I put on my shoes and get up, I run into a wise, all-understanding smile.

"Are you still angry with me?"

"No."

"My God, I loved you so much then!"

I walk out into the hallway and put the kettle on. I can't go back into the room — she's standing in the doorway.

"I loved you so much! But you didn't understand a thing. You were kind, noble, affectionate, but you didn't understand a thing."

Right, right. And what other twaddle have you got for me?

"What was I supposed to understand? Let me through."

She moves aside.

"You were very naïve." She follows me.

"But how?"

"No, really. You were clever. A lot cleverer than me. But there were some things you just didn't feel or understand."

"For instance?"

"I loved you so much!"

"Would you like tea?"

"Yes… But you didn't understand that my fate was being decided. You remember what I used to be like? I had to break free of all that somehow, no matter what. And he was the first man who'd ever wanted to marry me. I realised this was destiny, my chance to change my life!"

How well she has learned to express herself now! A real orator! As if she spent all those years doing nothing but preparing to turn up here one fine day and impress me with her eloquence. But I know the reason for this belated upsurge of feeling, this note of fervent sincerity in her voice. I just wonder how she's going to get down to business, how she's going to jump over the ditch that she dug without getting mud on her dress and the heels of her shoes. She's made a very elegant beginning, coming at it from a distance.

"Did you think what would happen to me if we broke up? Did you ever think about that?"

"And what if we hadn't broken up?"

"I couldn't risk it."

"That's the whole point. You prefer to play safe."

"I wanted to be a real person. Like everyone else. He promised me that."

"Well, have you become one now?"

The surge of inspiration that was buoying her up seems to be subsiding now. She lowers herself wearily on to the chair.

"You hate me."

"And just why should I love you?"

"Was I the reason you never married?"

"I don't know."

"How are all your beauties?"

"Thanks, I do all right."

"Are there many of them?"

"Enough."

"I have two children."

"I know."

"I graduated from college."

"I know that too."

"Will you help him?"

Here we go! Now it's started!

"No."

"No?" She walks up to me. "Do you really want to take such petty revenge on me?"

"It's not revenge. I simply can't help him."

"That's not true. Your director said that everything depends on you."

"He's lying. There are another twenty men working there apart from me."

"They take their orders from you."

"Yes."

"Then order them to do it."

"No one has any right to order them to do it. They can only be asked."

"Then ask them."

"So that your husband can have his doctorate as well as everything else?"

"As well as what else?" — her lips curl in a sneer accentuating the wrinkles — What has he got? You don't understand anything."

Yet again there's something I don't understand! What a family! They're the only ones who have everything clear, and the rest of us simply can't get by without their explanations.

"Do you think everything in our family is fine, everyone gets along just wonderfully? And all that's needed to complete our happiness is a doctorate?"

That's not exactly what I think. I know a few things about their life, but there is some truth in what she's saying, so I say nothing and wait for what's coming next.

"Unfortunately, that's not the way things are at all. He did everything he promised me, but it just didn't work out. We're simply strangers, with nothing in common." — she speaks about it as if it's some unfortunate circumstance of no great importance — "The children are bored stiff by him, he's always at odds with his father, he's lost contact with his friends — with a little help from me. And why did we come back here? He always dreamed of managing without his father's help. That was why we went away then. That was another of his obsessions — total independence … We spent the whole ten years wandering from place to place. At least he managed to complete his post-graduate work, but then it turned out that everything depends on this idiotic experiment. We had to make peace between him and his father. We let our principles go hang and came back, confessed that we were wrong. His father arranged things with the ministry, they sent him to your section and …"

"And they ran across me."

"They didn't run across you, he asked for you."

"Why?"

"We hoped that you'd help us."

"You were wrong."

She loses control, a multilayered defence cracks open and just for an instant I glimpse the naked fear deep inside her.

"Are you sure that his suggestion won't work?"

She waits for the answer with such frank anxiety that I start feeling like a doctor who has to tell a patient that his disease is incurable.

"No… but I'm not sure that it will, either."

"But there is some hope?"

"There's always hope."

"So you will help. I'm sure you will! You're not that kind of man …" She moves closer — so close that I can feel her breath.

"I behaved very badly then … But, believe it or not, you were the only one I loved. And whatever I was doing all these years, I always wondered what you would think about it, whether you would approve or not. Do you believe me?"

"No."

"Well, of course, it's convenient for you not to believe it now… and anyway …"

"Anyway what?"

"I suppose whatever I say now makes no difference. It's all ancient history, all forgotten, nobody cares any longer."

Now that all the levers have been pushed, the flames in the firebox are consuming the final grains of truth, and I am filled with the vapours of memory, she falls silent in the hope that the pressure will send me hurtling in the direction that she has indicated. I have to do this if I'm a real man and an honest citizen. This is what my former friend and my former love expect of me, and if their hopes are deceived they will feel very hurt.

"Everything you've said is lies!" I say calmly. "You don't really think you're to blame for anything. It's all forgotten ancient history for you too. And you only remembered about it because you need it *for some purpose of your own.*" The last phrase is pronounced with special emphasis.

It's clear now that the train has set off in the wrong direction. There's panic in the station.

"That's not true," she says, trying to conceal her alarm.

"Perhaps you still love me." I can't resist the temptation to squeeze the very last drop of deception out of the tube.

"Yes … I love you!"

"That's a lie too!"

"I've loved you all these years …"

"Liar."

"Every time I closed my eyes in loathing …" — the ultimate, most taboo weapons are being brought to bear now — "… the only thing that saved me was thinking about you …"

"That's a disgusting lie!"

She finally realises the real meaning of what she's saying. But strangely enough, that only makes her even more vehement. And there's no way to stop her.

"What I'm saying is disgusting, but it's true. You can't possibly imagine what it's like to be physically intimate with someone for ten years when you cringe at every word he says, every habit he has, every touch..."

I find this so impossible to imagine that I forget to accuse her of lying again.

She carries on, a little calmer now and backing her words up with a bitter smile:

"But it helps to keep the old feelings alive! All the things I felt for you weren't forgotten, they actually grew stronger, more intense, they obsessed me, tormented me, haunted me like ghosts. I couldn't leave him: I'd been through too much and it would have made it all meaningless, all those sacrifices... But I couldn't live like that any longer either. I was suffocating. Only you could help, like a breath of fresh air. Only you!"

I can't restrain myself any longer; in order to put an end to this intolerable torrent of lies, I say what I had decided ought to be left unsaid.

She is shaken by what she hears, but she still tries to wriggle out of it — like a petty thief, who denies the charges simply because he wasn't caught red-handed during the robbery.

"What could you know?"

"Everything."

"But how could you?!"

"Don't even bother trying to lie about it."

"You mean to say that you know everything... You know how I..." She searches feverishly for the words... You want specific facts?"

"I don't want anything."

"How could you know anything about me?" There's a pause intended to squeeze at least one word out of me, so that she can understand how much I really do know, but I say nothing. "But

I suppose… If that's the way it is, my behaviour…" — once again the right word fails to come to mind immediately — "…during all these years has been far from flawless."

I can't help grinning.

"Far from flawless?"

Vika's doubts are finally scattered. I definitely do know something about those years of her life when she needed me like "a breath of fresh air". When she realises that, she starts to cry.

"I'm telling the truth. I swear. I was waiting for you… And the way I lived… I had no choice… Otherwise they would have fired him… He could never get along with anyone, anywhere… We just wandered from one place to another.

"You mean there were several of them, those bosses?"

"Please, don't … Don't remind me about all that filth! But I love you. Whatever happened, you were still the only one I loved."

"Don't cry…"

"I had to do it… You don't know what a family's like… You have to live somehow, find a way out… For better or for worse, he's the father of my children … But he's absolutely helpless … You think that I've come here and I'm telling you all this to persuade you to help him. It's true, there's no point in denying it, but it's also true that I have loved you all this time. Otherwise it would mean there's never been anything real in my life! But that can't be true! Of course, I'm lying. I didn't remember you every night… Sometimes I didn't remember you for months at a time… And I didn't remember anything like that at all, I had so much to cope with: children, illnesses, moving house, money, examinations — there was no time for problems of the heart. But didn't I sometimes suddenly feel a pain for no obvious reason, completely out of the blue? Didn't I cry in the middle of the night? Or when we went out visiting. Didn't all that happen? Doesn't that mean that I still loved you?"

Sobbing and sniffing, wiping away her tears coloured with mascara, she waits for my answer; now I'm the one who has to reassure her that she carried on loving me, despite everything.

"Or did I? Was there really nothing? Did I just imagine it … I don't know … Perhaps … I'm totally confused. But there's one thing you're definitely right about: I came here and I'm saying all this in order to persuade you … There's certainly no doubt about that." Now her desperation and shame drive her to the opposite extreme. "I don't know if there was any love or not, or if love even exists, I don't know, I can't swear to it, I don't have any right. But it's a fact that it depends on you whether my children will have a hundred roubles more each month."

"And what about science, the oil industry, the country? He told me he was concerned about the interests of the state."

Before she can answer, there's a knock at the door. But I already know without her that in pushing through an experiment that his family needs so badly, Eldar is absolutely convinced of his own selflessness.

"It's him."

She must have recognised the knock. Perhaps she even knew that he was coming. For some reason she walks across to the door to open it herself. Now everything will finally be made clear …

He's so dumbfounded to see her that all my doubts instantly evaporate: of course, meeting here at my place is a surprise for both of them. He avoids looking at her and seems very tense. He only speaks to me:

"So, I asked my father … he made enquires at the municipal soviet. You need to get out of here as soon as possible. There isn't going to be any park here. This is reliable information. He looked at the development plans himself. So you should accept what they offer you. Later they'll move you further into the suburbs. He can have a word with the right people if necessary."

"Thank you," I say, making it clear that I'm not in need of protection.

"He suggested it himself. You know the way he feels about you."

"Yes, I know."

"Well then, that's all, really. I just dropped in to warn you."

"Thank you."

Now what's going to happen? How will they extricate themselves from this messy situation, if meeting at my place was a surprise for both of them?

"I thought you were here." As I expected, she's the one who starts first. "So I decided to call in."

Maybe she feels awkward lying in front of me, or maybe there's no need, but she's absolutely unconcerned about whether he'll believe her.

"I phoned and phoned, but you weren't there …"

"We almost arrived at the same time, I got here literally just a few minutes before you," she tosses out casually.

Even nursery school children make more of an effort when they try to deceive. But he's so glad to hear this that he has no desire to doubt anything. The few words she has spoken, supposedly in self-justification, have a positively intoxicating effect on him — he's so wildly happy that he can't help sharing the feelings that are simply bursting out of him.

"We usually let each other know…" he explains, to make sure that I understand his agitation at the very beginning, when he came in.

"All right then … It's time we were off," she interrupts him rather rudely. "I'll be going, then?" she says, practically asking my permission, and smiling guiltily as she does it, as if apologising for him and for herself and for everything that has happened.

Then she takes him by the arm.

We say goodbye...

But when he is already at the door, the need to tell me something important overpowers his habit of obeying her and he deftly twists his elbow free and dashes back to me. She stays by the door, biting her lower lip in annoyance.

"I'm sorry … I've been wanting to tell you for a long time… we're very grateful to you. You're still a bachelor, and you don't know what family life is like," he says in a strange, hasty kind of half-whisper, as if to let me know that, although he's expressing their joint opinion, he's afraid she might be embarrassed by my presence: it's one thing when the two of them discuss such intimate matters alone, but quite another when he tells a third party, basically an outsider, about them. "To be honest, we don't really approve of your lifestyle: it's time you dropped anchor, so to speak. But some day you'll get married and you'll realise how important it is to have, not just a wife, but a friend and companion, a soul-mate who supports you with her love and devotion every day."

She comes over to him and takes him firmly by the elbow — the other one this time, since he's waving his right hand about in front of my face for greater emphasis.

"Yes, yes, let's go. Just another couple of words … Please, it's very important!" He manages to move just a little bit closer to me. "Of course, I wronged you. But you must understand me. I can only love one woman … That's the way I am. I can't squander my feelings. It's all or nothing for me, you understand? And when I hear her say 'I love you' every day, I don't need anything else. This is for life, do you understand? Once and for all. She's the same, believe me…" It sounds like a confession of love — addressed to the woman clutching his elbow. "She's an amazing person. Incredible integrity."

"We have to be going." That sounds so stern that he immediately breaks off and trudges after her to the door.

I show them as far as the gate. He leads her respectably by the arm, as if they have just paid a friendly family visit to his best friend. And not a single glance, not even a cursory one, at the first-floor windows. As if he never spent all his childhood here! Look round, will you! If only out of sheer curiosity? Maybe the gaping windows that make the place look like a bomb site might arouse some doubts in you about the correctness of your actions?

No, he doesn't look round…

I call to them when they've almost reached the road. Both heads turn in simultaneous haste.

I ask the question in an emphatically cool voice. I don't want to let them think that they've moved me to pity. But after all, he's not the only one who can be concerned about the interests of science, the oil industry and the country as a whole!

"Are you sure that the increase in oil output will be significant?"

"At least twenty per cent," he replies immediately, without any hesitation. Well, whatever else, he's certainly not short of confidence.

"All right," I say. "You can tell them in the office that I agree. I'm working tonight, so I'm not likely to catch any of the management in."

He tries to come dashing back to me again, but his wife has a firm grip on him.

"Good man!" he shouts to me from a distance. "I knew it, I never doubted it. Vika will tell you! She was worried, but I wasn't… I knew I could convince you."

I go back into the yard and close the gate behind me. I suppress a yawn. How long did I sleep? It's about twelve now, that makes it almost five hours. Well, that's plenty."

Before I start my run, I put the tablecloth on the table in the yard. Just in case. She might just turn up.

After just a few dozen strides I'm covered in perspiration. At the end of the second circuit I can feel the poison of last night's spree flowing out through my open pores with the drops of sweat; I break through the smothering shroud of lethargy, back into my usual state of lightness and freedom — this run is pleasurable, and it can go on and on.

I do six circuits to the frantic whining of the stone-cutting discs (for some reason they sound especially frenetic today), then slow my pace to a fast walk. I linger at the gate for a while to do my breathing exercises and finally step into the yard. I see a young guy with long hair sitting at the table — one of that trio — and immediately something hot comes crashing down on my head. As if I've been scalded with boiling water. My legs buckle, my knees touch the ground, and for a moment blackness engulfs everything around me, including the long-haired guy and the table. Then he appears right beside me in a strange pose, with his foot drawn back. I manage to duck, and the ribbed sole of his shoe scrapes past my ear and ends up behind my back: now he's sitting on my shoulder. I throw him off with a sudden jerk and get to my feet. I can't see what's happening behind me, but someone scorches the back of my head with a second blow and everything is suddenly engulfed in darkness again. In the brief flashes of light that break through it, I lash out, landing blows on everything that appears in front of my eyes.

When I come round, the yard is empty. The dull ache in the back of my head is echoed at the front, and at the slightest movement everything goes dark. The terrible pain in my ribs makes it hard to breathe.

I grunt as I make my way to the tap and stick my head under the cold water.

What do they want from me? What is it they're after? The question keeps pounding away in my head, which is splitting with the pain.

It's very hard to breathe, I want to straighten up. I try taking my head out from under the tap, but it's steaming, as if it were red hot. The pain is unbearable. I stick my head back under the water... What do they want from me? What do they want?

And now the pain in my side gets worse, creeping up from one rib to another, towards my shoulder blades, towards the back of my head... The circle is closed...It all seems to join together into one big wound, from my ribs to my head, and the water can't help. I drag myself over to the table. I lie on it on my stomach. I feel the roughness of the starched tablecloth on my cheek. The whiteness that my eye is thrust up against is gradually covered by dark, wet spots. From the drops of blood.

Now what do I do? How can I find them? And what if I do find them? I can't kill them! And *he* never even looked round. As if he'd never lived here at all. Never been ill with the deadly tuberculosis bacillus. He used to sit right here, on this very spot! He's forgotten everything... But what good does it do when you remember? It just makes things harder!

Well, it's time to get up. I can't lie here forever, can I? I have to take a look at what they've done to my face.

It's a long way to my mother's tall mirror, it's in the room, I can't get to it. I can see my face in parts in the little mirror under the stairs. Everything looks alright; nothing hurts when I touch it. So they didn't beat me on the face. Or they missed. That's good. Everything else can remain my business: the pain, and the insult, and the memory... But the face is trickier. Other people have rights to it. You have to explain, make excuses, invent things. Or sit it out. At home. And I can't do that right now. I've got a shift in the evening. And if I don't turn up, they'll think I've done a runner. It's going to be hard enough to explain anything to the lads anyway. But that way, they'll think I've betrayed them and I'm hiding.

And what is it that's eating these guys? Why all this rage? Surely not just because she's taken a fancy to me? And how do they know about that? Who are they anyway? They don't look like students. Although you can't tell nowadays. There's no difference. Workers, thieves, students; they all look the same. Why hasn't she come? She promised to. And the way she promised! That means something stopped her. A person like that couldn't lie. She shouldn't. No one forced her to promise. She came and she promised of her own free will.

I have to tidy up the yard. And change the tablecloth. At least they didn't use the dumbbells — they'd have split my head open.

There's quite a serious swelling at the back of my head. What did they do that with? Must have brought something of their own, I suppose. Some kind of club. The pestle from a mortar, for instance. A very handy little instrument.

Right, now I can sit down for a while. Order has been restored to the landscape after the battle. Very tidy lads, they hardly broke a thing. I wonder if I managed to break anything? At least one nose out of three? That would be great. But what is it that's got them so furious? There has to be a reason. Well anyway, I'll sit and wait for a while. Everything ought to be cleared up today. She arrives in the afternoon, in that warm tender hour just before evening, which has given me a chance to rest and recover a bit. She's carrying a large bundle wrapped in newspaper.

I like the familiar way she talks to me, and in general I like everything about her — the boyish face, the strong thighs in the frayed jeans, and the breasts, with their nipples slipping across the soft material of her short blouse. And that strip of body that's exposed between the jeans and the blouse every time she moves her arms. And I like the fact that she has brought me a present.

I carry on watching her as she unwraps the present. In some elusive fashion she resembles Vika. It's not her appearance — they're not at all alike — and it's not the way she behaves ... It's something deeper and more mysterious, but something I can sense very clearly. And I'm not surprised: it's been clear for a long time already that basically I've been dealing with the same woman all my life. The age, the appearance, the character, the habits — these all change — but it's the same person every time.

"Do you like it?" She unwraps a huge sheepskin with long wool.

"Very much." I put my arm round her shoulders. "Thank you."

If she tries to break away, or even expresses surprise at my behaviour, it means I'm mistaken and it's not her after all. But she looks up at me affectionately and nuzzles my shoulder.

"I just couldn't make it the day before yesterday, I tried my best."

"I know."

She glances up and shakes her head.

"I saw you in the restaurant."

"I know."

"Did they come here?"

"Yes."

"I'm so afraid…"

"But who are they?"

"I'll tell you everything. But not right now, all right?"

"All right."

"I'm divorced, but he won't leave me alone." She looks round the yard. "I really like it here… And you live here on your own?"

"Yes."

"All alone?"

"Yes."

"And you haven't got anyone?"

I smile:

"Why? I've got friends."

She's enraptured by the yard and the things I say.

"Only it's very noisy. Is that the quarry?

"Yes."

She's disappointed. The noise is appalling.

"I didn't notice it at first."

I hug her against myself. Kiss her on the forehead. Closing my eyes, I whisper in her ear:

"They're going to close it, fill it with water. And there'll be a park around it. With a restaurant and boats."

She closes her eyes too. Her arm hugs my waist tenderly. A small, warm breast thrusts against my armpit. We sway to the rhythm of my words. And we both imagine the same picture: a pond with white boats sailing across it, a wooden restaurant on the bank, and a park, a lush green park, stretching out in all directions, all the way to the horizon. To the very ends of the earth.

THREE

The Rector

The face of the woman riding in the bus was so garishly made up that at first glance all her features seemed quite separate from each other — the exhausted eyes in a funereal frame of mascara, the thickly-rouged cheeks and the rapacious scarlet mouth. She was holding her two sons of five and six by the collars of their white shirts, and they were struggling to break free with all the stubbornness of young puppies unused to the leash.

Her mind was focused sombrely on the conversation to come and she paid no attention to the passengers watching with stern disapproval as those two wriggling, jerking, suspended bodies struggled to break free from her grasp. The woman was indifferent to the unspoken indignation of the people around her, but even if she had been sensitive to the opinions of others, she would have behaved in the same way on this September morning that was as hot as summer, taking no notice of what was going on around her, so deeply was she absorbed in her own thoughts.

There was one more stop to go before the institute — the educational establishment where the meeting that she expected to decide her family's fate was due to take place; the woman jerked her children closer to her, gathered herself as if she were about to jump into deep water, scratched an inopportune itch on her chin with her shoulder, screwed up her lips and blew upwards across a cheek polished like an apple to brush aside a strand of hair that had fallen on to her forehead. There were small drops of sweat sparkling in the dark fluff on her upper lip — not so much because the day was already hot as because she had been one big bundle of stress ever since she made the decision to take active measures. She had no doubt that she would be able to make the man she was going to see help her. Whoever he might be, this rector of the institute, and no matter what he might think of her demands, the method of persuasion she had in store for him was absolutely infallible. The important thing was to achieve her end, and make sure that they left her husband alone.

As the bus stopped, the passengers swayed violently and lost interest in everything but the effort to stay on their feet. The woman was dragged through the passenger compartment by her boys, who made a dash for the open front doors of the bus as if they were escaping from a metal cage in which they had been locked for years.

The entrance to the institute, which was flanked by plaques immortalising the memory of several alumni of the technical college who had gone into politics, was under strict guard. The doorman from the extra-departmental security service attempted to stop the woman with two children who certainly didn't look like students, but failed — the boys almost knocked him off his feet as they burst through into the building after being granted their long-awaited freedom at a precisely calculated moment; the woman paraded through after them, majestically swaying her remarkable hips. She seemed not to notice the fat doorman, who had gone dashing after the children.

"Citizen! Where are you going? Wait!"

The woman completely ignored the fat man's howls; after casting a rapid glance over the notice board hanging beside the door of the assembly hall and peeping into the deep shadow inside it (there were students moving something about on the stage) she negotiated yet another flight of stairs, walking soundlessly up the carpet runner, and then followed the runner to the rector's waiting-room.

At this time the man whom the woman had come to see, Fariz Agaevich, was still at home, unhurriedly scraping the foam off his face one strip at a time. Even after the age of fifty the contours of his face had retained enviably neat and clean lines. His greyish-blue eyes — an unusual colour for an Azerbaijani — keenly watched his hands perform the habitual movements they had been making for more than thirty years now, ever since he had finally been allowed to shave the coarse, bushy growth off his chin and cheeks — for some reason his father thought it necessary for him to be at least sixteen, although the razor that the Doctor had given him had been awaiting its first encounter with the early growth covering his face for a long time by then. As he shaved, he recalled how he had helped his father mix up mortar to build the wall which the Doctor, their neighbour, was putting up to screen off part of his long glazed veranda to make a bathroom. It was the first bathroom in the yard where he was born and grew up. Throughout his young life everyone who lived in the yard had gone to the bathhouses to wash: the Azerbaijani bathhouse where, after you got undressed, you were supposed to cover your nakedness with a piece of faded red cloth that was handed to you by the skinny bath attendant (you could see every bone under his bluish skin) and the Russian bathhouse, where you could sit in the steam room for a while. The courtyard of his childhood had been approximately the same distance from both bathhouses, and so there was always a debate over which one to go to every time several families set out to get washed. He preferred the Russian bathhouse with the steam room. He and his friends used to sit on the very lowest wooden bench and the steam made their faces sting, so they would dunk them in a basin of cold water in order to stay in the steam room as long as possible, as a dare. The grownups disappeared into the swirling steam to occupy places higher up, right under the ceiling. But the Azerbaijani bathhouse had its advantages too, for instance a shallow round pool of warm water for rinsing off your feet on the way out of the large bath hall.

They usually went to the bathhouse on Sundays, and most often it was the Doctor who led these expeditions. But now he was building himself a bathroom at home, he and his son, Sultan, who was in the top four at holding out longest in the Russian steam room, wouldn't be taking part in the collective bathing sessions any longer.

Carefully steering the razor round the mole on his right cheek, which had grown thicker and darker over the years, he was surprised to be remembering events that had happened so long ago, events that hadn't surfaced from his memory for the last thirty years, like everything that had to do with the early part of his life, spent in that small, two-storey building on the corner of Shemakhinka Street and 1st Parallel Street.

He only had a few more passes with the razor left to make, after which he usually spent two minutes, no more, applying a hot compress — the white linen napkin was already waiting for him, soaking in boiling water in a special little stainless steel dish; his younger son's wife never forgot to prepare it in time. As he buried his face in the hot cloth, he felt a sudden strange sense of alarm that made his chest contract and his breathing accelerate, and he realised it was connected to the unexpected upsurge of childhood memories. The involuntary comparison that his imagination had suddenly thrown up between the modest little cubicle screened off at the end of the Doctor's veranda, and the bathroom in which he was now standing — a slab of marble below the mirror, gleaming nickel-plated taps, an illuminated ceiling and white-tiled walls — intensified his surprising sense of sadness. He also found himself remembering how the Doctor used to invite guests to celebrate his son's and his wife's birthdays and May Day, which happened to be the Doctor's own birthday. They used to bring a huge slab of ice and chop it up with a crowbar and hammers. They put the large pieces in an ice box lined with zinc-plated iron sheeting or tipped them a tin bath to cover the half-litre bottles of lemonade and the quarter-litre bottles of beer that it already contained;

Fariz and the other boys from the yard would snatch up the small chips that were sent flying in all directions by the hammer blows.

The Doctor's wife would set out for the market in the morning and come back loaded down with full baskets, while the Doctor's son, Sultan, trudged along sulkily behind her, carrying four chickens with their legs tied together, two in each hand.

None of the neighbours from the yard were invited to the celebrations in the Doctor's house, and that was only right, because he couldn't invite everyone, and if he favoured anyone the others might be offended (on ordinary days the doors of the Doctor's flat were open to all).

His smart-looking guests would gather in the evening, most of the men wore spectacles and white linen suits, and as soon as they had taken their seats at the table, Sultan would come down to his family's room on the ground floor with a large plate of spare pilaf. His mother threw her hands up and thanked him fussily for being so kind, and Sultan would ask her to empty the plate and give it back to him at once. At first she wouldn't, but he never left without the plate — it was the tradition in that courtyard that any plate left in a house had to be returned full, with some kind of reciprocal gift, so the Doctor's wife made things simpler for everyone by warning her son that he should never come back without the plate.

How did his father happen to be in the Doctor's flat on one of those birthdays? Most likely because they had asked him to fix the tap in the new bathroom — it used to leak. His father had taken it apart with his wrench several times and changed the washer, cutting one out of the sole of an old shoe. It usually took at least half an hour to do it, but that evening his father had come back down from the first floor very quickly, looking pale and agitated. He threw his wrench on the dining table covered with oilcloth, sat down on a wooden stool and lit a cigarette.

"What's wrong?" his mother asked, gazing in surprise at

the wrench lying beside the empty Vaseline jar that served as an ashtray in their house.

His father didn't answer, just smoked his cigarette in silence.

Of course, half an hour later the tap on the first floor was fixed — the Doctor himself came for his father and spent a long time persuading him to come back upstairs. The rest of the family wouldn't find out until years later what had caused the quarrel, but on his way out the Doctor winked mischievously at *him*, a boy of only sixteen, to make it clear he considered *him* an accomplice in this absurd dispute. But Fariz was proud of his close relations with the Doctor's family, who treated him as if he were their own son, they were always showing him how they felt …

Like everyone who lived in that yard, he worshipped the Doctor; he found everything about him delightful: his height, his powerful voice, his gold-framed spectacles, but most of all the way he was able to rise above the people around him, without even trying. Even when he found himself in situations where the very logic of life seemed to condemn him to humiliation. Like that time in Bilgya when the Doctor needed some kind of certificate from the village Soviet and his father had a day off work, so he took Fariz along and all three of them went to collect the certificate together.

First they had a dip in the sea, and then they walked along the sandy road hemmed in by low stone walls to the village Soviet, which was in a two-storey building where the Doctor's family had lived until nineteen twenty-seven. The Doctor, his wife, his son and his younger brother, who later became a professor, had moved into their yard when Fariz was eight years old — he had just started school that year.

The village Soviet, which was on the first floor of the Doctor's old house, was closed for lunch, and they went back downstairs, into the canteen. The small hall in the semi-basement contained several tables and in one corner there was a counter with a plate of honey cakes standing in a fly-spotted display case. They sat down at the table furthest away from the counter.

There were some collective farm workers eating lunch beside them, his father and the Doctor said hello and initially they replied without getting up, but then they obviously recognised the Doctor, hastily got to their feet, and bowed. There was a young man with high cheekbones who hadn't shaved for some time sitting at another table with a bottle of champagne and a large plate of bozbash mutton soup in front of him. He was local too, and he recognised the Doctor, but he didn't get up and responded to his greeting with a casual nod.

The silence in the room was only broken by the clinking of spoons on plates and the chomping sounds made by the young man every time he raised the spoon to his mouth.

"How are you getting on, Doctor?" one of the farm workers asked.

"Well, thanks to your prayers," the doctor replied with a smile.

"Everyone alive and well?"

"Yes, thank God."

"We often talk about you."

"And I often talk about you."

"God grant you good health."

"Thank you. And the same to you."

The conversation dried up of its own accord and they fell silent again. But not for long. The young man who was eating the soup took a gulp of champagne and spoke.

"Doctor, I'm drinking champagne!" he declared with a triumphant grin below the ginger moustache on his face.

"Good health," the Doctor replied in his usual mild, benevolent manner.

"I'm sitting in the canteen and drinking champagne," said the young man, still smirking, "see how everything's turned out."

"I see," the Doctor replied. "I'm pleased for you."

"I'm sitting in your house," the young man persisted.

"Shall we go?" Fariz's father asked the Doctor in a quiet voice.

"We'll go in a moment," the Doctor answered just as quietly.

"Why don't you say something, Doctor?" the young man asked. "Feeling annoyed, are you? You used to drink the champagne before, now I'm drinking it."

"But I," said the Doctor, getting to his feet, "never drank it with bozbash!" His quiet voice was full of contempt.

Perhaps the young man understood the Doctor's implication, or perhaps he simply responded to the tone of voice, but either way he didn't say anything else and the Doctor emerged triumphant from a situation in which someone had done his best to humiliate him, seemingly without having made the slightest effort.

"Goodbye," he said to everyone in the room.

The young man drinking champagne with bozbash half-rose to his feet when they started walking towards the door.

The Rector wiped his face with a dry towel, unaware that the woman and her two agile little sons had already broken through his secretary's impregnable defences and burst into his office. He would have found this event amazing in any case — people who came to see him usually sat in the waiting room for as long as he thought necessary and only crossed the threshold of his office when they were invited — but all the experience that he had accumulated in twenty years as head of the institute would not be enough for him to apprehend the true significance of this woman's visit and its consequences.

The same, indeed, applied to the other events in store for him that day; although each of them was insignificant in itself, they nonetheless required the expenditure of a certain amount of energy and we all know no one has inexhaustible reserves, even if he's in good shape.

Another memory from his earlier life, this time from a later period, just before the war, was about to surface, but with an effort of will he turned his mind away from that episode which, unlike the other things he had remembered so far today, was liable to spoil his mood.

He walked out of the bathroom, into the dining room, and saw his daughter-in-law and grandson through the open door of the balcony.

"Vika's here," his daughter-in-law told him, "she's talking to mother …"

"And where's your husband?"

"He'll be here in a moment. He was working all night."

"Why don't you sit down?"

He was fond of his youngest daughter-in-law, and she knew it; before taking a seat at the table, she poured tea for him and his grandson.

"She wants to talk to you."

Who does?" he asked, spreading butter on a slice of bread.

"Vika."

"Are you upset about something?"

The daughter-in-law didn't answer and lowered her eyes guiltily. But in any case, he could guess what was likely to spoil anybody's mood in this house. His suspicions were confirmed the moment his son walked into the room.

His son said good morning and then, reaching for the teapot, he announced: "Your daughter-in-law wants to leave us. She can't take the pressure." The smile trembling on his lips was on the point of slipping off.

His daughter-in-law carried on studiously examining the cup standing on the table in front of her.

"What's happened?"

"The usual story," his son said with a dismissive gesture. "She won't go for long… Just for a week, maybe two. She'll take a rest with her family and come back."

The Rector glanced at his daughter-in-law and then looked away, because she could scarcely hold back her tears.

"It's your business, of course," he told his son, "but in general a wife ought to live with her husband, not with her own parents."

"She won't be gone long."

"You already said that."

"Well, what's to be done? Mum's become quite unbearable. You know it yourself…"

The Rector got up and walked over to the balcony door.

There were yachts and launches swaying on the gentle waves at the wooden quayside that had reappeared in the bay — the quayside had been demolished and then rebuilt, like other structures on the boulevard that looped around the bay. Every time the municipal administration changed, the new men regarded it as their duty to commemorate their period in charge by rebuilding part of the coastal boulevard.

He went out on to the balcony. His Volga was standing down there beside the main entrance to the building, in among all the other cars, but he couldn't see his driver. A man in a dark suit was leaning out over the stone rim of the pool round the fountain, trying to catch something in the water, which looked silvery from up here because of the slanting rays of the sun. The monument — the heroic figure standing on the stones in the middle of the pool and trying to hack through the long-tailed monster that had attacked him with his sword, would have been squinting if he could — the sun was shining straight into his eyes. The man leaning over the rim of the pool straightened up, revealing the bucket that he was holding in his hands: when he started carrying the bucket towards the cars standing by the entrance, the Rector recognised him as his driver.

When he reached the Volga, the driver sluiced the water over it and set off back to the pool. Only people who had known the Rector for a long time would have been able to tell from the slight narrowing of the eyes following the driver's movements that he disapproved of the way of obtaining water that his driver had discovered. Of course, his son and daughter-in-law noticed the expression on his face as he walked back through the dining room without a word on his way to the entrance hall. Before going into his study to get a file of papers, he hesitated for a moment, walked a few steps further and stopped in front of the blue-painted door of the bedroom, behind which he could hear the voices of his wife and his elder daughter-in-law, Vika.

"It's absolutely out of the question," his wife said in her usual capricious and domineering tone, "he's my son and he must make the decisions."

"You're absolutely right," replied her daughter-in-law, who was sitting on a chair beside the other woman's bed. She hastily got to her feet as soon as he appeared in the doorway.

"Did you want to have a word with me?" he asked after saying hello.

"Yes."

"Then wait in the study, please, and I'll be there in a moment."

"All right," said his daughter-in-law and left the bedroom with the precipitate haste that many people showed when he asked or instructed them to do something.

"How are you feeling?" he asked his wife, moving closer.

"The same as ever," she said, grasping the metal rail set into the wall for this precise purpose and lifting the massive body that bulged out of her linen nightdress up higher on to the pillows.

"Shall I help?"

"No, thank you," she said adjusting a pillow so that she was half-lying. The fringe of short, silvery-grey hair suited the stubborn expression of her face perfectly. "The neighbour downstairs had guests who stayed late again."

"Tamila wants to go and live with her parents for a while," he said.

"Good riddance."

"And who's going to take care of you?"

"I'll manage."

"You know perfectly well that nobody will put up with you for more than two days, for any money."

"Did you come in here just to upset me?"

"I came to let you know the problems that your unpleasant disposition has caused again, and to say that if you don't make it up with her, I won't lift a finger to find someone to look after you."

"I'm ill."

"You've been ill for many years, and no one's preventing you from carrying on being ill."

"Why can't I say what I think is right in my own home? She's slovenly and she drops everything.

"I'm sorry, but for months she has been taking out your chamber pot, feeding you with a spoon, and you…" He could barely restrain himself. "Well, anyway, I've warned you." He swung round sharply and walked out of the bedroom; in the hallway he stopped in front of the mirror and waited for his left eyelid to stop twitching before going into his study, where his elder son's wife was waiting. She hastily got up off her armchair. "Sit down, sit down," he said, lowering himself into the next armchair without looking at her. How are the children?"

"Fine, thanks."

"We don't see much of them around here," he said, trying to speak more politely, suppressing his dislike for this woman who had become his relative by chance.

"We did call in, but you weren't here."

"How old is the eldest now?"

"Nine."

"Is he in the third class?"

"Yes."

"Bring them both round next Sunday morning if you can."

"All right," she said, as usual looking off to one side, unable to bring herself to meet his gaze, and pulling the hem of her dress down over her exposed knees, as if she felt ashamed of the way her striking appearance had blossomed with the years.

"You always agree, every time," he said with a cold smile, "but I hardly ever see them."

"You know what he's like," she said, meaning Eldar, her husband.

"And what am I supposed to know?"

"You know his nature…"

"My meetings with my grandsons have nothing to do with

your husband's character." The Rector spoke in his usual cool, calm manner, but his left eyelid had started twitching again. "What did you want to say to me?"

"I'm sorry for taking up your time." She glanced briefly at him and turned her eyes away again. Her hand let go of her hem and started straightening her hair (he had guessed straight away that she had come with some request, and that gesture to check that her hair was neat and tidy — the gesture of a woman used to relying first and foremost on her appearance — confirmed his guess). "But we have a difficult situation. Eldar doesn't know that I'm here… it took me a long time to decide to come… He needs help… You know what he's like. If he finds out I came to you, he'll kill me."

"I doubt he'll kill you," he said, forcing a smile, "especially if I do what you ask. So how can I be of help?"

"He's finished his PhD thesis. The theoretical part. Now he needs to hold a field experiment. But they refuse to let him."

"Why?"

"I don't know. He doesn't tell me everything," she said, expressing herself more and more briskly, "but you know the way things are done nowadays."

"How are they done?"

"Well, how shall I put it, he needs someone to push things along… to ask for him."

"Ask whom?"

"The Ministry of Oil."

"Why?"

"So that they'll hold the experiment."

"But why can't the institute where he's doing his post-graduate work obtain official permission for the experiment to be held?"

"They tried, but they were refused."

"Why?"

"I don't know."

"And what makes you think they won't refuse me?"

She laughed as if she thought what he'd said was a good joke.

"You?"

"Yes, me. Not to mention the fact that I can't ask them when I have no idea what we're talking about. You'll have to send your husband here so that he can explain what I have to ask for."

"But you know he won't come." She was standing now as well, and speaking without her former reticence. "He's not that kind of man."

"Then why in hell's name are you asking for him, if he's not that kind of man?!" Without even noticing it, the Rector almost broke into a shout; it was his old anger with his elder son showing through. "You demean him by acting like this! The man wants to achieve everything in life by himself, without any help from anyone! And you put him in this idiotic position!" Something constricted his breathing again, he heard himself shouting and fell silent.

There was an oppressive pause during which he breathed heavily, trying to do it without making any noise, but failing, and his son's wife stood in front of him in a pose that expressed guilt and alarm, not knowing what to do: leave, in order not to annoy her father-in-law any more, or stay so that he wouldn't take her departure as a deliberate insult.

"I beg your pardon," he said when he finally managed to master his voice and his breathing, "my nerves are playing up."

"No, I beg your pardon," said his daughter-in-law, sidling towards the door. "Goodbye."

He watched her leave and then went over to the desk. Lying on the painstakingly polished and cleaned surface, between his typewriter and his calculator was a notepad with a list of tasks planned for the day. Number three, at ten thirty, immediately after his lecture in the engineering faculty, was a meeting with an investigator from the republican public prosecutor's office. At precisely eight o'clock he stepped out of the door of his flat and started walking downstairs (when he came home in the evenings, he usually took the lift). After he had taken a few steps, he heard voices: a man's voice, speaking rapidly and therefore not very clearly, and a woman's voice, speaking quietly with intermittent bursts of laughter. It was the neighbours on the next floor down talking: the widow of a professor who had died of a heart attack many years earlier and a man the same age as the Rector's elder son, a Muscovite who had recently swapped his one-room flat somewhere in Biruliovo for a three-room flat on their staircase. Izik, his younger son, who had helped arrange the exchange, had told him these details over breakfast one morning.

When they saw him, the neighbours stopped talking, as if they had run into some insurmountable barrier at full speed.

"Oh!" said Lyalya, as everyone called the widow, although her full name was Lyatifa, "I'm not decent." And she darted in through the door of her flat.

There was nothing particularly wrong with her appearance, except perhaps that her hair was gathered into a bun under a headscarf instead of hanging loose over her shoulders in her usual fashion.

"Good morning," she said from behind the door that wasn't quite closed.

"Good morning," he replied affably, although he disliked the way they had broken off their conversation when they saw him, and the hasty way she had taken cover, as if she had been caught doing something reprehensible. If you don't like the way you look, you shouldn't go out onto the stairs at such an early hour!

Seimur, as the new neighbour was called, stepped aside to let him go down the stairs.

"Fariz Agaevich," he said in a solemn voice. "I would like to apologise."

"What for?"

"I had the lads round again yesterday. Was it very noisy?"

"I'm sure you have an idea of that yourself," he replied without turning round. His neighbour leaned down over the banister

"My repairs start tomorrow."

The Rector nodded without speaking. He did not like the former Muscovite — he was only too familiar with the tacit impertinence of characters like that: perfectly civil and even respectful in their behaviour, but absolutely convinced of their own superiority over the people with whom they occasionally had to play at being polite.

For some reason there was a smell of paint, although the greyish-green walls of the staircase had not been painted for many years. One of the neighbours must be having some repair work done. And indeed, on the next floor down a large part of the landing was taken up by two buckets of paint and several sacks of cement standing outside the door of the former Rector of the Industrial Institute, whose flat had been taken over by numerous distant relatives immediately after he died. Who would have thought that only fifteen years after the building was first occupied, almost none of those who had been honoured with the right to live here would have any use for the place any longer? And that the flats that had been fought over for so long with such cunning would fall into the hands of outsiders?

As he stepped round a heap of cement that had spilt out of a sack, the Rector smiled wryly to himself at the casual way he had started thinking about time — "only fifteen years!" Easily said — fifteen years! But only recently a year had seemed like an immense period of time to him. "Only recently?" He laughed to himself again as he caught himself repeating that casual approach. And even earlier, fifty years ago (half a century, that was, and how it had flown by!) a single day had seemed like an eternity, never mind a year — how much you could fit into it from morning to evening, how many events and impressions! He used to remember everything quite clearly, as if it had been imprinted on his memory, with all the details, the smells, the colours, the mood, the taste of the food. Then in some imperceptible way time had started moving faster, and everything had started swirling and spinning along, the weeks and months and years had gone flickering by. And a lot of what had happened seemingly not so very long ago had started dropping out of his memory, and if he did remember it sometimes, it was only vaguely, like the shadow of the past or, rather, like some formal protocol that contained nothing but the bare facts.

Fifteen years! A third of his life had been spent in this building. His elder son was twenty years old when they moved in here; and although no one had asked his opinion, he had been categorically opposed to the move. The Rector's wife had greeted the news about the new flat without any particular enthusiasm (she could still stand on her feet then, but it was getting harder and harder to get her to go out and visit anyone). He himself hadn't really been desperately keen to live here, even though at one time he had gone to great lengths to be kept on the list of potential tenants, which comprised some of the most respected names in science. Circumstances had forced his hand: his not getting the flat could have had other consequences — as he had only just become rector, he didn't carry very much weight in the institute as yet, and a failure with the flat would have been taken as a sign that he didn't have the unconditional backing of the leadership. And then his enemies would immediately have started crawling out of the woodwork...

Usually when he walked out of the front entrance, the driver immediately started the engine, and he and the car arrived at the edge of the pavement at exactly the same time. But today this ritual, perfected over many years of working together, was disrupted: there were two young men chatting in the carved stone archway of the entrance, clearly silhouetted against the light background of the street, and for some reason they didn't move out of his way as he approached, but just carried on standing there without budging, as if they hadn't noticed him.

"Excuse me," he said, interrupting their conversation.

The young men moved apart with insolent slowness, leaving a narrow gap between them that the Rector could hardly squeeze through. His right elbow touched an absurdly protruding belly as round as a melon and he could smell stale alcohol fumes on the left. Of course, he ought to have asked them to move further apart, if they couldn't find any other place to have a chat, but a glance at one ugly mug with gold-capped teeth (you couldn't possibly call that insolent unshaved assemblage of features a face) was met with a fierce stare from a pair of narrowed reddish-black eyes, and so he said nothing, which spoiled his mood even more as he took the several steps required to cross the pavement.

He opened the door and got into the front passenger seat of the car that was already standing at the kerb. His driver's cap was generally regarded as the largest owned by any chauffeur in town — a genuine "International airport" among mere local "aerodromes", as such peaked caps were known. He smiled to himself every time he saw it.

"Make sure that doesn't happen again," the Rector said when the car had rounded the fountain pool with the stone figure of a great hero and driven out on to the broad avenue. The driver inclined his head respectfully, he understood immediately what the boss meant (he called everyone whose official car he drove "the boss").

"There was no water in the tap," the driver said. Before changing lanes he looked in his mirror and arched an eyebrow in surprise. "That Zhiguli was following us yesterday too," he said, and speeded up, sending the car dashing along the embankment: the trees flashing by on the right emphasised just how fast they were moving.

Turning the rear view mirror towards himself, the Rector saw the two young men who had been standing in the entrance a minute earlier sitting in the Zhiguli that was hurtling after them; as if they could sense his gaze, the one who was driving suddenly swerved sharply without reducing speed and turned into one of the side streets; the shrill squeal of brakes startled the people sitting on the benches in the seafront park.

At the doorman's post at the entrance of the institute, he found all three provosts — for science, academic matters and general matters — waiting for him. The fat doorman was telling them something and waving his arms about excitedly. When he saw the Rector he froze in a theatrical posture, with an absurdly polite expression on his face to demonstrate his great respect for the head of the institute.

"Good morning," the provosts for academic matters and general matters said together; the provost for science, Ramazanov, who towered over the other two, greeted him a second later, and his tone of voice lacked the intense respect of the preceding duet.

Replying to them all with a single nod, he walked on towards the stairs without stopping. His deputies followed him — the "duet" fell in on his left, while Ramazanov lengthened his stride and walked on his right.

"We have an emergency," the provost for general matters told him in an anxious voice.

He turned his head slightly to the left to indicate that this information interested him.

"A woman has broken into your office. She won't listen to reason. She has two children with her. We decided it was best not to use force."

"We decided to wait for you," put in Gumbatov, the provost for academic matters, patting into place the sparse hair carefully combed across the top of his head, which had parted to reveal the pale dome of his bald patch. "To avoid any unfortunate incidents."

"How did she get into the building?" he asked.

"Literally forced her way in. The doorman wouldn't admit her."

"She wants to talk to you," said Ramazanov. His calm tone of voice sounded defiant.

"What about?"

"She refuses to explain. You're the only one she'll see." Ramazanov even permitted himself a smile.

They walked along the corridors of the institute, nodding in response to greetings from students crowding around the doors to lecture halls. In the glass corridor connecting the old block with the new one they were greeted by a student in a white cap. The Rector slowed down (his deputies, who had not anticipated a halt, were carried on for several steps by sheer momentum). He shifted his gaze from the student's face to the cap, which was immediately removed.

"I'm sorry, I forgot to take it off."

"Tell the dean to issue you a reprimand."

"Yes, sir."

They walked on through the connecting corridor, across a foyer and into the third block that was under construction. The foreman and his builders were waiting for them there.

"Well, what good news do you have for me?" The Rector's question was addressed to the foreman, who was holding his wide-brimmed hat in his hands.

"Everything's okay so far," said the foreman, with a glance at Ramazanov, who had been made responsible for overseeing the progress of construction. "But we might have to stop in two or three days…"

"Why?"

"We're short of joinery and boards. They only delivered part of the paint too. We're almost out of whitewash and a few other things. I handed in a list."

"How long ago?"

"It would be about a week now."

"Why don't I know about this?"

"We were hoping to deal with it ourselves, without your help," said Ramazanov, "and then…" He hesitated, unwilling to speak in the presence of the "duet". "There's another reason, I wanted to have a word with you about it, but you've been very busy recently."

"Who is supposed to issue the materials required?"

"State Supplies Department, but they don't have them in stock. They're expecting them in the next quarter."

"Let me have the list."

"Very well. Could you spare me ten minutes of your time today?"

He remembered that during the last few days Ramazanov had requested a meeting with him several times, but had been refused for lack of time. The two other provosts, who didn't know the background to this story, felt that Ramazanov's insistent tone was tactless and assumed expressions that made their disapproval evident to all.

"Come to me at eleven fifteen."

"Thank you."

"And it would be a good idea to use copper cables instead," said the foreman. "The ones we have will pack up before long,"

"Put the cables on the list of materials too," he said with nod to the foreman, and set off back to the old block: the provosts took their places on his right and left, following just slightly behind.

Eighteen years ago, when he became Rector effectively by pure chance, who could have foreseen what great results he would achieve?

When he was awarded his PhD at the age of thirty-eight (after withdrawing from Party work) and took the position of dean of the faculty of general electrical engineering, he could not possibly have imagined that in four years' time he would be in charge of the entire institute. It seemed especially impossible because the man whose place he eventually took was a scientist with an international reputation, a monumental figure whose position seemed impregnable. But times had changed, and so had the way things were done, they had changed very rapidly, and the outstanding scientist had not kept up with them, in fact he had not even tried to keep up. The result was a bolt from the blue, an order from the very top that the administration of the institute must be consolidated with personnel who possessed a more modern mindset. He was the secretary of the institute's

Party organisation at the time, and was just gathering momentum. It emerged later that his aggrandisement was greatly facilitated by a certain incident, rumours of which had reached all the way to the very top. Later, the whispers greatly embellished the story and transformed it into one of the institute's legends, but the rumours were basically true. On the day of the institute's general Party meeting, he took a colleague home — one of the lecturers. At that time he still lived in the old flat in the yard on Shemakhinka Street, where he was born and grew up and left for the first time when he joined the army. His colleagues in the department had heard a lot about his mother's abilities as a cook, and the lecturer had practically begged to be invited when he heard that she had made pilaf. The lecturer had been just as insistent when he saw a bottle of vodka standing on the old oak sideboard. Since they were taking advantage of an almost two hour interval, or "window", as the students called it, for their lunch, they were able to dine at their leisure, and as the host, he could hardly refuse his guest a glass or two of vodka; he didn't touch a drop himself of course. But three hours later, as secretary of the Party organisation, he was obliged to note the fact that certain members of the Party had returned to the meeting in an inebriated condition. Subsequent rumours added that the invitation to lunch had been intentionally planned in order to compromise a talented scientist and administrator who was a potential contender for the post of Rector, and that was the form in which the story became a legend. In actual fact, however, at that time Fariz was not even dreaming of becoming Rector; he only accused his colleague of being drunk because he behaved in a very impertinent manner at the meeting, and, of course, there was no way he could have foreseen that a few months later, when the old Rector was dismissed and the contenders for the vacant post were being discussed, that in addition to his merits as a front-line soldier and a Party worker, someone would also recall this story as an example of his firm principles. Or that it would make everyone present smile, which in itself encouraged them to decide in his favour.

His secretary Mina, who had been sitting outside the door of his office for the last ten years, used to work for the militia immediately after the war, and this had left its mark in the way she received those rare professors and representatives of the teaching staff and the body of students who tried to get in to see him. But evidently these occasional visitors were so timid and docile that Mina's skills had been considerably blunted — there was no other explanation for her embarrassing failure with the woman he found in his office.

"You'll get fifteen days, sweetheart. And if anything goes missing, we'll pursue criminal charges. And disorderly conduct goes without saying," said Mina.

"You're the hooligan here," the woman in the office replied in a slightly gruff, brazenly calm voice.

"And you'll answer for affronting an officer in the performance of her duty too!" Mina said with an offended sniff.

When she saw the Rector, she screwed up her tearful face and came dashing towards him.

"Fariz Agaevich, I beg you, don't go in there. She's insane. She was going to throw herself off the balcony when we tried to get her out!" she blurted out in a torrent of sobs, tears and whispers. "It's dangerous! Believe me!!"

He stepped round his secretary, who was trying to block his way into the office, walked over to the door and saw a swarthy woman in gaudy makeup who gave the impression of being tall, even though she was sitting down. She was not alone in the office — she had a little bull-calf writhing in each hand, and the boys' faces were so red from struggling against the tight collars she was using to restrain them, it looked as if they would choke to death right there in his office if they weren't released immediately.

The woman assumed a thoughtful air. Neither the children and their convulsive attempts to break free of her grasp, nor Mina, who was inventing threat after threat, seemed able to distract her from her thoughts.

"What's the problem?" the Rector asked sternly as he stepped into the room: this question, pronounced in a low, cool voice, usually had a compelling effect on everyone who knew him, because it indicated that he was extremely annoyed. Venerable professors, hardboiled administrators, reckless students — everyone in the institute understood the significance of that question.

Mina smirked triumphantly, now she could be certain that this insolent creature who had temporarily bested her would be put in her place; she knew what those words implied, especially when they were spoken in that tone of voice.

But the woman seemed not to have heard the stern question. Fixing the calm gaze of her dark-lined eyes on the short male figure that had appeared before her, she opened the fingers of both hands. Was happened then was rather like a collision between two billiard balls, which sends them flying apart in opposite directions: one urchin dashed across to the Rector's desk and instantly tossed everything that was lying on it onto the floor, while the other ran out on to the balcony with the obvious intention of jumping down into the street. It was only Mina's rapid militia-trained reactions that saved the institute from an inevitable scandal — uttering a howl that brought everyone walking along the street to a sudden halt, she just managed to grab hold of the boy's leg when his body was already outside the balustrade.

The Rector froze in the middle of his office, wondering what he ought to do — go dashing to help Mina or pull the other brother away from the desk, where he was already rifling through the drawers.

Their mother was calm and impassive.

"Aslanchik, stop fidgeting like that, my love," she said affectionately to the son who was emptying out the desk and then, evidently recalling her second child, lazily turned her head towards the balcony door. "What are you doing there, son? Come over here."

"Who are you?" he asked, with the same breathless feeling he had had earlier that morning, only this time it was caused by a sense of outrage. "How dare you come here uninvited like this?"

"Are you the Rector?" the woman asked.

"Yes, I am. And who are you, if I might be so bold as to ask?"

"Aslanchik, don't, my sweet. You can see the man's angry." As she spoke these words in the same quiet, detached voice, the woman looked up at the owner of the office and a strange glimmer of menace appeared in her eyes and stared slowly growing brighter.

Mina finally dragged the child she had rescued back into the room, slammed the balcony door loudly and dashed towards the desk, uttering another howl, which could not be heard in the street, but must surely have frightened anyone who happened to be walking along the institute corridor just at that moment.

"Come to me, my love," the woman said to her son, "come to mummy."

Struggling to recover his usual confidence, the owner of the study stepped over the second boy, who was rolling about on the floor, struggling to get away from Mina, and took his usual place at the desk.

"Who are you?" he asked again in an extremely stern tone of voice.

"Tell her to leave," the woman said instead of answering. She pursed her lips fastidiously and jabbed her index finger towards Mina.

"Perhaps I should call the militia?" Mina asked as she forced the writhing body of her small opponent down against the floor.

"I don't advise it," said the woman. "You'll be sorry."

Astounded by her insolence, Mina gazed tearfully at the Rector, expecting him to give vent to his wrath and put their common enemy to shame, but he surprised her.

"Mina, go out please," the Rector said in a low voice. "And take the children with you."

The woman nodded in satisfaction, apparently approving of his rational behaviour.

"Boys, go with the lady," she said. "The lady will give you a chocolate."

Either the boys had a very sweet tooth, or when their mother really wanted, they became perfectly obedient, but Mina had no trouble at all in getting them out of the room.

"Well, I'm listening," the Rector said dryly, leaning his elbows on the desk.

Instead of replying, the woman put her hand into her handbag and took out an unlabelled half-litre bottle containing a clear liquid. It was sealed with a polythene stopper.

"What's that?"

"Petrol." The woman pulled out the stopper and the smell of petrol filled the air. "Have you opened a whorehouse in the institute?" she asked, and her face contorted malevolently, removing any need to ask what she needed the petrol for. Clearly for burning something: either him, or herself, or the whole institute if she could manage it! "Do you want to destroy my family?" the woman asked, taking a cigarette lighter out of her handbag and reaching for the bottle with her free hand.

"What are you doing?" he asked, trying to maintain his composure.

"You'll see soon enough," she replied, "I'm going to burn myself in front of you." The cigarette lighter in her left hand clicked.

"Stop, are you crazy?!" He got halfway to his feet, trying to work out if he could reach the woman in time if she really did try to commit self-immolation in his office.

"If you don't give me back my husband, I'll set myself on fire." She clicked the cigarette lighter menacingly again.

"What husband? Please explain what it is you want."

"Ten years together. Two sons by him. Why should I let that whore have him?"

"Does your husband work in our institute?"

"Of course, where else?!"

"In which department?"

"Electrical engineering."

"What's his name?"

"Gasanov. Doesn't it bother you that two children will be left without a mother? If that whore wanted a man, why should I have to suffer? Aren't there enough unmarried men about?"

As if in response to this exclamation the door of the office opened slightly and the agitated face of the provost for general matters appeared in the crack.

"Close the door," said the Rector, realising that the appearance of another person in the room might jolt the woman into sudden action.

His deputy's head obediently disappeared and the door closed.

"As far as I understand it, your husband is involved with another woman. Is that correct?"

"As if you didn't know!" the woman laughed. "She works in your department. Sofa Imanova."

"Imanova?!" the Rector exclaimed, unable to conceal his surprise. Imanova was the only one of the previous year's graduates they had kept on in the institute. She was a quiet, plain girl, nothing like the typical married man's mistress. And it was hard to imagine Gasanov, the husband of this woman who was threatening to burn herself alive, in the role of seducer. "Are you sure you're not mistaken?"

"Me, mistaken?" said the woman, putting the bottle down on the desk. "He told me himself. I'd guessed, of course. He's been neglecting me badly just recently — you know what I mean... Then he didn't come home for the night at all a couple of times. And three days ago he announced that he'd fallen in love with someone else, with this Imanova, that is. And he disappeared. But I'll find him! I'll drag him out of his hidey-hole! You can tell him that."

Now that everything had been clarified and the imminent

danger of the woman setting fire to herself in front of him there and then had passed, he had to appease her somehow and get her out of the office.

"How can I be of help?"

"It's all in your hands. In the first place, he's frightened to death of you. In the second place, he values his job very highly. And in the third place, what's happened to public opinion in your institute? Hasn't it got anything to say?"

"It hasn't got anything to say because this is the first time we've heard about this business."

"I phoned your deputy," the woman sneered, "the provost as you call him, a month ago."

"And what did he say to you?"

"He promised to check the facts," the woman said, still sneering as she put the bottle of petrol back in her handbag. "Apparently he's still checking."

"Well, that's strange, but in any case, you'll have to write a statement. To set matters moving, we have to have formal grounds."

"I've got a statement," the woman said, and took the bottle of petrol out again, so that she could rummage in her handbag more easily; eventually the statement, written on a sheet of lined paper from a school exercise book and folded in two, was found. "I've written it all down, all the facts."

"Very good. Give it to my secretary."

"So I can hope, then?"

"Your statement will be considered very carefully."

"Only I warn you — leave him alone. That whore's to blame for everything."

"The necessary measures will be taken," he said, getting up.

The woman realised that the visit was over and also got to her feet.

"They didn't let us out from under the veil so that we could break up other people's families, did they?" she said. "You know I'm right."

He nodded briefly in reply — he had to indicate some minimal level of agreement now, so that she would finally get out of his office.

"Don't forget that," he said, pointing to the bottle, when the woman had already said goodbye and was heading for the door.

"Ah, yes…"

The moment she left the office, his phone rang.

"It's me," said the voice of the provost for academic matters. "Perhaps we should call the militia?"

"Come to my office," the Rector said and hung up; the situation had now been sufficiently clarified for him to select the optimal measures to neutralise any possible consequences.

Of course, had the provost for academic matters taken the matter in hand in good time, they could have got by with "therapeutic" measures, but now, unfortunately, it was impossible to avoid more aggressive intervention. It wasn't the first time that Gumbatov had confused and complicated the simplest of problems by failing to make timely decisions because of his cowardly tendency to avoid taking responsibility.

The Rector looked at the clock — there were only a few minutes left until his lecture — and got up. In the doorway of the office, he ran into Gumbatov, puffing and panting from hurrying there, so they spoke as they walked along.

"Did Gasanov's wife phone you?"

The provost for academic matters had obviously been expecting this question.

"I wasn't sure that it was his wife. Anyone can make a phone call…"

"Did you know about Gasanov's relationship with Imanova?" the Rector asked as he walked unhurriedly across the waiting room: Gumbatov walked after him, about half a step behind, but he seemed to be moving faster, almost running; the long hair combed across the top of his head had fallen into separate strands and needed to be put back in place to restore the hairstyle.

"Well, you know… How can I put it?"

"Just tell me the way it is."

I guessed, and I wasn't the only one. A lot of people knew."

"A lot of people aren't responsible for educational work."

"You're absolutely right."

"Ask Gasanov to come and see you. Show him the statement. Let him resign of his own free will. Explain that in the situation that has arisen, they can't possibly work here together." He left Gumbatov in the waiting room and went out into the corridor.

The bell that shrilled through every floor of the institute, from top to bottom, was still ringing as the Rector entered the lecture hall. Several other people slipped in through the door after him as he walked to the desk.

The attendance register was lying in its place, but he started calling out the names without bothering to open it: the students were very impressed by his ability to remember all the names in a group after only one meeting.

"Airapetov, Aliev, Akhmerov, Bagirov, Bobrov, Burstein," he recited, extracting one name after another from his memory. "Here", "Yes", "Yes", "Here" they answered from various parts of the lecture hall; after the name "Vezirov" there was a pause.

"Vezirov," he repeated.

"Vezirov's not here," said the group prefect, a Korean who had come to the institute from the Russian Far East under the non-competitive entry programme.

"May I come in?" a breathless voice asked. A sturdy young man in a striped polo shirt appeared in the doorway.

"No, you may not," he replied, opening the register and entering the letters "ab" beside the name Vezirov to indicate that Vezirov was absent from the lecture, "nobody is allowed into the hall after the bell."

He waited for the disappointed Vezirov to close the door behind him and continued the roll call, declaiming the names from memory. When he finished, he stood up and, before going across to the blackboard, said:

"This is the second time we have met. At the first lecture I didn't think it necessary to warn you, I hoped you would be conscientious. But now, so that there will be no grievances or misunderstandings in the future, I am warning you: you can only miss one of my lectures. If you miss a second one — regardless of whether you have a valid reason or not — the next time we meet will be at the examination. Please inform Vezirov that he has already used up his right to miss one lecture."

Having delivered this ultimatum in a cool, dispassionate voice, he walked towards the blackboard; the lecture hall was absolutely silent, and if he didn't know otherwise, he might have imagined there was no one there but him.

The solution of the linear equation describing the operation of a static regulator fitted neatly into the only space left on the board — the bottom right-hand corner — just as the bell announcing the end of the two-hour session sounded. His ability to time a lecture so that the final words written on the full board coincided precisely with the bell also had a chastening influence on the students. Many years of teaching had convinced him that the most powerful impressions were made during the first two or three lectures, which determined the way the students regarded both the lecturer and the subject that he taught. And so it was important to make the right psychological impact on them from the very beginning. As he walked out of the lecture hall, he thought that he had succeeded rather well yet again.

He walked through the crowded corridors, and the sense of satisfaction he felt after giving his lecture was reinforced as a passage through the living mass of students opened up before him, as if someone were running ahead with the quiet, but awesome warning of his approach. And immediately the booming din of the corridor declined, then faded away completely, and was not renewed for a long time behind him; the Rector seemed to be carrying along the zone of silence and low whispers that his appearance had produced.

He moved through the corridors of the institute to which he had devoted the last twenty years of his life, the corridors of his institute, and the expression on the faces of those who greeted him — a complex combination of reverence, respect and timid curiosity — confirmed that he had been right to invest so much hard effort in the work that had become the central meaning of his life.

At the same time, one floor lower, someone else was fighting his way through the bustle of the corridors, someone for whom it was very important to reach the Rector's office at least a few seconds earlier than he did. Barging straight into the students he couldn't walk round, the skinny, clean-shaven thirty-five-year-old man in spectacles frowned and apologised, but didn't slow down. It had been explained very clearly just how important it was for him to see the Rector as soon as possible, and he was trying as hard as possible to comply with Ramazanov's instructions.

Things went well at first — he managed to reach the waiting room before the Rector. Now he had to meet him in the doorway and persuade him by any means possible to hear him out. The secretary Mina, whom he feared no less than the Rector himself, was sitting at her place when he glanced into the waiting room (one of the chairs lined up along the wall was occupied by a stranger with a black attaché case leaning against his legs); there was no point in trying to negotiate with her — he knew that himself, and Ramazanov had told him so as well, so he immediately pulled his head back out and closed the door.

The small square hallway with several ceramic pots containing cacti standing on the floor and two portraits hanging on the wall was quiet, in contrast with the uproar of the corridors he had just walked or, rather, run along. It seemed to be cooler here than in the other spaces in the institute, although there was no possible explanation for that but the psychological impact of silence and space — the hot August air coming in through the open windows here was the same as everywhere else.

The man took a handkerchief out of his pocket and carefully wiped his sweaty face and neck, he tucked his shirt into his trousers and adjusted his tie. Just as these preparations were concluded he heard confident footsteps and the Rector's short figure appeared round the corner of the corridor.

The man in spectacles started, as if he had not hurried so desperately to get to this meeting, but had unexpectedly run into someone he had been hiding from for a long time.

When the Rector came close enough for the man in spectacles to attract his attention, the man discovered that he had lost his voice — his lips moved, his tongue moved, his larynx tautened, but the only result was a few faint, muffled sounds.

And yet these muffled sounds were perhaps the very reason the Rector slowed down and gazed in amazement at the man who was making them. In fact, there was no doubt that it was only the surprise of seeing this assistant lecturer from his department so dumbstruck that he took him into the waiting room, even though talking to the assistant lecturer had not been part of his plans. If the assistant lecturer had not acted so strangely, the response he received would have been limited to a nod in reply to his greeting, and any attempts at explanation would have been cut short and redirected to the provost for academic matters.

In the waiting room the Rector nodded to the only visitor, who for some reason did not feel it necessary to get up on seeing him, and cast an enquiring glance at Mina.

Gasanov started making sounds that were louder, but still inarticulate.

"The comrade from the republican prosecutor's office," said Mina, standing up in a way that seemed to hint to the visitor that he ought to get up off his backside as well.

"Wait here," the Rector told Gasanov and walked into his office without even glancing at the impudent investigator.

Mina followed him through the door.

"Has he been waiting long?" the Rector asked, taking his place at the desk.

"Ten minutes."

"Ask him in."

The attaché case was a good match for the fashionable lightweight, light-coloured suit that fitted the investigator so well. The tiny red collar of the blue shirt, combined with the grey speckled tie, lent his appearance an elegance untypical of men in his profession — in those long-ago years when fate had briefly cast the Rector up into a high position in the ranks of law enforcement, not even the lawbreakers had dressed like that.

The investigator cast an appraising eye round the office, looked at the Rector seated in state and approached the massive polished desk without being asked.

"I'm here about the Kalantarov case," he said, stopping beside the chair for visitors.

"Go on," the Rector said dryly.

"Perhaps you might allow me to sit down?" the investigator asked. "This will not be a brief conversation."

"I can only give you a few minutes."

The investigator shrugged, sat down on the chair and took a notepad out of his attaché case.

"Can we invite in Kyazimov, Galustyan and Shirakhmedov?" he asked, putting a ballpoint pen down beside the notepad.

"Who are they?"

"Students involved in the Kalantarov case and mentioned in the anonymous statement that you forwarded to us."

"There is nobody with those names registered as students here," said the Rector.

"How can that be?" the investigator asked in surprise. "They were admitted into the institute by decision of the admissions committee."

"But they were expelled from the institute by order of the Rector."

"When?"

"As soon as we received the anonymous statement."

"All three of them?"

"Yes, all three."

"On the basis of an anonymous letter?"

"The secretary of the admissions committee has been arrested on the basis of that same letter."

"The case is under investigation. The money found at Kalantarov's home does not prove that those particular students gave him bribes to accept their applications."

The Rector frowned.

"I am not concerned with the degree of criminal responsibility of Kalantarov or the students he favoured. This is the first time anything like this has happened in our institute. We discussed the warning that we had received and took the appropriate decision. Kalantarov will not work in our institute again, even if he avoids punishment under criminal law. A higher educational institution is an ideological establishment and people suspected of illegal activities have no moral right either to teach or study in it."

"Suspicion not confirmed by facts is not proof of guilt," the investigator objected.

"You and I are talking about different things," the Rector said dryly. "You are thinking in terms of the criminal law, but I have something different in mind — the right to call oneself a Soviet educator or a Soviet student."

"And what if the anonymous letter that you received is slander?"

"I shall be only too pleased if that can be proved."

"But you have already expelled these students!"

"And you have arrested Kalantarov!"

"We were acting in the interests of the investigation."

"And I was acting in the interests of the institute's good name."

Finally realising that it was hopeless to continue trying to shake the other man's certainty that the decision he had taken was correct, the investigator stood up.

"Where should I look for them now?"

"Ask for their addresses in the academic office."

The investigator nodded and walked towards the door. When he had opened it, he looked back.

"Perhaps I underestimate the importance of the interests of your institute, but it is still my opinion that the decision you took was premature. And let me warn you: since this matter concerns the futures of three young men, be careful. At that age people can act very rashly."

"What do you mean?"

"Nothing specific. But better safe than sorry." And with that the investigator stepped out of the office and closed the door behind him.

The Rector pressed a button on his intercom.

"Mina, ask Gasanov to come in."

His left eyelid had started twitching again, and he wanted to rub it with his hand, but Gasanov had already slipped in through the half-open door. He took a step forward, stopped and suddenly started backing away, as if he had decided to go back into the waiting room.

"I… if … a bit later …" he said in a barely audible voice, looking down at his feet.

"Stop," the Rector said sternly, and Gasanov stopped. "Come here."

Gasanov approached the desk hesitantly.

"Sit down."

The impressively large Adam's apple below Gasanov's skinny chin jerked up and down several times, as if he were trying to swallow something that was stuck in his throat.

"Don't sack me," he said in a strangled voice.

The business had taken a most undesirable turn — the last thing he wanted to do now was launch into explanations which he had made the responsibility of the provost for academic matters.

"I have two children."

The Rector's hand reached up and started rubbing his left eyelid, which was still twitching.

"Why don't you sit down?" he asked, not knowing what else to say.

At this point there was a very timely knock at the door and Ramazanov looked into the office.

"May I come in?"

"Please do," said the Rector.

"Don't sack me," Gasanov repeated.

The Rector exchanged glances with Ramazanov who walked over to the desk and picked up one of the two phones that had both started ringing simultaneously.

"Nobody's firing you," the provost said to Gasanov, "just calm your wife down so that she doesn't cause any scandals here. Hello…"

The second phone fell silent as the Rector reached out for it, Mina must have answered the call in the waiting room.

"Your case will be decided in the academic office," said the Rector, as if he hadn't heard what Ramazanov said. "You should make inquiries there."

"It's from the dean's office in mechanical engineering," Ramazanov told the Rector. "They want to know how to admonish that student in the cap, the one you rebuked — write a report on him or just reprimand?"

"Let them decide."

Immediately after these words, Mina appeared in the office and started leading Gasanov to the door, holding him tightly by one arm just above the elbow and speaking quietly but very forcefully into his ear. Gasanov followed her submissively and only turned back in the doorway to cast a melancholy glance of farewell at the Rector.

"Poor fellow," Ramazanov sighed sympathetically.

"Did you know he was involved with Imanova?"

"I guessed. But we can't sack him for that."

"Are you suggesting we sack Imanova?"

"Certainly not! She's our best programmer."

"Then we'll have to let him go: if his wife does something

to herself, and she is quite capable of it, the staff of the institute will be collectively responsible."

"She's only trying to frighten us."

"One of them has to leave the institute," the Rector said in a tone of voice that indicated the subject was closed. "What did you want to tell me?"

Ramazanov reached into his pocket and took out a sheet of paper completely covered in writing. The Rector squinted at the tall grandfather clock standing in the corner of the office.

"I came about the new building," said Ramazanov. "Is the decision to use it for teaching final?"

The Rector's left eyebrow shot up: for those who knew him well, this was an indication of great surprise.

"Why would you have any doubt about that?"

"Please, don't take this the wrong way." Ramazanov began, speaking rapidly and excitedly, as if he sensed that he might be interrupted at any second. "Your decision has been approved in the Ministry of Higher Education, and it's not easy to change anything now. But I have to try: you know as well as I do what working conditions are like in the institute's Research and Development centre — people are literally sitting on each other's heads. There's nowhere to put the equipment and instruments, and that makes it impossible to develop contract work on the proper scale. And anything that does get done requires a hellish effort. And yet, knowing all this, you suddenly accept the ministry's proposal to double the intake of students. You yourself have said many times that they're expecting us to solve a whole range of scientific and technical problems of great importance for the national economy. And then suddenly you give away the science laboratory block, without which any expansion of research work is absolutely impossible, to be used for lecture halls. Is it really all that important to have more students than any other institute of our kind in the entire country?"

The Rector's first impulse was to put an end to this conversation immediately, but this unusual display of determination by one of his subordinates (although, admittedly, the most independent of them) induced him to act more cautiously. But he had only one goal in mind: not just to tweak his upstart deputy's nose, but to hit him hard with the full weight of his fist, to put paid to any desire to pester him with questions once and for all.

"Generally speaking, I shouldn't have to give you explanations," he said in a quiet voice, with a cold reserve that marked very precisely the distance that separated them. "But, I'm not going to live forever. The time will come when one of you will be sitting in this chair; and it's about time you understood how important it is for a leader to take decisions that produce strategically important results, not just immediate ones. You're right, we won't have decent conditions for research and development for another two or three years. But in the next Five-Year Plan we'll get three new blocks all at once: we have done the ministry a favour by increasing the student intake now, and it will respond by increasing our capital investment fund in the future. Not to mention that the three hundred students taken in over and above the Plan are desperately needed by the national economy that you are so concerned about."

The Rector felt his arguments had made the impact that he had intended, primarily because they had been addressed to a man who did not have the institute's true interests at heart, and was therefore incapable of correctly understanding the meaning of any sacrifice made for their sake. But nevertheless, he waited for an answer to his words. He waited in order to move on to the conclusion of the conversation, which was absolutely unavoidable, regardless of how far they had understood each other, or failed to understand each other so far. But Ramazanov was in no hurry to reply — his expression and his posture expressed profound disappointment at what he had just heard.

"That's easy to say — two or three years," he said eventually in the voice of a man obliged to give the funeral speech at the burial of his own dream. "Those are years in the lives of human beings, not abstract immortal entities. It means postponing for two or three years or, realistically speaking, four or five, the realisation of specific scientific ideas, plans, calculations, projects. And at the same time the lives of dozens of people are wrecked."

"Their careers, you mean," the Rector corrected him.

"Put it that way if you like," said Ramazanov, jerking his head back testily. "It's very hard to separate one from the other. Of course, you mean me in the first place. But you didn't dispute the theses of my dissertation. Why are you opposed to them being applied in practice? Tens of millions of roubles a year are just thrown away because the mathematical models of most industrial plants are not adequate to their physical reality. It has been proved by dozens of examples. We talk about using data processing machines to manage production, but for that we have to…"

"You want to turn the institute into a testing ground for mathematically re-equipping an entire sector of industry," the Rector said, interrupting Ramazanov. His tone was as calm and cool as ever. "That is the job of scientific research institutes, but we are a higher educational institution. And our primary goal is to train specialists, in the greatest possible numbers. And as long as I sit in this chair, I will not allow an educational institution to be transformed into a site for the application of its employees' scientific ideas, no matter how interesting they might be. And I advise you not to abuse your official position to promote your own scientific advancement. You can pay a heavy price for that sort of thing, including your Party membership. Do you understand me? I didn't start this conversation, but since it has taken place, make a note of this and pass it on to the others. As long as I am Rector here, scientific research will only be carried out to the extent necessary to maintain the high quality of education for students, and that is all!"

Ramazanov stood up, and the expression on his pale face expressed his determination to have his say.

"The quality of the students' education is directly dependent on the level of scientific research work conducted in an educational institution. That was proved long ago. And not to use the scientific potential we have for the needs of industry is nothing less than sabotage!" These last words were spoken in the voice of a man who has decided he has nothing left to lose, since every goal that gave his life meaning has turned out to be impossible.

The Rector had the same feeling he had had that morning while he was shaving — as if there was no air for him to breathe: the oppressive sensation started in his throat and darted into the left side of his chest, towards his heart, which started fluttering and leaping in an effort to resist the sudden pressure.

"A surprising point of view," he said, after taking several inconspicuous gulps of air. "And, above all, a candid one. I'll think about it. But don't be surprised if the outcome is that you have to leave the institute." The Rector smiled ironically and pressed a button on his intercom. "You may go."

Mina glanced into the office.

"It's time for your lunch. The car's waiting," she said with a glance of disapproval at Ramazanov, who was still standing by the desk; there was something else he wanted to say — either to clarify the meaning of the torrent of words that had come pouring out of him, or to apologise for the excessively emotional way in which they had been spoken. But the Rector no longer seemed to notice his deputy; as he talked to Mina, he lifted up one of the phones and started dialling a number. Ramazanov glared at him for a while, with his head lowered, then gave up and walked towards the door.

The Rector waited until Mina also left the office, put down the receiver and threw his body against the back of the chair. He took several deep breaths in and out. His eyes were closed, his left eyelid was twitching as if someone were pricking it with a needle. But he walked out into the waiting room perfectly calm, not even Mina's penetrating glance could detect a trace of agitation in him.

"Have you taken your medication?," she asked, getting up.

"I'll take it at home. After lunch."

"When shall we expect you?

"At about three."

"I'm worried about that car."

"What car?" he asked, thinking it necessary to sound surprised.

"The one that was following you today. Your driver told me about it."

"I think it's all in his imagination…"

He left Mina at the door of the waiting room and walked through the institute's empty, deserted corridors (another double lecture period had started), down to the ground floor, past the fat doorman standing respectfully to attention, and out into the street. The car drove up to the pavement at the very moment he appeared on the marble steps of the institute's entrance.

It was a difficult day — problems suddenly appeared that he had simply not foreseen. Although, of course, he should have expected Ramazanov's reaction to the decision to use the science building for lecture halls; perhaps not in quite such a tempestuous form, but some kind of conversation on the subject had certainly been bound to take place. And if he hadn't foreseen it, then he was to blame, not Ramazanov, who was right in his own way. Only in his own way, though, as a scientist, for whom the most important thing was scientific results. But there were wider considerations that took into account other aspects of the institute's life, and circumstances of which Ramazanov was not aware or, even if he had heard of them, he didn't think had to be taken seriously. He didn't have to make the rounds of the offices, deciding the institute's problems. But never mind Ramazanov; if he didn't have the wits to calm down, he would have to leave the institute; there was no other alternative. Far more difficult to neutralise was the wife of that quiet one, Gasanov. He felt sorry for the lad, of course, but with a wife like that he could have behaved a bit more prudently.

They drove home by the same route they had followed in the morning, at about the same speed; this time the trees on the embankment were flickering past on the left.

And beyond them was the thick inky blue of the sea.

There had been a time when he really loved the sea; he suddenly remembered the long-forgotten sensations of a body immersing itself in the cool caress of sea water, it was like quenching your thirst. And this surprised him, in the same way as he had been surprised by events and people he had completely forgotten about starting to surface in his memory that morning. Well, if he hadn't completely forgotten them, at least he hadn't remembered them for many years. The number of times he had driven along this boulevard and seen the sea behind the trees, and he looked at it almost every day from his balcony, but every time he only saw it as one part of an attractive landscape, together with the lawns, the avenues and the arbours on the embankment.

When he was a child, nothing had given him greater pleasure than the sea. But he had abandoned it for a very serious reason: of course it was hard to accuse an inanimate medium of treachery, but as he gulped down the water in terror, feeling with his foot for the bottom that wasn't there, it was precisely the bitterness of betrayal that he had tasted as he sank down into the water's bottomless depths. That was the summer he thought he had learned to swim. This assurance had come to him at the Young Pioneer camp at Pirshagi, where they were taken to the sea every day. Choosing a spot where it was deep enough, he had floundered about in the water for a long time, trying to stay horizontal and hoping that he was moving along the line of the shore. When he got tired, he reached down with his foot for the safety of the bottom to take a rest and then carry on practicing.

While he was at the camp, his friends from the yard had been sneaking off to the municipal swimming pool (visiting it without an adult was strictly forbidden). And when he came home and announced that he had learned to swim, he found out that his friends had been putting their time to good use as well.

The very next day the whole yard had set out to the swimming pool to compare their achievements. The white wooden tower of the pool, a monument from the times of Tsar Nicholas, had been demolished later in the sixties, a few years after the municipal health authorities had prohibited swimming in the bay. Time was short, so they ran all the way from the house to the embankment, and when their bare feet were already pattering across the battens of the decking on the wooden gantry, they all chipped in for the tickets.

The fourth pool, where they swam during their rare visits to the swimming pool with their parents, was no deeper than the place at the Young Pioneer camp where he thought that he had learned to swim. But while he was away, his friends had moved up to the deeper, "open" pool. Here there was a springboard three metres high and the occasional daredevil even jumped from the "burner" — the solarium on the roof of the baths, which was fenced off with a wooden balustrade. On one side there were rows of so-call "numbers" — separate cabins where you could get changed or simply pass the time which had short stepladders running down to the water. While they were still hurrying to the ticket office, one of the lads thought he caught a glimpse of the Doctor in the crowd moving along the gantry. But since everyone in the yard knew that the Doctor had gone away on business a week ago, they decided it was a false alarm. Sultan asked if his father was alone, but then felt surprised at his own question — as the Doctor's son, he knew better than anyone else that the Doctor was out of town.

They didn't jump off the wet springboard with its tricky bounce, let alone the sunbathing roof, but walked down the wooden steps, holding on to the banisters, and jumped into the water one by one: even back then it was already covered with a film of oil shimmering with all the colours of the rainbow. And Fariz went with them, not the last, but not one of the first either — the doubt in his ability to negotiate the ten-metre wide strip of water to the steps of the nearest "number" arose simultaneously with the foreboding that the bottom of this opaque, greenish water was somewhere very, very far down, and he wouldn't be able to push off from it if he needed to, as he had done at the beach in the camp.

He couldn't bring himself not to jump, although at the last moment, when he still had time to change his mind, he finally realised that he was deceiving himself and his friends — floundering about in the water as he had been doing all summer at the camp was absolutely nothing like knowing how to swim.

Later, when he had grown up, he had only once experienced such a stark feeling of fear again. It wasn't at the front, where in three years the need to act independently had never arisen — the general command was given and he had acted along with everyone else, but on both occasions the fear had been worsened by the fact that he could have refused; after all, no one had forced him to do what seemed so dangerous; in both cases he had had a choice.

But anyway, he jumped. The water seemed to scorch his skin — it was deeper here and much colder than at the beach in the camp.

What made him follow all the others? Certainly not courage, he knew that now. He was probably driven by fear. Not the kind that can be overcome with an effort, but a different kind, more powerful — the fear of losing people's respect. In the first case it was children, in the second grown-ups, both times he had not done what he wanted to do, but acted according to the dictates of the situation. The first to notice that he was drowning was Sultan, who had already swum to those distant steps. And of course, he immediately jumped into the water to help. But how can you help someone who's drowning when you can barely swim yourself? If the grown-ups hadn't come dashing out of their "numbers", they would both have drowned, because none of his screaming friends had decided to follow Sultan's example.

The story would have had a perfectly happy ending if only one of the people directly involved in saving them had not been the Doctor, who was supposedly away on business, and if a woman had not been discovered in his "number", where the half-drowned boy was taken to be given artificial respiration. (His friends told him later what she looked like. He hadn't been in a fit state to admire female charms but, according to the description, the Doctor's companion in the cabin was young and beautiful, and her close-fitting bathing suit emphasised the sumptuous forms of her body and the whiteness of her skin, which was highly prized in those days in the southern city of Baku, where even today many woman carefully avoid getting a tan).

Many years later the Doctor had joked that the future Rector had risked drowning in order to do him a good turn: infatuated by that woman with the glorious breasts, the Doctor had been going away on "business" more and more often, and there was no telling how it would all have ended if he had not been exposed by the incident at the baths. Sultan's mother had taken action immediately after that, and unlike certain modern-day women, she hadn't created any public scandals, but simply applied certain highly effective domestic measures to restore conjugal fidelity.

"I can't see them," said Amanulla, breaking the silence.

"Who?"

"They drove up to the institute twice. The doorman took down their number."

"And who told him to do that?"

"Mina."

"You're great masters at creating a mountain out of a molehill."

"Then why did they drive off as soon as the doorman went over to them?"

"There could be plenty of reasons. Are you sure it was the same car that he went over to?"

"The same colour, the same model… And there it is!" Amanulla exclaimed. "Look, over on the right."

The Rector glanced round, realising that he was doing so with untypical haste. As if it realised it had been spotted, the white Zhiguli that was rapidly gaining on them turned off at a crossroads, just as it had in the morning.

"Did you see?"

"Yes," the Rector said somewhat uncertainly, since he hadn't got a clear look at the men in the car.

"We ought to give the car's number to the militia," said Amanulla, "so they can find out who they are."

These words reminded him of the investigator's visit and the warning he had given him: if the two men in the Zhiguli were on the list of students that the investigator was interested in, it clearly made sense to take precautionary measures.

The car pulled in to the kerb and stopped: the Rector stepped out on to the pavement, but he didn't walk to the entrance. Instead, for the first time in many years, he walked across to the fountain that he often admired from above, from the balcony of his flat. His attention was caught by the solitary figure of a man standing on the small area of square tiles surrounding the watery site of eternal battle between the mighty knight and the scaly-tailed monster. He noticed something familiar straight away, at first glance, and the closer he came to the fountain, the stronger the feeling became that he had met this broad-shouldered young man quite often. But where and when?

"Hello," the young man said, and the husky voice set his heart racing for the fourth time that day, as if he were grasped in someone's slowly but surely closing fist. Again he had the feeling that there was no air to breathe, as if he had just been on a long, exhausting run, and he had to take several deep breaths.

The young man could easily be one of tens of thousands of graduates from his institute. But for some reason, as the Rector said "Hello" he carried on straining his memory in an attempt to find a more convincing explanation.

"Don't you recognise me?" the young man asked.

"Of course I do!" he objected, and at that very moment the

search taking place in the depths of his memory was completed: Marat! The Doctor's grandson, Sultan's son. "Your mother?" he asked uncertainly. "How's your mother? Is she still…" As soon as he asked the question he remembered that several years earlier he had driven to his childhood home in his Volga for the carrying-out of her body.

"My mother passed away. You were at the funeral." In the years since they last saw each other, Marat had become very like his father. And his grandfather too, especially the voice — the Doctor had had that same husky bass.

"Yes, yes, of course, I'm sorry. She was a remarkable woman."

A picture flashed into his mind and disappeared again: his elder son, wrapped in an army greatcoat, sitting on a stool beside the door of the flat they used to have on the ground floor, with a basin at his feet for hacking up tubercular phlegm. And all around there were healthy boys of the same age, including Marat.

What year was that? Forty-six? Forty-five? Yes, forty-five, immediately after he came back from the front. Marat and his mother still occupied the Doctor's entire flat on the first floor — the Doctor and Sultan were no longer alive: Sultan was killed during the first months of the fighting near Moscow, and the Doctor had died even earlier, in thirty-seven.

"Do you still live in the same place?"

"Yes."

"How many of the old neighbours are still there?"

"None. I'm the only one left."

"The only one left? In the entire yard?"

"Yes, the building is due to be demolished."

"Oh, I see. And when are you going to move?"

"I'm holding on for the time being," Marat said with a smile, and a fold appeared beside his mouth in his right cheek, just like the one the Doctor used to have when he smiled. Sultan used to get one too, only it wasn't so noticeable.

"Your father and I were very close friends," said the Rector.

"I know."

"You were still very young."

"My mother told me."

"And how's that other one getting on? Your friend, he was a bit older than all of you…"

"Alik?"

"Yes, Alik."

"He's doing well. He's got a flat."

"Did he get married?"

"A long time ago. He has three children."

"Well, thank God." He was surprised at his own tone of voice — it had the ring of genuine interest in the life of a neighbour he hadn't seen for about twenty years. "And what are you doing here? Taking a walk?"

"Waiting for Eldar."

A simple act of deduction led him to conclude that his elder son had paid a visit to his parents and at the present moment was in their flat on the third floor.

"But why are you waiting for him here? Why didn't you go in?"

"Thank you, but he won't be long."

"You're right there," said the Rector, "if he comes at all, then it's not for long. Well, goodbye."

As he stepped into the road and waited for several cars to go by, the Rector looked round: Marat was watching him go, with his shirt sleeves rolled up to the elbows, revealing the strong, tanned arms folded across his chest — the Doctor's favourite pose. How exactly nature had reproduced the Doctor's appearance, first in his son and now in his grandson! Only did he have the same character? But then, why shouldn't he? His mother had been the same, even though she was Russian. She had agreed so easily to the exchange of flats, she hadn't even let Fariz finish what he was saying. It was only nine months after he got back from the front, no more than that; his elder son was dying of tuberculosis, his younger son was just about to be born. In the little room that they still shared with his parents and one of his sisters (fortunately the other two had got married) it was hard to find space at night even on the floor; he used to sleep in the cold corridor, with the glass wall looking out into the yard prudishly covered with muslin curtains.

Where had the idea of the exchange come from? Who had been the first to think of it? Not his father, of course, and not his mother or himself — they had lived all their lives in this yard and accepted the order of its life as inviolable, they could never have had such an idea, even faced with the threat of losing a son, and infecting the second child who was expected any day. Only his wife, whom he had brought into his parents' home just before the war began — she was the only one capable of coming up with such a way of saving her children. Of course, he compensated Marat and his mother for the difference in floor space — with money, and food, and clothes; he worked in the "service" as they used to say then, meaning State security, so he had the means to thank them. Although he had tried to help Sultan's widow and her son even before that; it would have been strange if he had come back from the war alive and not given all the support he could to the family of his dead friend. Not to mention the fact that his friend was the son of the Doctor, to whom the entire yard, including himself, owed so much. But even knowing that he could more than compensate financially for the uneven exchange, he hesitated for a long time before approaching Marat's mother with the suggestion. For several evenings in a row he sat in the yard after work, glancing up at the first floor balcony and trying to persuade himself to walk up the old stone steps with the rough wooden banisters that he and Sultan used to slide down when they were children, and knock at the door with the plaque that said "Doctor Agakhanov, Internal Ailments". Perhaps he would never have been able to make himself do it, if Marat's mother hadn't helped him to start the conversation. Much later, after he finished his PhD and got a job in the department of electrical engineering, he had read something by a foreign author about the concept of provocative behaviour by the victim of a crime, which was taken as a mitigating circumstance in determining the punishment for a person who committed a crime as a result of such provocation. Something of the kind had happened then, although, of course, he hadn't done anything criminal in responding to her sympathetic enquiries about his son's illness and what he was going to do after the second child was born by forcing himself to utter the words that he had prepared long before.

She hadn't even let him finish — she had agreed to move out of three rooms into one as if it was something that didn't really matter to her, as if she were simply giving away some medicine that she hadn't needed for a long time anyway.

On the other side of the street the Rector walked into the entrance and pressed the lift button: the doors clanged open to reveal his elder son, who was far from delighted by this unexpected meeting with his father and stepped aside to let him pass.

"What brings you here?" the father asked.

"I'm looking for my wife."

"Is that the only reason you dropped into your parents' home?"

"What do you want me to reply to that?" the son asked.

"Just tell the truth."

"In that case — yes."

"Well, no one could accuse you of being insincere."

"And what could they accuse me of?"

"What reply can I give to a man who isn't even interested in his mother's health?"

"She's perfectly well."

"She hasn't got out of bed in months ..."

"Not everyone has that opportunity."

"What's opportunity got to do with it?"

"She wouldn't have been lying there for so long if she wasn't waited on hand and foot."

"And what do you suggest?" despite the cruelty of his son's words, they contained a certain element of truth that the Rector didn't wish to challenge, so he changed the subject. He wasn't sure that his daughter-in-law's visit in the morning had been made with his son's knowledge, but even so he spoke about it as if the couple had taken the decision to ask for help jointly. "Oh, by the way, since we've run into each other, I didn't quite understand what it is that you need? Your wife doesn't know the details, and it's not easy to help without knowing the essence of the matter."

"She asked you for something?"

"Yes."

"You?"

"Believe it or not. But I explained to her that a proud and independent man like you shouldn't allow his wife to go asking favours of all and sundry."

"You're right, father," said the son, displaying remarkable self-control, but turning so pale that it was obvious even in the poorly lit entrance. "She shouldn't have bothered you: I've warned her over and over again that it's better to starve to death than accept a crust of bread from the hand of someone like you." The son's voice, which had so far been calm, suddenly broke and he turned away sharply and walked quickly towards the bright rectangle of the doorway, in which the Rector could see a sun-drenched corner of the seaside park.

Perhaps they didn't get on because their characters were so alike, although their son had plenty of his mother in him too, or perhaps the reason lay in the exceptional amount of attention the boy had received because he was ill as a child, but one way or another, many qualities that had only manifested themselves in the Rector's character at a mature age and as a result of the circumstances of life, had become noticeable very early on in his son. The Rector had had the patience to act for most of his life in accordance with his own rather limited abilities. Now, however, he had achieved his goal, everything that had been denied to him during the first half of his life, he had received in abundance later, as the result of many years of effort. But in the meantime how hard it had been for him to maintain a relationship of mutual respect with his own father! Of course, he had to give the old man credit for the tactful, almost casual way in which he had ceded the role of head of the family. And the Rector himself had always treated his uneducated father with irreproachably correct filial respect. After all, by modern standards, his father had done nothing for him (and how could the poor devil have done anything, when his pay was barely enough to feed his wife and six children?). He had achieved everything in life for himself: school had been difficult enough, then he had struggled to manage the classes in the evening college, and it had taken him three years longer than other people to complete his PhD dissertation. Why had he been so stubbornly attracted to science? Was it because it felt more reliable, more stable than the job in "the service" in which he was already quite successful, after four years in state security?

The Doctor had spotted this ambition of his to acquire an education, no matter what the cost, and had often held him up as an example to Sultan, to whom everything came easily. The Doctor had been the first to take notice of the future Rector, he had singled him out from the other lads, and the things the Doctor occasionally said to mark his modest successes had meant a great deal to him, because they came from a man who was respected in their yard.

Of course, Sultan also respected his father greatly, although he never made a point of emphasising it, and sometimes even allowed himself a few critical remarks. But just how much Sultan loved his father only became clear later, when it came to deciding what college he should study in. Everyone in the Medical Institute knew the Doctor, and in order to avoid any possible complications after what had happened a year earlier, it was suggested that Sultan should formally — "on paper"–

disown his father. Then the Doctor's brother (who by then had become a popular physician) could have "adopted" Sultan, thereby making it possible for the admissions committee to allow him to take the entrance exams.

Fariz was present at that conversation. The picture of a semi-naked woman in a cape offering a jug of water to a weary hunter was no longer hanging on the wall of the large room in the Doctor's flat (the Doctor had bought the picture in nineteen-nineteen at a second-hand market in Petrograd, and it had turned out to be an original work by some 17th century Italian artist), the two huge Chinese vases with dragons had disappeared and the windows were bare — the maroon velvet curtains had also been sold to one of the neighbours.

Sultan's mother asked him in a hesitant voice to write a few words, saying that he repudiated his father, and Sultan, sitting at the round table with his father's portrait in a plain wooden frame, kept repeating the same thing over and over again: "I can't do this, mum, I can't. Surely you understand that?" The Doctor's younger brother was supposed to arrive to collect the declaration at any minute, but he didn't show up. Not that evening or later. He never again set foot inside the home where he had been raised and educated. So the question of Sultan's "adoption" effectively resolved itself. And soon afterwards the war started.

Amanulla drove along, occasionally glancing into the rear-view mirror, and although he did it with an air of great concern, it was clear that the strange business of the Zhiguli he was watching out for so carefully had introduced a little welcome variety into his boring driver's life.

"I can't understand what it is they want," he said, launching into a lengthy monologue. "What are they trying to achieve? Do they want to spend the rest of their lives in prison? They've chosen the wrong person to trail! I'd give good money to get a look at their faces. Eye to eye. And of course, if you allowed it, I'd give those characters what they've got coming to them without any help from the militia! They wouldn't go following other people's cars around again." As he spoke, he kept glancing into the mirror, but the white Zhiguli still didn't appear.

The institute building appeared on the far side of Progressive Workers Square, and a few seconds later the car pulled up at the entrance.

Imanova was waiting for the Rector in the small "cactus hallway" outside the office, on the same spot where Gasanov had stood only a few hours earlier.

"I beg your pardon, Fariz Agaevich," she said, stepping towards him, "but could you please spare me a few minutes?"

"Unfortunately I can't just at the moment," the Rector replied, opening the door of the waiting room. "I have other things scheduled. My reception day is Monday."

Imanova followed him into the waiting room.

"I'm afraid that Monday will be too late," she said in a quiet voice, and something in her intonation, some hidden threat, made him gesture to stop Mina, who was already advancing on his visitor.

"Gumbatov is dealing with your business," he said, looking into the narrow space between Imanova and Mina.

"If you won't see me, I shall have to resign," Imanova said.

"You've been told, go and see Gumbatov," said Mina, deciding to intervene anyway.

"Why you?" the Rector asked. "As far as I'm aware, it was Gasanov who…"

"He can't leave his job, he has two children."

"He should have thought about his children sooner," said Mina.

The Rector squinted at her in annoyance and walked to the door of his office.

"If you had ever loved anyone," Imanova said before he could step inside, "you wouldn't act so heartlessly."

The Rector closed the door and leaned back against it for a

moment with his eyes closed, then he walked across to his desk and dialled Gumbatov's number.

"It's me," he said in his usual cool, calm tone of voice. "If Gasanov refuses to write a letter of resignation, have his behaviour discussed at a meeting of the department's staff."

"He's already refused," Gumbatov replied in a tearful voice.

"In that case, don't put the meeting off any longer." The Rector put the phone down and called Mina in. "I have a meeting scheduled with Nuriev from *The Baku Worker* at three thirty."

"He's in the waiting room."

"Ask him to come in."

The correspondent Nuriev, well known everywhere for his ability to gain access to the most highly placed individuals, no matter how often they might be replaced, apologised for being three minutes late and produced several narrow strips of paper out of his briefcase with the gesture of a conjuror: the article about the institute and its prospects in the years immediately ahead had already been typeset.

"I'm busy until six o'clock," the Rector told Mina, "no matter who calls."

"Very well," she said and left the office.

"Can we manage it in three hours?" the Rector asked, picking up the galley-proofs of the article.

"Basically, the article's ready," Nuriev said with a condescending smile, "and as you can see, it has already been typeset. It only needs your approval…

"I think you've been over-hasty," the Rector said as he glanced through the text of the proofs. "This article is going out under my signature, and I haven't even read it."

"That's precisely why I'm here."

"Thank you," said the Rector, setting aside the strips of paper that Nuriev had brought and taking several sheets of typescript out of the drawer of his desk. "I have prepared my own version. I think it gives a more accurate picture of the important aspects of the work of our institute and its immediate prospects." He held the text out to Nuriev, who took his spectacles out of his pocket before taking it. "We are going through a very special stage here — at very short notice, in accordance with the demands of the time, we intend to almost double the numbers of students training at our institute for professions that are essential to our national economy. And it seems to me it is precisely this feature of the current stage in the life of our institute, which will make it one of the largest educational institutions in the country, which should be the central focus of the article. Everything else should be secondary to this truly historical turning point in the work of our institution."

Nuriev frowned in annoyance even as he nodded his head in agreement with what he heard — he was far from pleased by the unexpected need to do more work on an article that had already been written. The Rector left the institute at about nine in the evening. The car was there at the curb the moment he stepped out into the street. On receiving instructions to drive to the doctor, Amanulla turned the car round and drove off along an avenue that led uptown.

It had been a stressful day, many things had happened — the Rector made himself comfortable on the back seat and set about analysing the decisions taken in the course of the day.

A little later, he noticed that Amanulla had driven past the crossroads where he normally turned off the avenue. As if he could sense his boss's unspoken question, Amanulla turned his head to look back and said:

"The road's dug up there, we'll have to drive round."

"Look where you're going," the Rector said, and when the car emerged on to an intersection with a street that climbed steeply upwards towards a series of single-storey buildings on the left, and dived down towards the city centre if they turned right, he suddenly ordered: "Go uphill here."

Reacting with impressive speed, Amanulla swung the wheel to the left, even though he had been about to do the very opposite. Of course, he would have liked to know the reason for such an unexpected change of route, but that would have violated the long-standing arrangement under which he carried out his boss's instructions, no matter how strange they might be, without any explanations. The car strained a little to mount the slope before emerging on to a plateau covered with newly built houses, some of which were not even inhabited yet.

"Straight on," the Rector said, and Amanulla drove the car along the neat row of buildings. "Left here."

Now they were driving though an open space that seemed boundless in the twilight; lights had already come on here and there in the buildings that they had left behind, and they twinkled mysteriously high above the ground.

Then there were two more lights, but they were almost level with the ground, on the far side of a dark space. The car drove towards them, avoiding the bumps and potholes in the dirt road.

"Stop the car," the Rector said when there were about ten metres away from the two-storey building in which only one window on the ground floor was lit; a second light bulb lit up the gates leading into the yard.

The Rector got out of the car, took several steps and stopped. Then, seeming to overcome his doubts, he walked to the gates of the building. But he suddenly turned around, walked resolutely back to the car, opened the front door and got in beside Amanulla.

"Let's go…"

After they had driven away from the dark space of the waste lot, bordered on one side by the lights of the newly built houses and on the other by the dark gaping hole of the quarry, he said:

"I was born in that building."

He spoke the words out loud, but Amanulla seemed not to have heard them — experience told him that the boss was occupied with thoughts of his own, and the words about the house were part of them.

Why did I come here? the Rector thought. And once I got here, why didn't I say goodbye to the yard where I spend the first half of my life, except the four years I gave to the war? Why, knowing that the building is due to be demolished, didn't I go in one last time, into that dark entryway with the row of four black iron rubbish bins and the steps up to the first floor, with the only toilet in the yard underneath them…

Before he could answer this question, the episode that he thought he had brushed aside that morning surfaced in his memory again. Like everything else to do with his childhood, his school years and his life after the war up until nineteen fifty-four, when he had moved to a new apartment, this episode was screened off by other important events from later in his life, but for some reason ever since the morning his memory had been throwing up all those things that had lost any meaning for him long ago. And for some reason on this very day he had met Marat, whom he hadn't seen for many years, even though Marat was a friend of his elder son. And finally, this unplanned detour because the road was being repaired had taken him close to the courtyard where he had spent his childhood. Although, of course, he actually visited the same doctor quite frequently — he was the only one of his former neighbours with whom he maintained any kind of contact. Perhaps that was because this doctor, who was the younger brother of the Doctor they all admired so much, and who had become a well-known professor and medical practitioner in his own right, had left the yard in the early nineteen-thirties, and didn't know about many of the things that had happened there after that.

After his family moved up from the ground floor into the Doctor's flat, and the "Dodge", a war trophy, had started coming to collect him in the mornings, the neighbours' attitude to him had changed quite markedly. Even Sultan's wife (she hadn't married again after her mother-in-law died in forty-nine, although she was still attractive, even after the age of forty) tried to make way for him when they occasionally met at the gates of the yard. Of course, he never allowed it, although he did take a certain satisfaction in these gestures, taking them as a sign of the yard's growing respect as everyone followed his achievements with keen interest.

Only one family seemed not to notice the changes in his life, even when he broke off all contact with them for that very reason. The head of the family, Nadir, who had married a girl from the courtyard, was also a front-line veteran, and during the years immediately after the war the two families had been very friendly, especially the wives who had eaten together, taken trips to the beach in summer, gone shopping together. The fact that their children were the same age had also made them close; his neighbours' son, who had the terrible nickname "Lucky", used to spend days at a time at their place (as did Sultan's son, Marat), even after the grown-ups had broken off all contact.

The Rector had never liked Nadir's over-familiar, backslapping manner. But it had started to annoy him intensely after he moved into Party work, when a completely different type of person had started visiting their home — reserved, respectable individuals who were circumspect in their choice of new acquaintances.

Hints had failed to produce any effect, and he had been obliged to find a pretext for quarrelling with Nadir, after which his former friend had taken several liberties demonstrating a clear reluctance to accept the changes in the Rector's circumstances. And so, in the heat of the moment, the incident involving his young son had been taken as another provocation of the same sort — dashing out into the yard when he heard his son screaming, he had seen him crying and struggling in the grip of Nadir's wife, and decided that he couldn't let this woman's actions go unpunished — she had had the presumption to insult his son in front of the whole yard. Not because he felt sorry for the child (although, of course, that was part of it too) and not at all because Nadir's wife deserved to be rebuked, on the contrary, unlike her husband, she was a person who knew how to behave. But the point was that she had hit his son, at first he had thought that was why the child was crying, and that had undoubtedly been taken by the yard as yet another expression of disrespect for him and his family.

He hadn't pushed her away from the little boy very hard. But either she had been taken by surprise, or she had tripped over something, and she fell against the banisters of the balcony and, as he had discovered later, hurt her side quite badly. He took his son and went back into the house.

That evening he heard that the "victim's" brother, twenty-year-old Alik, who lived in the same yard with his crazy mother, intended to intervene on his sister's behalf; for all his swaggering pushiness, Nadir would never have dared to. And since he had watched this Alik grow up, the Rector knew, as the entire yard did, what he was capable of — it was enough to recall the time when Alik (who was only fifteen years old at the most) almost stabbed Nadir with a kitchen knife in nineteen forty-eight, after he found out that Nadir was involved with some other woman and was planning to leave his wife. No one could say if he would have used the knife or not, but when the decorated soldier Nadir, who had gone all the way from Moscow to Berlin, found himself backed up against a rubbish container in the entrance, he had promised the fifteen-year-old boy to leave his mistress immediately, and to love the boy's sister to the end of his days.

Of course, he could have taken timely measures, made a phone call to the right place and had the boy removed from the yard before he left to go to work, but for the neighbours that would have made him a coward and — more importantly — it would not have solved the problem. In a day or two the same thing would have happened all over again — the boy was not the kind to cool off quickly.

His wife begged him not to leave the flat, but at six thirty he went down the steps as usual and walked towards the gates. As a precaution, he was accompanied by his driver and two employees from his former place of work (he had listened to his wife's arguments and made that phone call after all). But even the presence of such a substantial escort wasn't enough to deter the madman, who overtook Fariz at the gates and said something in a low, calm voice — he didn't really hear it, because he was too agitated, it was something about it being easy to hit women, but hitting men was much harder. And then, quite unexpectedly, it took Fariz, and the men with him, and all the neighbours watching what was happening from the doors and windows of their flats by surprise, Alik flung back his right arm — Fariz caught a brief glimpse of the widespread fingers — as if he were trying to catch something flying past. Then the hand moved forward and there was a loud hollow smack, like someone clapping their hands. It was a moment or two before Fariz realised he had been slapped in the face in front of everyone in the yard. Later his cheek had swollen up and turned red, and for a day or two there had been a noise in his ear, as if water had got into it, but at the time he hadn't felt any pain, in fact he hadn't felt anything at all, except shame: his two sons and his wife, and everyone who lived in the yard had seen him get slapped, and he felt the mark of that slap on his cheek for many years. He already knew, even then, that nothing could ever bring him consolation, even though they would twist Alik's arms behind his back and take him away to the militia station, and they would beat him there in the heat of the moment and he would get several years in prison for assault (of course, at the trial they brought up a few other things that Alik had done, including attacking his own sister's husband with a knife — Nadir hadn't dared to deny something that everyone in the yard knew). And a little while later he realised that for the rest of his life he was doomed to be woken in the middle of the night by dreams in which various people slapped him on the cheek. In different circumstances, with or without any good reason, in public and in private he was slapped, slapped, slapped. And every time he saw that upraised young hand with those thin, widespread fingers.

It had taken many years for the healing power of time to weaken and blunt the pain, to push it aside and screen it off with new events, new cares, disappointments and joys. But even so, the memory of it often broke through and he saw the incident in every humiliating detail. Like today. He got out at the small park in front of the doctor's house without saying a word to his driver — that meant the car had to wait for him.

The Doctor's brother was a widower and he occupied an entire three-room flat on the third floor all on his own. The stone steps that the Rector walked up ended at a massive door with a cast-bronze handle and a bronze plaque with the occupant's name and title. The bell was bronze too, and it jangled when he turned the decorative handle protruding from the spot where there should have been a push-button.

The door was opened by a man of about forty with his shirt unbuttoned to the waist.

"The professor is not receiving today," he declared politely but categorically, after greeting the Rector.

"But he is at home?"

"Does that make any difference?" the man answered with just the faintest hint of irritation and fastened a button on his stomach.

"Obviously it does," the Rector replied calmly. "Please tell him that Fariz Rzaev is here."

The man shrugged and went to discuss the situation with the professor. The Rector stepped into the hallway with its two mahogany armchairs and closed the door behind him. While he was wondering whether to sit down or not, the same man appeared in the hallway and said in frankly annoyed tone of voice:

"Come through."

The professor whose shirt was also unbuttoned received the Rector in a spacious drawing room, one corner of which was occupied by a brightly lit round table. In his right hand the professor, who must have been eighty years old at the most conservative estimate, was holding something that looked like playing cards.

"Come through into the office," he said affably, "we were just having a bit of fun in here…"

The people sitting at the table were all different ages — the intense light of the chandelier that had been lowered right down glittered on venerable heads of silvery hair, glistened on bald patches, gleamed dully on thick heads of young hair. In all there were seven people sitting there, including the man who had opened the door.

The professor led the Rector through into the office and told him to take off his shirt, then went back to the drawing room. The Rector admired the sight of his own naked torso still muscular and by no means old-looking, in the mirror on the antique desk with numerous drawers.

The sound of voices in the drawing room was an even murmur, he couldn't make out what they were saying. There was quiet music playing.

The Rector's left eyelid, which he could see clearly in the mirror, started twitching again, as soon as he heard a single loudly spoken phrase, which obviously referred to him.

"I'm amazed at you!" said the voice of the man who had opened the door. "He put your brother in prison and you still treat him!"

"Those were difficult times, my friend," the professor replied, trying to keep his voice down. "It's easy to judge people now." The last words were very clearly audible, since the professor walked into the office immediately after them; evidently realising that the Rector had overheard the conversation, he put one hand on his shoulder. "Take no notice," he said.

"Who is he?" the Rector asked.

"Don't worry about him… Has the eye been twitching long?"

"A few days."

"What else are you complaining of?"

"Shortness of breath, I can't get enough air… And it feels as if someone's squeezing my heart when I get a bit worked up."

"Let's have a listen," said the professor, taking his stethoscope out of one of the drawers in the desk, "and my basic advice to you is — take a rest. It's a typical case of nervous exhaustion."

The investigator, a red-cheeked Ossetian with close-cropped hair by the name of Gudiev, who was later a production manager at the cinema studios for many years and once even came to see the Rector to ask for permission to shoot some footage in the institute, behaved in a very friendly fashion and welcomed him like a long-awaited guest. (He hadn't been officially summoned, they came to meet him at the security point of the metallurgical plant where he was working as a handyman while he studied in night school.)

"Well done… very good… sit down… take the pen… this is where you have to sign…" The investigator leaned his bulky body right across the desk and pointed to the bottom of the sheet of paper, where the typed text came to an end.

"Can I read it?" Fariz had asked, feeling awkward for not doing as his affable host asked straight away.

Gudiev laughed out loud — a sound like one of the plates of sheet iron that he carted about every day at the metallurgical plant clattering as it fell on the floor.

"Of course you can! So you would have signed without reading it? Good lad!"

He smiled in reply and ran his eyes over the text lying in front of him. As he suspected, it concerned the Doctor, who had not come home from work two months earlier.

Basically everything it said was true: every now and then the Doctor did rail against collective farms and the collectivisation policy as he drank his tea on the balcony in the yard in the evenings and looked through the newspapers; all the neighbours had heard his ironic comments, and so had Fariz.

"Agakhanov has confessed to everything," Gudiev told him. "Well, have you read it?"

"Yes."

"Why don't you sign it?"

"I'll sign it," he said in a quiet voice, "only don't tell the Doctor.

Gudiev started rumbling again, his entire body shook with laughter.

"Well done... Good lad. You have a great future ahead of you!" Still laughing, Gudiev got up from behind the desk, ruffled Fariz's hair and walked out of the office.

The pen was lying beside the sheet of paper that he had to sign, but he couldn't make himself pick it up and do what was required. In the final analysis, everything it said was true, and in all probability it had been confirmed by the other neighbours and, most important of all, by the Doctor himself; so his testimony wouldn't add anything or take anything away from what was already known. What then was preventing him from picking up the pen and writing his name under the printed text? At the time, and even now, more than forty years later, he was under no illusions about the reason for his doubts: if it had been anyone else but the Doctor, he would have regarded the need to give testimony as fulfilling his civic duty, but what made the situation horrific was that he had to sign a document against the Doctor, who had saved his life, given him the same pocket money as he gave his own son, cured his infection of the middle ear, taught him Russian... Against the Doctor, who had taken part in the Revolution in 1917 — he had seen the awards, the letters and the documents in the desk, Sultan had shown them to him.

He heard voices in the corridor and Gudiev came into the office, followed by the Doctor, who had lost so much weight that the grey jacket and striped trousers he always wore were dangling loosely on his body. One detail that caught his eye was the broken bridge of the gold-rimmed glasses, tied together with black thread.

"Ah, Fariz ..." the Doctor said quietly. "I was wondering who else there could be."

Gudiev laughed and sat down at his desk. He looked at the sheet of paper lying in front of Fariz.

"I told you it was a surprise. Sit down," he said to the Doctor, speaking in a very familiar fashion.

The Doctor sat down on a chair beside the window: Gudiev cast another brief glance at the interrogation report, saw that the signature he needed was still not there, frowned and uttered a phrase that made the Doctor cringe, as if in anticipation of severe pain.

"You feel sorry for him," said Gudiev, "but he didn't feel sorry for your father."

"Please..." the Doctor's quiet voice sounded as if someone had crushed his fingers in a door and forbidden him to cry out.

"He didn't feel sorry for your father," Gudiev repeated, "first he dragged him into his organisation, and then he betrayed him."

"Don't listen to him, Fariz," the Doctor said in a near-whisper.

"What was that you said?" Gudiev asked, staring at the Doctor with withering contempt. "Getting uppity again, are you?"

"No, no," the Doctor protested with a strange, subservient urgency, "you misunderstood me... But why does the child have to be here... That was what I meant..."

"He called you a child," said Gudiev, turning jovial again, "but at your age he was already carrying out assignments for the enemy."

The conversation that followed made it clear that the Doctor had begun his counterrevolutionary career in Moscow, when he was still a student, continued it during the Civil War and then really spread his wings when he came back to Baku and moved into their yard: the members of the organisation that he led used to meet in his flat several times a year, and at these gatherings, which were described to the naïve residents of the yard as birthday parties for the Doctor and members of his family, criminal plans directed against the state were discussed and approved. Fariz's father had also attended one of these meetings (it must have been the time when the Doctor asked him to mend the tap), at which he had been recruited, to which the Doctor had confessed under the pressure of evidence. After that, right until his father died in forty-nine, Fariz and his family had been afraid that the old man might be taken away any day.

Of course, he signed that sheet of paper typed by the future production manager Gudiev and felt no guilt for doing it — in comparison with what the Doctor had signed, his testimony was the very model of truth and objectivity.

But how had the card-player in the unbuttoned shirt found out about all this, and why had his words been taken so calmly by the professor, who had his ear pressed against a little trumpet, the broad end of which was tickling the skin on the left side of the Rector's chest, in the region of the heart that his memories had distressed so badly? But then, there wasn't really anything strange about that — the professor had cut all ties with his brother's family as soon as the Doctor was arrested.

Instead of bringing him relief, the visit to the doctor had ruined his mood completely. He knew perfectly well that he had been overdoing it, he hadn't had a chance to rest in the summer because of the entrance examinations, and now he was too busy with commissioning the new building.

On the way home Amanulla kept glancing in the mirror, but the white Zhiguli that had followed them so persistently during the day didn't show up again.

"Stop," the Rector said when the car drove out on to the embankment, "I'll take a walk. Tomorrow as usual," he added when he was already out of the car.

"Yes sir," Amanulla said and as a token of a driver's respect, he waited until his boss had walked some distance away from the car before driving off. The Rector crossed the street and strolled unhurriedly towards the building along the furthest alley of the seaside park, then he crossed back over the street opposite his house, walked past the fountain with the mighty hero, which was more impressive in the evenings because of the carefully designed electric lighting, although for some reason it wasn't working that evening.

There was no light in the entrance and, naturally, the lift wasn't working for the same reason.

The short walk hadn't tired him very much, but the need to drag himself up to the third floor was annoying.

The entrance was lit up intermittently by the headlights of passing cars, but on the staircase it was pitch-dark and he had to feel his way along, shuffling his feet up the invisible steps.

The Rector took a short break after the first flight of stairs and then moved on. He clutched the banister with his left hand and held his right hand out into the darkness in front of him so that wouldn't run into any invisible obstacle. This apparently superfluous precaution was suddenly justified on the landing between the first and second floors, when his fingers touched something soft and undoubtedly alive, because he heard a rustling sound, as if someone had moved aside to allow him past

"Who's there?" the Rector asked and took another step, with his right hand held out ahead of him again, but this time it didn't encounter any obstacle. "Who's there?" he asked again, because he had quite distinctly heard someone breathing — someone who wasn't hiding, but for some reason kept silent, just breathing calmly very close to him. "Do you hear me? Who's there?"

The only response to these questions that betrayed the extreme agitation of the person who asked them was the same calm breathing.

That morning's visit from the investigator and his warnings, the strange Zhiguli, the darkness in the entrance and now this calm, somehow expectant breathing all came together in a single interconnected whole. He recalled the names of the students he had expelled with absolute clarity, one after another: Kyazimov, Galustyan, Shirakhmedov. Which of them was standing there in the darkness? Or were all of them there?

"I'm warning you," said the Rector, making an immense effort to speak in his usual cool, restrained manner, "my driver is following me up."

That declaration also failed to produce any change in the situation — he could still hear that regular, slightly snuffling breathing behind the dark silence. Like someone preparing to make a decisive movement.

"Right, out of the way!" the Rector shouted suddenly when he thought the breathing had moved closer and he could feel it as well as hear it. He leaned backwards and swung his arms about to defend himself. At that moment the light came on and he saw a dishevelled-looking man standing in the corner of the landing with his eyes closed and swaying regularly backwards and forwards, asleep on his feet. Or else he was completely absorbed in thoughts that were profoundly private and very far removed from the surrounding reality. He didn't notice that the light had come on, it had no effect on the state he was in. "What are you doing here?" the Rector asked. "What's wrong with you?"

But these questions also went unanswered. He heard voices downstairs and the door of the lift clanged.

Making an effort to overcome the sudden weakness in his legs, the Rector walked up another flight of stairs. On the second floor he listened to the sound of the approaching lift and realised that it would stop there.

His unwillingness to see anyone just then forced him to climb another flight of stairs. From the landing between the floors he heard the lift stop and people get out of it — several men talking in loud voices.

"And what great jazz musicians we used to have! Top class! We supplied all the orchestras in the Soviet Union."

"There are some pretty good ones now too..."

"There are pretty good ones," the first voice agreed, "but I'm talking about really outstanding ones."

A door opened and swallowed up the voices.

The Rector lived on the third floor and he only had to walk up another half-storey to get home, but without even asking his permission, his legs set off downwards, something that had not been part of his plans for the evening. The sudden urgent need to share everything that had happened that day, as though he had been trying for many years to tie all the widely separated threads of his life together into a tight knot and today was the day when he had finally managed it, made him walk back down to the second floor and ring the doorbell opposite the door that the noisy group had entered.

And as always, she was there in the doorway as instantly as if she had been waiting by the door for him for hours — this person whose important place in his life had been determined many years earlier, although by no means at first sight, it had taken time. Closing the door behind her, she leaned back against it and gazed into his face for a few seconds.

"What's wrong?"

"Nothing, everything's fine."

"You look awful." She put her arms round his waist and drew him into the room, where she took his jacket off and then sat him down in the armchair by the television, pulled off his shoes and put soft slippers on his feet. "You need to take a bath. Has something happened?"

He gestured vaguely with his hand, leaned back in the armchair and closed his eyes.

"I'm sorry about that scene on the staircase this morning. He phoned to ask for a broom and then started telling me a joke. It would have been rude to interrupt, and then you came along, and there I was looking like that, so like a fool I came rushing back in... Shall I light the water heater?"

He was still sitting there in the same position when she came back from the bathroom.

"Will you have something to eat?"

He shook his head, and for the first time that day he had feeling of transcendent calm, as if he had finally landed on a soft sandy shore after a long battle with the waves.

"The tea's ready. Shall I pour you some?"

He moved his head again very, very slightly, afraid of shaking himself out of his newly acquired state.

"Has something happened?" she asked again, and there was so much anxiety in her voice that he simply had to answer.

"Yes."

"What?"

"Everything… At work, and at home, in general…"

"Ramazanov?"

"And Ramazanov too."

"What happened at home?"

"The same as always…"

Every time he was amazed by this woman's ability to listen to him as if there was nothing in the world more important than his concerns, even the most petty and insignificant of them. It had taken many years for him to believe that this was no pretence, no deliberate exaggeration of how much she cared about everything to do with him, but the rare ability to devote herself completely to another person, to become so attached to him that she perceived everything that happened through his eyes and his feelings. There were probably some men who didn't like that kind of woman, who wanted someone independent beside them, someone who lived her own life and maintained her own point of view. But this was the woman he needed. And fate had given her to him: a gift of fate was the only possible name for the way everything had happened. The Leningrad professor Klyatsko, who had married one of his students, had to apply for the vacant post of head of the department of electrical measurement at the Baku institute, he had to get the job and move into a flat on the same stairwell as the Rector, and then suffer a fatal heart attack soon afterwards; his widow had to come to see the Rector to ask him to give her a job, and a vacancy had to appear in his department just at that moment and, finally, they had to work together for several years so that he could feel this woman's love and her willingness to make any sacrifice for the sake of that love, and then it had taken about the same number of years for him to respond with feelings that he only discovered within himself after he was convinced of her absolute devotion to him. "My eldest son amazes me," he said, breaking the silence, "he actually quivers with hatred, as if it's my fault that he wants to manage without my help and can't."

"You have nothing to blame yourself for."

"They demanded an increase in the student intake, and I gave them the science block that we've been building for five years to use for lecture theatres," he said, with his eyes still closed.

"Why did you do that?" she asked quietly.

"If only I knew…" he said even more quietly.

"I'll bring the tea," she said and left the room.

He opened his eyes, glanced round the room and then lowered his eyelids again: his position on the armchair was comfortable and familiar — he was half-lying, with his legs outstretched.

"I was at Agakhanov's place. Just had him take a look," he said when she came back in and set the tea and jam down on the little table beside the armchair.

"Bring me the phone, please." He asked with his eyes still closed. When he was handed the phone, he opened them and dialled Gumbatov's home number. "What did you decide about the meeting?" he asked when his deputy's nervous voice enquired who was there.

"We set it for four p.m."

"Tomorrow?"

"Yes."

"Does Gasanov know?"

"Yes."

"All right. Try to leave Imanova out of it."

"Very well."

"Goodbye," he said and hung up. Then gave her a guilty look.

"Drink your tea," she told him.

"A crazy business," he said, "two people love each other, and because of some appalling bitch I have to sack them. She just drove us into a corner."

"Who?"

"The wife of one of our staff. She came bursting into the institute and threatened to set herself on fire. We barely managed to get her out."

"And you decided to sack her husband?"

"What else can I do? Can you imagine what will happen if she really does do something to herself?" He closed his eyes again.

"Please," she said.

"I'll drink it now…"

"I don't mean the tea," she said, touching his arm affectionately. "Please, I beg you. What do you need all this for? You're not the right kind of man for this, you deserve a different kind of life. You're suffering, you're in pain. I can see how much all this costs you! I beg you: leave it. Hand in your resignation and leave."

"Altogether?" he asked.

"I don't know. Perhaps just for a while. You need a rest."

"That's what Agakhanov says too."

"Better leave altogether. Keep the department, give lectures. Why do you need the Rector's job?"

He reached for his tea without answering.

"I think I'll take a bath," he said after taking a few sips.

"Everything's ready."

"Thank you," he said and got up. "Thank you for everything, I don't know what I'd do without you."

"Don't be silly." She came closer to him and he pressed her head tenderly against his chest. "My darling. I'm the one who waits for days for you to come…"

"You be careful, there's some kind of drunk hanging about in the entrance."

"I've seen him. He's from the next stairwell his wife won't let him in."

"He gave me a terrible fright," the Rector said with a smile. "The lights were off, and I ran into him."

She laughed.

"I thought I was going to have a heart attack."

"My little coward."

"You've no idea how frightening it was. I ask: 'Who is it?' I ask: 'Who's there?' He doesn't answer. Just breathes. You can't imagine!"

"Yes, I can," she said, still laughing, and pushed him towards the door of the bathroom. "Go and get washed."

She closed the door behind him, carried his half-drunk tea out to the kitchen and washed the glass, plugged in the iron, walked back to the bathroom door and listened.

"Give me your trousers," she said in a voice loud enough to be heard above the sound of the water. "I'll iron them while you're getting washed. They've got really creased."

She waited for a moment, then repeated what she had said, then listened again to what was going on behind the door. The only thing she could hear was the sound of running water.

The Doctor had been very fond of dictations: he knew a lot of poems, and he would declaim them loudly, striding round the room, while Fariz and Sultan wrote down the text in special exercise books — they each had their own. Then the doctor would check their efforts and go through their mistakes with them.

The Doctor very often recited poems by Pushkin. The Rector remembered some of them for the rest of his life. Unlike Sultan, he went to an Azerbaijani school, so naturally he made more mistakes and found it harder to memorise the poems. But there were some things that he managed to remember, like the line from "Winter Evening": "Now howling like a beast, now crying like a child …"

It had taken him a long time to grasp the way the word "now" was used in this line, so he wasn't able to memorise it, he had unconsciously substituted "and", so that the line became "and howling like a beast, and crying like a child". The Doctor carefully explained the difference to him every time — he had really wanted Fariz to learn Russian properly.

"Can you hear me?" she asked and opened the door without waiting for an answer.

He was lying across the bath in a strange position, half-undressed, but he hadn't managed to take off the trousers that she wanted to iron. His jacket and shirt were hanging up, but he was still wearing his trousers. Lying there, naked to the waist, in the pose of man felled by a sudden shot from round a corner. And he was trying to say something — his lips were moving.

He wasn't heavy and she managed to hoist him out of the bath quite quickly. Struggling to hold his body in place on the wet, slippery edge of the bath, she tried to understand what he was trying to say, but the sounds that he thought were words were so incoherent that it was impossible to make anything out. "All right, all right," she said, pretending that she could make sense of what he said. "Straight away, my love. There now, there now." With an immense effort she moved him along the edge of the bath, away from the water heater that was still burning, and sat him up against the wall. "Sit here like that, you mustn't move, my darling, it will soon pass. It's your heart. Can you hear me?"

He opened his eyes and then closed them again, as if confirming that he could hear her.

"Where does it hurt?" she asked, barely able to hold back her tears. "Your heart? Here?" she touched his chest. He tried to say something again and she could see that the attempt cost him a great effort.

"Don't talk, don't talk," she said, struggling with all her strength to hold back the tears. "You mustn't strain yourself."

But he carried on moving his lips.

"What? What?" she asked. "Do you want to lie down? Water? Call an ambulance?" But he repeated something that she couldn't understand. "Straight away, straight away, my dearest! Don't worry. I'll understand. Get someone to come? Phone someone? No? What is it you want?" she asked, peering at the movements of his lips. "Your clothes? You want me to put your clothes on? You mustn't move. You need rest, rest, do you understand? You can't take any risks with your heart." His lips moved demandingly again. All right, all right, I'll try." Weeping floods of silent tears, she wiped down his shoulders and chest with a towel and started to dress him: she moved him to a chair, put one arm into a shirt sleeve, and then the other one, then she did the same with his jacket. "And now what?" she asked, when his shoes were on his feet again. "Is that all? Are you happy now? I've done what you wanted, you're dressed." He said something again, and this time she understood him almost immediately. "You want me to take you out of here? Yes? Am I right?"

Yes, she was right — he confirmed that with a movement of his eyelids. But before carrying out this strange request, she made an effort to dissuade him.

"You mustn't move. Do you understand? It's your heart. I explained it to you. You can't take the risk. I'll take you out later, when you feel a bit better. No? You want to go now? But I can't do that!"

He half-opened his eyes, and the reproach in them was so intense that she had to obey his silent command. She threw his right arm round her neck and started moving towards the door of the flat. Slowly, step by step, they crossed the several metres of hallway. Pushing open the door, she led him out of her flat on to the brightly lit landing and leaned him against the wall.

"What do you want now?" she asked. "Shall I take you upstairs?"

He shook his head. It was a very slow movement, but at least he was able to make it.

"Are you feeling better?" she asked.

He replied with a very faint nod.

"Yes," his lips said; it was quiet "yes", but he managed to say it.

"Shall I take you upstairs?" she asked again.

"No," he whispered.

"What shall I do?"

"Go home," he said; the letter "g" sounded strange and breathy, almost like a "k".

"You want me to leave you here?

"Yes."

"You want to go up to the third floor on your own?" She finally realised what he was thinking and was horrified

"Yes."

"I beg you, don't do that, you'll kill yourself... You're a bit better already, but you mustn't move."

"Go home," he repeated in the same breathy voice. She tried to protest, but when she met the gaze of his greyish-blue, almost steely eyes, she withdrew submissively to the door of her flat.

For a few moments it seemed as though his legs would buckle under the weight of his body, but by the time she stepped inside the door, he had forced himself to take a step towards the stairs. Through the half-closed door, she saw him take a few more steps on stiff, wooden legs... Then he suddenly swayed forward and leaned his left hand on the banister. After standing like that for a moment, he put one foot on the stairs.

He managed three steps and then fell. From the way his body hit the stairs, she realised it was the end. And when she dashed to him and turned his head towards her and looked through her tears into those dead staring eyes, she knew for certain that it was all over.

After that she acted as if she were obediently following his orders: wiping away her tears, she tucked in the shirt that had come out of his trousers, walked over to her neighbour's door and pressed the doorbell. She had to do it several times before the neighbour finally appeared in the doorway with a glass in his hand.

"A-a-a-a," he drawled, glad to see her, "come in..."

"He rang my bell," she said almost calmly, "he felt unwell and he rang my doorbell..."

It was only then that the neighbour noticed the Rector's body lying on the stairs.

"He was walking past," she added, "and he rang my doorbell."

"Sabir, Enver," the neighbour called into his flat, then he went towards the body lying face down on the stairs.

Two days later there was a civil funeral service in the assembly hall at the institute. A guard of honour with black and red mourning armbands stood beside the coffin on the stage. The hall was full, and she was there among all the people who had come to say goodbye to the Rector. The neighbour from across the landing — he was sitting beside her — explained who was in each shift of the guard of honour; she listened carefully to what he said, every now and then wiping away the tears running down her cheeks.

In the wings Gumbatov was readying the next six-man shift of the guard of honour.

"Well now," he exclaimed mournfully and sighed as he handed an armband to Gasanov, "they say the Lord moves in mysterious ways. Who would ever have thought it? Now you don't need to worry, the problem has solved itself, so to speak."

"I wonder what's going to happen to the new building now?" said a stout, bearded man standing beside them.

Gumbatov glanced at him in annoyance, but didn't say anything.

The funeral proceedings were opened by Ramazanov, who was now the acting Rector.

"We have lost a man," he said, "who gave many years of his life to our institute. The successes achieved while Fariz Agaevich was at the head of our collective transformed our institute into one of the leading education institutions in the country. An eminent scientist and outstanding scientific manager, a demanding leader in all the responsible posts entrusted to him by the Motherland, Fariz Agaevich Rzaev will always be remembered here as the model example of a man of our time…" Ramazanov spoke at length and very convincingly, he displayed sincere feelings and demonstrated his skill as an orator. He was followed by the minister of higher education, the secretary of the institute's Party committee and a third-year girl student who broke down and cried in the middle of her address and couldn't carry on.

Immediately after the meeting Gumbatov asked everyone to leave the hall in order to allow relatives and close friends to bid farewell to the deceased, and Lyalya walked out of the hall with all the people who were not relatives or close friends. The neighbour Seimur and the driver Amanulla walked behind the coffin with her as it was carried for a few city blocks. Amanulla had a black eye, his right one. In answer to Seimur's questions he said he'd had a fight with some hooligans over a girl he was involved with. It turns out the car that had been trailing him and the Rector for days wasn't the expelled students at all, but a jealous boyfriend wanting to teach Amanulla a lesson. Amanulla was fond of exaggerating his amorous exploits, but this time his voice sounded sadly sincere.

Lyalya walked behind the coffin of the man who had been dearer to her than anyone else in the world, struggling with every ounce of her strength not to let anyone guess what terrible grief had overwhelmed her — it was what the dead man had wanted, he had paid with his life to keep their relationship secret.

Two days later a bus drove along the route to the institute, carrying a garishly made-up woman who was clutching two squirming young bodies full of energy, one in each hand. The boys were struggling desperately to break free. The expression on the woman's face suggested that she was in a very determined mood, and the hands grasping the boys' collars testified to an indomitable strength that was surely not only used on the children.

There was one more stop to go before the educational establishment and her meeting with the new rector. She jerked her children closer to her and gathered herself as if she were about to jump into water. Gloomily intent on the forthcoming conversation, the outcome of which (she believed) depended primarily on how decisively she acted, the woman took no notice of the disapproving looks that the other passengers in the bus were giving her.

She had no doubt that she would be able to make the man she was going to see help her. Whoever he might be, this new Rector, and no matter what he might think of her demands, there was no way he could hold out against the means of persuasion that she had in store for him. "They come and they go," the woman thought, clutching her children by the scruff of the neck — but they didn't let us out from under the veil just so that we could let some whores take our husbands away!"

FOUR

The Golden Ratio

Narrated by Seidzade

The investigator with the round face and noble shock of grey hair continued to behave like a man very interested in resolving the situation in a way that would please everyone. After several hours of vain attempts to extract the answers he wanted from me, this benevolent attitude could not possibly be sincere. But I caught myself thinking that it was precisely his sympathetic tone that was making it harder and harder for me not to give him the confessions that he was after. It would have been better if he hadn't concealed his perfectly justified irritation — that would have simplified the situation greatly; but this way it looked as if he was doing everything within his power to help, while I was obtusely resisting, insisting on petty details that hindered the completion of necessary legal formalities.

His pronunciation betrayed his rural origins — he had most likely been born in the Agdam region. In answering his questions, I sometimes switched into Russian. He didn't object at all, but he himself spoke only in Azeri, flaunting his fluent mastery of the standard literary language.

He looked about five years younger than me, his likeable face seemed familiar, and the feeling that I had seen him somewhere before came to me immediately, just as soon as we found ourselves in the tiny, scantily furnished office where he was now interrogating me, sitting with his back to the window that was as narrow as a loophole. When it was almost midnight, it suddenly came to me: I realised that we had never met, but my former classmate, Marik Haikin, who had become a well-known defence attorney, had told me about him. Among the numerous cases Marik had won, there was one of which he was especially proud — he had managed to get an investigator from the public prosecutor's office out of jail, where he was serving time for taking a large bribe. It was a sum of hundreds of thousands of dollars, which had been paid to the investigator by a man accused of the murder of a well-known scientist. But Haikin had found and brought another man to court, who claimed that he had shot the victim. This turn of events had allowed Haikin's defendant to go free and return to his duties as an investigator. Haikin swore to me that the killer he had found was the genuine article, but for a long time rumours circulated in Baku that neither the man originally accused of the murder, who had been obliged to pay the bribe, nor Haikin's volunteer had killed the scientist. Hearsay confidently named the individuals who had actually organised and carried out the murder, but what the entire city knew remained a secret for public justice. The investigator whom Haikin had got out of jail went on to work in the Ministry of Internal Affairs and was now interrogating me.

The silence of the night outside the window was broken only occasionally by the sound of passing cars. The skin under my hair smarted and stung where it was stretched tight by the crust of dried blood and my entire right sight ached painfully after all those kicks.

"I understand your doubts," he said, leaning against the low back of his old wooden armchair. Then he inclined his head towards his right shoulder, gave me a sympathetic look and said: "But believe me, we can only reconstruct the true picture of what happened if we work together."

"I've told you everything I know," I said in a tone of voice that sounded almost apologetic — I actually was feeling a bit bad about having contradicted him for several hours. He gave a slightly weary, slightly condescending smile, making it clear to me that in his long working life he had heard those words many times from different people, but in the end they had all come to realise that they were mistaken in believing that they had supplied all the information he required.

"During the two hours since I saw you last, I've managed to find out a few things." He pulled several sheets of paper covered with close handwriting closer to himself. "And you know, I regret sincerely having to say that your testimony simply does not fit into the overall picture." He paused, evidently expecting me to say something to him, but when I didn't, he went on:

"The opposite parties testify that the man who died fell and hit his head on the edge of the pavement following a blow from Alexander Krokin, Alik as you call him, and that was how he received his fatal injury. You'll be able to see that for yourself at the line-up."

"What about the couple who were the reason for the fight in the first place, have they been found yet?"

"Unfortunately not."

"And what does Alik say?"

"So far nothing."

"What do you mean, nothing?" I asked.

"Precisely that!" he said, deploring Alik's behaviour with a melancholy sigh. "He's not saying a word, and that's all! He didn't see anything, he doesn't know anything, he didn't hit anyone. But a man died as a result of a blow suffered in that fight, and that blow was certainly struck by one of you five. There were five of you, weren't there?"

*

The previous day, thanks to Eldar's efforts, we had all got together for the first time in months. Even Lucky managed to stop off on his way to the airport.

We sat down at the table at about eight o'clock and by ten Rafik, in whose flat we decided to meet, was already well oiled — the alcohol in his blood had reached a level at which he was quite capable of pulling any crazy stunt, even though he appeared perfectly sober otherwise– he was simply talking more loudly than usual and his eyes glinted aggressively. The most frequent target of his frenzied abuse was the government, regardless of who was running it. On the New Year's Eve of 1980, for example (he was still living in Moscow then, and whenever any of us arrived in the Soviet capital, we used to stay at his studio flat in Chertanovo), in the middle of the traditional television address to the people by the head of state he suddenly jumped up from the table in an alcoholic frenzy: before the startled eyes of his wife's female friends and their husbands, he unzipped his fly with a sweeping gesture and directed a powerful jet of urine, which had evidently been accumulating for quite a long time, straight at the Leader's face and chest, which was covered with various medals and decorations. The furious torrent of abuse that came bursting out of his contorted mouth was interrupted by a terrifying sound as the overheated television exploded like a blast-bomb on contact with the cooler liquid. His frightened guests tumbled off their chairs, but Rafik broke into a denunciatory harangue about the poor quality of Soviet electronic goods and threw the television out of the window, fortunately without killing anyone, as he lived on the ground floor.

Yesterday he spent several hours castigating the communists, the democrats, the Popular Front and himself — for moving back to Baku with his Armenian wife after living in Moscow for twenty-five years. And of course, we came under fire for not talking him out of this decision: by January 1990 it was obvious that it had been a rash one.

*

"Yes, there were five of us," I said.

"And where's the fifth one?"

"He got on a plane. We were on our way to see him off when it all happened. I told you."

"Yes, you told me," the investigator confirmed, "but we'll be going back over some points a few more times ."

We saw Lucky as far as the steps of the plane, since he was boarding through the VIP lounge, and as we all took turns to hug him, none of us suspected that in three hours' time we would be arrested.

*

"Where did he fly to?"

"To Istanbul, and from there to Stockholm."

"And why does he have that nickname, "Lucky?""

"It goes back to his childhood."

"Was there any particular reason?"

"Does that have any bearing on why I'm here?"

"In a certain sense, it does," said the investigator, still speaking in that wise, gentle tone of voice. "I'll explain to you later."

"I don't know," I said with a shrug. "It's just that he was often lucky."

"Like this time," the investigator muttered to himself, making a note of something on a separate sheet of paper. "Was he the one who asked the driver to stop the car?"

"No."

"Then who did?"

"I think it was Eldar."

"Rzaev?"

"Yes, but there's nothing illegal about that! A violent crowd attacked a young man and his girlfriend, we intervened, and now we're the guilty ones?!"

"Who was the first to jump out of the car?" he asked, after waiting for me to finish speaking.

"I don't remember, I'm sorry. But what's the point in repeating the same question over and over again?"

*

The first one out of Lucky's official Volga was Alik; he was sitting beside the driver. I was next. There were about ten of them: they had surrounded a tall, thin youth in a leather jacket and the boyish girl in a mini-skirt who was cringing back against him, and they were just about to start beating them — a hand had already been swung back ready to strike, there was swearing, and the kicks that had forced the poor couple back against the wall left no time for hesitation.

The car stopped about thirty metres from them. It took me a moment or two to overtake Alik. While he was trying to break free of my grip, Lucky and the others caught up with us and overtook.

*

The reproach in the glance that the investigator gave me conflicted with the benevolent expression on his face. He knew quite well without me telling him which of us had been the first to leave the car, but for some reason he wanted to hear me say it.

"And what about you?" he asked and paused for a long moment, but I still didn't answer. "Did you stay in the car when it stopped?"

"No, of course not. I told you."

"Were you the first to get out?"

"No."

"The second?"

"Yes."

"So, someone jumped out of the car, and you were next, right? Do I understand you correctly?"

"Yes."

"And what did you do?"

"I ran."

"After your friend who was running ahead of you?"

"Yes."

"He was running ahead of you along a well-lit street, and you don't remember who it was?" He laughed, but not because he was glad to have demonstrated my obvious lie: on the contrary, he seemed embarrassed for me because I had tried to deceive him.

"I understand that you are reluctant to name your friend. But apart from the fact that you are obliged to tell me the whole truth, there is another circumstance which I think you fail to appreciate. One of you five struck the blow that resulted in a man's death, and if the identity of that person is not established in the course of the investigation, the burden of the charge will be laid equally on all five of you."

"What are you trying to say?" The question betrayed just how perplexed I was.

"Just exactly what I said: either one of you is guilty, or you are all guilty together. And so, to be quite honest, not only would you *not* be betraying anyone, you would be helping to save four people, including yourself, from a false accusation."

"I didn't see Alik hit him," I muttered and turned my head away resentfully: my gaze fell on a Soviet-style military greatcoat with major's epaulets hanging on one of the coat hooks on the wall.

"We'll come back to this point." The investigator's voice was as gentle as ever, but suddenly I could sense an inner tension in it, like the note of a string that has been stretched too taut and might break at any moment. "But meanwhile I ask you to remember who was running in front of you after you jumped out of the car."

There was no way I could avoid naming Alik now.

"Krokin," I said, still examining the greatcoat on the wall: in addition to the badges of rank on the chest there was the small rhomboid form of a university badge. Out of the corner of my eye I saw the investigator pull over a fresh sheet of paper for recording testimony.

"So," he said, giving no sign of his satisfaction at having

achieved a result, "I write that when the car stopped, you saw Krokin jump out of it first and run towards the scene of the incident?"

"Yes, but he only reached the scene of the fight after it had already started …"

The investigator put his pen down and gave me a special, thoughtful kind of look, as if he had discovered something new in a familiar object that he had already studied thoroughly.

"You already told me that."

"Yes, and I ask you to enter it in the record."

"Certainly," said the investigator, leaning against the back of his chair, "but first I'd like to make sure that you're telling me the truth." He paused, but carried on studying me. "Tell me, where were you when the militia came to get you?"

"We went out for a walk," I said, expressing no resentment at his frank refusal to believe what I had said — I was hampered by the fact that only a minute earlier he had quite easily caught me out in an attempt to deceive him.

"With Krokin?"

"Yes."

"And how did you come to be at the scene of the incident? By chance?"

"No."

"You had reasons to be there?"

"Yes."

"What were they?"

"I lost my folder during the fight."

"What folder?"

"A folder of manuscripts — it has nothing to do with the case. It contained some papers that mean a lot to me, and when I realised I'd lost the folder, Krokin and I decided to look for it at the scene of the fight."

The investigator leaned down and took my folder out of the bottom drawer of the desk.

"Is this it?"

"Yes," I said, half-standing and reaching out for it across the desk.

"We'll give it back to you as soon as we conclude the investigation," the investigator said, but he left the folder on the desk. "Pardon me, but I took a look inside it — these texts are stories?"

"Yes, and a screenplay."

"And you wrote them?"

"Yes."

"But you're a doctor by profession?"

"Yes."

"In Sabunchi?"

"Yes." My curt replies were intended to let him know that I objected to talking about anything that was not directly connected with the investigation he was conducting. And it seemed to have at least some effect, as after a last glance at me he turned his attention to the papers on the desk in front of him.

Taking advantage of the fact that the investigator was otherwise engaged in writing something — evidently the report of the interrogation — I pulled over the folder with my manuscripts and started reading the screenplay, which was on the top; Never Grab a Scorpion by the Ears was what it said on the title page. Then came a text that seemed more and more dubious as I ran my eyes over it: the writing style was too American and some scenes were altogether too candid.

Of course, even in Soviet times you had to swallow plenty of insults and humiliations before you could get anything published. The bitterness of years of waiting in the queue of authors laying claim to their tiny slice of the common cake, the painful procedure of the rape of the text by semi-literate editors, the petty bribes, arrangements and presents to overcome the snags at the printing works, the symbolic fees that were barely enough to pay for a party to celebrate the publication of a scrawny little volume — and there had only been three of them in my life. All those sad memories from the recent but already forgotten past seemed almost pleasant now. At least in those days you were dealing with the state: your application was made to the state, your resentment was directed against the state, and your conflict was with the state when you refused to surrender and carried on doing things the way that you thought was right. But now the state no longer had any interest in you, it had given you a freedom that you had to pay for with far greater humiliations than before: now your fate was decided by "men with money" and unfortunately rich men are not the best part of humanity. Was that perhaps why my latest screenplay was so different from everything I had written before? Had I not tried too hard to extract money from one of these men in order to make a film?

As I read the screenplay I kept glancing at the investigator, who was busy with his own work. When he eventually finished writing the report, he felt a yen for further conversation. At one o'clock in the morning I would have thought this was mere eccentricity, except that I could sense some deliberate purpose that I couldn't understand yet behind what he was saying. Even though his voice sounded so interested, I simply didn't believe that he was really concerned about the fate of my miserable creative efforts. And even if he really was interested, what kind of shape was I in for literary discussions?

"I've read something somewhere… Were any of your stories published in the *Molodyozhnya Pravda* newspaper?"

"Very possibly."

"I'm a mathematician." It sounded like the confession of a carefully guarded secret. "I studied game theory."

"At university?"

"No, at university I studied law, as an extra-mural student. But I graduated in mathematics from the pedagogical institute first. You look tired…"

"I am."

"I can see you are. In that case, we'll take a half-hour break. You have a rest, and I'll have a word with your friends. I really need to finish questioning all of you before morning, so that I can discuss the matter of a warrant with the public prosecutor tomorrow."

"What warrant?"

"A warrant for your arrest. I explained to you already. If we can establish whose blow caused the man's death, we'll detain one of you, but if we can't, then I'm afraid…" — he shrugged and spread his hands as he walked towards the door — "…we'll have to arrest all of you. I'll be back in about forty minutes. If you need anything, there's a sergeant sitting in the corridor here." He was politely hinting that it would not be a good idea to leave the office.

Of course, he hadn't left me on my own so I could take a rest: and the warning that I might be arrested had not been accidental either. This benign investigator was trying to get something out of me, there was something about my testimony that he didn't like. And it wasn't just to do with Alik, there was something else, something that wasn't directly connected with the case that this district militia department investigator had inherited by chance, simply because he happened to be on duty at the station at the time. I had the feeling that he was interested in us for our own sake — in me and Lucky and Alik, in all five of us.

*

The museum-style interior of Lucky's flat had been adorned with new exhibits — a huge African boomerang and several spears with black iron tips. Lucky still brought back something to decorate his home from every trip abroad, and it was easy for anyone who visited to guess which countries of the world his host had visited on his latest trip.

"Decided to keep us waiting?" Eldar asked me, vainly attempting to conceal his irritation with irony. They were sitting in Lucky's study and, to judge from the number of cigarette butts in the ashtray, they must have been there quite some time.

"I was doing my house calls. I've only just finished."

"Did you see Alik?"

"No, I didn't have time."

I knew he wouldn't like this news, and he duly exploded with indignation.

"We've been sitting here for three hours, waiting, and you didn't have time! Have you no shame? You were right there. Was it too much trouble to ride two stations down the line?"

"Don't shout," I said, taking a seat at the desk. "There isn't a single train on his line between six and seven, and I finished at six. Was I supposed to hang about at the station for an hour?

My explanation slightly tempered his fury, but he carried on throwing out reproaches addressed at both Lucky and me.

"Am I the only one who cares?" It wasn't the first time in the last few years that he had asked us that question, full of ingrained bitterness and resentment. And we'd never had an answer for him; a long time ago Eldar had taken on the responsibility of organising the effort to maintain our friendship, and we'd simply got used to it. "Why do I always have to coax you? Surely you could spare one month after all these years for a friend in trouble? In any case it would be no bad thing for us all to sit down together for a frank heart-to-heart. Can't we forget our own mundane troubles, just for a while, and try to deal with this? Everything's collapsing around us!"

"Yes, of course we can," Lucky interrupted. "We can and we must."

"Then what's the problem?"

"I've got to go on an urgent business trip."

"Abroad?" Eldar asked with more than a hint of spite.

"Yes, to Stockholm."

"For long?"

"A week."

"When?"

"On Thursday."

"That leaves three days before you go, and when you get back from your trip, you can join up with us again," said Eldar, then he gazed at me. "What do you say?"

I plucked up my courage and told him I would be busy for the next two days.

"What have you got to do?"

"It's a long story."

"Try me."

"I have to rewrite a screenplay before Wednesday."

"Why Wednesday in particular?"

I could understand his doubts: I'd been writing for so many years, and there had never been any hurry, but now all of a sudden I had a strict deadline.

"Because the man who promised to find the money to make the film is leaving at the beginning of next week."

"Fair enough: you're all very busy, very serious people. I'm the only idle good-for-nothing." He grinned dourly at his own joke, "But at least one of us will have to go and see Alik — and today."

Lucky and I exchanged glances, as the inevitability of this visit to Alik became obvious to us both.

"And we need to do something about Alik in general," Eldar continued. "You don't see much of him, but I see him all the time, because I teach his son maths. And I tell you in all seriousness that he's fallen into a deep depression, all the changes in Baku have hit him harder than anyone. And I can't handle him on my own."

"I glanced at Lucky. He didn't say anything — he obviously hadn't seen his uncle for a long time either.

Lucky drove his Volga with the panache of a racing driver, overtaking the cars in front of us one after another, slowing down at points where we might run into the traffic police and then immediately speeding up again, as if by pure coincidence, just as soon as we were past the danger zone.

Soon we were driving along a narrow street without a single tree — it's one of our sad national peculiarities that trees are generally planted on people's own private land, and rarely in communal areas. Right at the end of this street was the small house that Alik built with his own hands when he came back from prison in the early sixties. While he was serving his sentence, Maya, whom he still loved, had become the leading actress of the theatre in Rostov. I saw her perform there when I went to meet her and hold negotiations that Alik knew nothing about — the membership of that delegation was decided by Eldar. She gave us a wonderful welcome, she still had the very warmest memories of our drama club at the Press House, and she was very glad to know that Alik had been released alive and well, but we had already missed the boat, as they say. The word was that she was involved in a longstanding romance with People's Artist of the USSR Bubnov.

A few years after he was released Alik married a girl from Zabrat and built his house there. He was well respected in the area: the local cutthroats took his opinions seriously, especially since they were expressed in Azeri with that remarkable accent that only natives of Apsheron possess.

For some reason Alik's wife, Nata, who had great respect for her husband, seemed alarmed by our arrival. In reply to our greetings she hastily informed us that Alik was not at home.

"Where is he?" asked Eldar, after we had walked in through the gate and followed the sandy path paved with bleached brick past the front garden and almost up to the two-storey brick house. Nata, who was obviously suffering agonies of doubt over whether to invite us in or not, came down off the porch to meet us. Her twelve-year-old son Georgy, Eldar's pupil, was standing behind her, phlegmatically picking his nose.

"I don't know," said Nata, looking round in a rather strange manner. "He told me not to tell."

"Not to tell who?" asked Lucky, giving her and Georgy a smile, which he tried to fill with all the genuine friendship and affection that he felt for Alik and his family but so rarely expressed.

"Anyone," said Nata, casting another rapid glance round the yard.

"He's in the shed," Georgy announced, still with the same vacant expression on his face.

Nata swung round deftly and tried to smack him on the back of the head, but Georgy avoided any contact with his mother's hand by elegantly swaying his body slightly backwards and to one side. The expression on his face didn't change one iota; he took his mother's lunge as something perfectly normal and not worth any special attention.

"Don't talk nonsense," said Georgy's mother, making a threatening face, but he wasn't scared.

"This is the third evening he's been hiding," Georgy told us, demonstrating his cool head and precise sense of distance once again as his mother's blows hurtled past, literally just a millimetre away from him.

"He's not hiding from anyone," said Nata. "He's depressed."

We looked at each other and set off towards the shed. Georgy went rushing past us and flung open the door — it was obvious that he definitely didn't approve of his father's melancholic mood.

Alik was lying on an old iron bedstead in the corner of the shed. An electric light bulb with no shade was burning just above his head. Our friend's face, picked out of the darkness of the shed by that patch of bright light, was incredibly still — he didn't even turn towards the sound of the door opening, just carried on lying on his back with his open eyes gazing at the ceiling of the shed. It was only when we walked right up to the bed that he started and jerked himself up, lowering his bare feet on to the floor.

"Lie down, lie down," said Lucky. "No need for any formalities with *us*."

An expression of embarrassment mingled with genuine surprise appeared on Alik's face: ever since we were children he had behaved with us as if he were our elder brother.

"Drag over the bench," Alik told his son, at the same time moving along to make room for us on the bed, which was covered with a light blanket. "Sit down."

"Who are you hiding from?" I asked.

"Well, not from you," Alik said with a smile and scratched the back of his head. "So what brings you here?"

"Nothing special, we just decided we should see each other more often."

Alik looked at him dubiously, then turned his gaze on me.

"We've agreed to meet at Rafik's place in the evenings, just in case. Because of Aida."

"You mean she hasn't left Baku?"

"No."

"This will end badly," Alik sighed. "But what are we doing sitting here!" He gathered his thoughts and got to his feet. "Let's go into the house."

"We're not staying long."

"Come on, come on, we'll cook up some *shashlik*. One of my neighbours sent me a young wild boar. They shot it this morning — fresh meat!"

Georgy appeared in the door with two stools.

"Take them back" his father told him.

We went out into the yard. Nata was standing there in the middle, wringing her hands and waiting to see how events would develop.

"What are you doing there?" Alik asked strictly "Lay the table."

Nata fluttered her hands in the air and dashed into the house without saying a word.

"Sorry, old friend, but we really can't stay long," said Lucky, putting his arm round Alik's shoulders. "Next time."

"Never mind next time," said Alik, shaking his head. "It'll be years before I see you again."

"I have a counter proposal," said Lucky, looking at his watch. "Let's take your boar and go to Rafik's place. We'll ring Marat and Eldar from there. Come on, get your coat on!" he concluded decisively. Lucky had a knack for dispensing with other people's hesitations.

Of course, in accusing us of not dissuading him from coming back to his homeland, so that he, in his ignorance of the situation, had made a tragic mistake, Rafik was being disingenuous, working off his anger at his own lack of caution. The exchange of his one-room flat in Chertanovo in Moscow for a newly renovated flat in the centre of Baku, with a substantial payment in addition, had only been possible due to an increased flow of people leaving Baku. And he must have realised that people didn't leave safe and happy places in such massive numbers. But on the other hand, who could have predicted then that life in Baku would take such a tragic turn?

Rafik had welcomed our suggestion of gathering at his home in the evenings, but while in their heart of hearts both he and Aida were proud of this demonstration of our friendship, they could not fail to understand that the protection we were offering was only for a few hours every evening and it didn't solve their general security problems.

And evidently that was why they drank during the day, in order to keep their spirits up, and kept a well-sharpened axe in the middle of the table crowded with glasses and bottles. This axe had been brought from Moscow and it was regarded as a family relic, because it had helped to lay the foundations of their marriage in the early eighties. Aida was Rafik's second wife. The first, whom he married after he graduated from Moscow University, had made a successful diplomatic career for herself, but only after their divorce. Rafik was two years older than us, he possessed exceptional mathematical abilities and as a child he dreamed of being an astrophysicist. In 1954 he was the first of us to finish school and go away to Moscow. In 1960 he married, when he was a junior research worker in some institute that he assured us specialized in secret matters of national security. By that time he was already a well known character in Moscow society, and he breakfasted every morning in the "Nationale" café (the next table was often occupied by Mikhail Svetlov, Yury Olesha or other famous poets whom Rafik was on first name terms with). He met his future wife at a reception — the poor soul didn't know then that she held the rank of lieutenant in the KGB — and he was pleasantly surprised to learn that in addition to possessing a brilliant command of English and a Moscow residence permit, the choice of his heart was also Azeri on her father's side, so he immediately proposed to her.

To do him justice, it must be said that, like every other woman that Rafik was ever involved with, Farida — that was his first wife's name — fell madly in love with him from the start. Either he was simply lucky and always happened to find passionate women, or he picked them out subconsciously (and afterwards cursed his fate), but there was never a case when he parted from his lady love calmly, on a basis of mutual and voluntary agreement.

They spent two years together and they were a wonderful couple — beautiful, well-groomed and impeccably dressed — and for all that time they were hardly ever apart.

We were used to them going everywhere together, so we were surprised when one day we arrived in Moscow and he turned up to meet us on his own. "I'm teaching her a lesson," he replied laconically when we asked him why he had come without Farida. Apparently Farida had not been ready to go out at the appointed time and Rafik had left on his own, telling her that he couldn't be late to meet his friends, who had travelled two thousand kilometers to see him.

When he got home after two in the morning, he found his wife at death's door — she had felt so hurt and rejected that she had slit open her veins, but fortunately not very professionally (what on earth do they teach those KGB officers at the Moscow

State University of Foreign Affairs?) and Rafik was able to staunch the sluggish bleeding that had been going on for several hours.

Afterwards, many years later, when he already knew about her second profession, he would remember Farida and say: "Just imagine what she could have done to me if she hadn't felt so sorry for herself". We nodded sympathetically, imagining the terrible scene of Rafik's death at the hands of the KGB lieutenant.

Aida appeared in Rafik's life twenty years after Farida. There was nothing remarkable about the other women who lived with him during that intervening period, except for their highly-strung amorous behavior. Things went from bad to worse for him; never having completed his doctoral dissertation, he gave up scientific research and started teaching, and the quality of the women he lived with declined year after year. Since many of the remarkable qualities of his brain remained intact, he could not fail to notice what was happening to him; even when he was drunk he was soberly aware of the true quality of his domestic partners, which must have been the reason he didn't remarry. After things had gone on like this for almost twenty years: we thought of him as a confirmed bachelor, so when he suddenly told us that he was going marry Aida, our total bewilderment prompted him to make a last ditch attempt to preserve his freedom. Aida, however, proved to have a grip of steel. When she arrived at Rafik's flat without warning one night to find that he was with some rival or other, she knocked on the door for several hours, insulting him with every obscenity known to man. When morning came and she realized that Rafik was not going to surrender, she borrowed an axe from a neighbour on the top floor and started breaking in the door. But even then Rafik wouldn't capitulate, he was sure that Aida would run out of steam at some stage before she could break down the door — it had been specially made to order. Only when the thick wooden boards started cracking and splitting apart did Rafik actually speak to her, explaining his behavior by saying that he hadn't heard Aida's shouting, or the doorbell, or the blows of the axe, because he was sound asleep. He opened the door, slapped Aida's face, led her into the sitting room and sat her down on a chair (meanwhile the frightened bird of passage flitted out of the bathroom and went flying down the stairs). They drank two bottles of vodka together and at noon the following day they handed in their application for a marriage license at the registry office. (The axe was not returned to the neighbor, as a lesson not to go poking his nose into other people's affairs).

After they had been together for about two years, Aida's flat was sold, and she finally moved in with Rafik, who by this time was suffering from acute homesickness. He had made attempts to move back to Baku in the past, but every time he had lived for a while with one or another of us and then left again, disappointed by the changes that had taken place in the city during the years he had been away. But from the mid-80s he begun suffering from what he called "the offensive manifestations of vulgar nationalism": Moscow, the city that he loved passionately, knew intimately and could talk about for hours at a time, suddenly seemed alien to him, and he applied himself with untypical zeal to the complicated, frustrating and time-consuming process of exchanging his Moscow flat for one in Baku.

We knew the Baku flat very well, because it had belonged to his relatives. Once upon a time it had been home to his grandfather Baladadash, who had a massive wineskin of a stomach that dangled right down to his knees, and his father's step-brother Amirgusein, a moneylender who was famous throughout the city. In our student days we all dressed ourselves on money borrowed on interest from Amirgusein: he usually lent at eight per cent a month, but as students we were given a fifty per cent discount.

In the post-war years Rafik's mother often brought us all to this flat with the three big rooms overlooking the sea and locked us into one of them before going on to work. Times were hard:

eighty-year-old Baladadash, half wasted away, used to wander through the other two rooms with his stomach getting tangled between his legs: he would walk out into the communal corridor that connected the flat with two others like it and go into the communal kitchen in the vain hope of finding something he could eat. As it happened he died at the age of ninety from twisting of the intestines after eating a huge pan of pilaf prepared in honor of his birthday. We were almost responsible for making Baladadash's constant desire to eat the death of him even earlier than that: one of us thought up a game during which we had to crawl under the table by turns and bleat like a lamb. I don't remember all the details of the game any longer, but bleating like a lamb was a compulsory element and that was what got old Baladadash excited: when he heard sounds that seemed to promise a piece of meat, the old man suspected that his daughters were hiding a lamb they had bought or someone had given them. He dragged a stool over to the locked door, stood a chair on top of it and then clambered up on to this rickety construction so that he could inspect the room through the top pane of the glazed door — the only one that wasn't blanked out with white paint. Baladadash was so upset when he saw Lucky bleating there, instead of a lamb, that he lost control of his body and went crashing down onto the parquet flooring from a very dangerous height for a man of his age. The three broken ribs that the old man suffered were described by the doctors as a most fortunate outcome for such a life-threatening incident.

And now the same group of us, plus Aida, who was already tipsy, were sitting in the room into which poor Baladadash had tried to peep fifty years earlier and one of Rafik's regular monologues was nearing its end.

"… And what do you think the result of all that is, who do I feel ashamed to look in the eye?" he asked, addressing the question to himself rather than us. "Her," he said with a nod in Aida's direction. "It's a paradox: *they* — the Armenians — have occupied our land, *they're* driving the people off it, abusing women, old people and children, and I feel ashamed to look her in the eye…

Aida seemed to be only half-listening: not knowing which way his thoughts would turn, she was afraid to react in the wrong way to what he was saying. The instinct of self-preservation had taught her long ago that after Rafik reached a certain level of intoxication, the vital thing was to grasp what he was driving at and agree with him as quickly as possible. The algorithm of their joint drinking sessions had remained unchanged throughout all their years together. For the first half of the session she controlled events. During these few short hours Rafik reacted considerately to her every wish: for example, every now and then he would demand that we ask her to sing for us and every time, after several refusals, she would switch off the light in the room and sing Norma's aria from the eponymous opera. Evidently this was an extremely difficult part to perform, because even in the darkness we could see how the strain of it distorted Aida's face, which was probably why she switched off the light. Later, when Rafik was even drunker, they swapped places, as it were, and he took charge of the situation.

"Why?" His question filled the entire space of the room and hovered in the air above our heads. "Why, I ask you, do I feel ashamed to look my Armenian wife in the eye? Because of the way we flee headlong from them is a disgrace, leaving village after village, kilometer after kilometer. Of course, they…" — he pointed his finger at Aida — "… are supported by the Russian army, there's no doubt about that, but they fight too…"

"Don't you point at me," said Aida, taking the risk of interrupting him. "I don't have anything to do with 'them'."

"I'm sorry…" said Rafik. He gave her a glance of loving sympathy and put his arm round her shoulders. "It's shameful and disgraceful! After the Russian troops arrived, on orders from Moscow we had to gather up all the guns, even the hunting guns, and hand them in to the state. And we left the people unarmed. And these "erazis" came running in from Armenia the moment the first drop of blood was spilled. Two hundred thousand of them! They abandoned their homes without offering the slightest resistance. And now they run riot on the streets of Baku, you can't even go out into town, they're so wild. They're even taking over peoples' flats."

"And what are they supposed to do, the poor souls?" Aida objected. "Where are they going to live?"

"They should be sent to fight in Karabakh."

"It's our government's mistake."

"They were only following orders from Moscow…"

Everybody started talking at once, and the talk went on until midnight. It was half an hour after that, on our way to see Lucky off at the airport, we got involved in the fight in which a man died.

*

When he came back into the office, the investigator put on the uniform jacket that was hanging on the wall and cleared all the papers off the desk.

"Right, what are we going to do?" he asked me in a theatrically cheerful voice, as if it wasn't really the middle of the night. "I need to go out for a little while. Would you like to have a chat with your friends?"

After he had carefully kept us completely isolated from each other for several hours, this suggestion sounded strange, but apparently the time had come when it could no longer hinder the progress of the investigation if we talked. It was also quite possible that the investigator thought he ought to give us an opportunity to consider our position.

"Who are they, these men?" I asked as he led me along a dark corridor to the stairs leading to the rear courtyard of the militia station. "They don't look like Bakuites."

"At this time of the night Bakuites are all asleep in their beds," the investigator laughed. "But these guys have nowhere to shelter, they're homeless."

"Azeris coming in from Armenia?"

"Yes, 'erazis' as you Bakuites call them."

We walked down a stairway that was fenced off with large-scale metal mesh and went out into the courtyard.

It was a small, cozy yard, with two white benches standing under trees that formed a short alley. Marat, Alik and Eldar were sitting on one of the benches.

"Well, how's the fresh air?" the investigator asked them. "I've brought your writer friend, you can enjoy it together." As he left, he clicked shut the lock on the door through which we had entered the yard.

I walked over to the bench and sat down between Alik and Marat.

"A fine business," Marat said gloomily.

"Yes, we're in deep shit," I agreed.

"Shhh," Alik whispered, gesturing to indicate that they might be listening to us.

"What have we got to hide?" Eldar asked in a loud voice.

"Did you refuse to give evidence?" I asked, turning to Alik.

"Yes."

"Why?"

He was surprised by the naivety of my question.

"I told them exactly what happened," said Eldar, still talking loudly. "In the situation that has arisen, the sooner the investigation is completed, the better."

"But you know that one of them died?" I asked.

"Yes."

"So what did you say?"

"That in the general ruckus anyone could have hit him."

"Lucky punched him," said Marat. "As soon as they attacked us."

"I didn't see that," I said. "Alik and I got there later, when the fight had already started."

"Really?" Eldar asked in surprise. "You two were the first to jump out of the car."

"Yes, but I held Alik back." There was no need to explain why I'd done it, we all knew about Alik's pugnacious character. "But how did the fight start?"

"I told them to leave that couple alone…" As Eldar spoke, he was obviously trying to reconstruct in his mind a detailed picture of how the unfortunate business had begun; I could see the effort of straining his memory in his eyes. "One of them swore and hit Lucky. So, of course, Lucky hit him back. And then they attacked us."

"And when Lucky hit him, did he fall?"

"No, I don't think so."

"He fell down later," said Marat. "And more than once. He was drunk …"

*

As I was fighting off blows from several men who had all attacked me at once, I stumbled over a man lying in the road and almost fell. One young guy in a bush jacket spotted his chance, lunged forward and started punching me methodically, blow after blow, first from the right, then from the left, breathing out each time with a hoarse, wheezing sound, as if he were chopping wood, and glaring at me with eyes as round as buttons, in which I could see no anger, only a kind of insane excitement. Fortunately the blows didn't land on my face, because I covered it with my hands: instead they hit the sides and back of my head. I swayed from side to side: slumping sideways from one blow I ran straight into the next one from the other side, and that was the only reason I didn't fall down — until I tripped over the body lying in the street again.

As I lay there with my hands still covering my face, I saw a foot raised over me and that same insane excitement in those button eyes. He stamped hard on my face, hurting my fingers very badly and grazing my forehead and one ear so that they bled. By some miracle I managed to avoid a direct blow until

Alik appeared from one side and knocked him off his feet by butting him with his head, like a battering ram.

*

"Fortunately," said Eldar, "the case is in the hands of someone sensible, who understands the situation perfectly and thinks those bastards were to blame for the fight. Although, of course, they claim just the opposite: they say we just attacked them for no good reason."

"Why did you tell the investigator that we'd been drinking champagne?" Alik asked.

"So he would know that we're not hiding anything from him," said Eldar, keen to show us that his evidence had been the result of a deliberate decision, which he believed to be the only correct one. "What's a bottle of champagne between five? Not even a full glass each. Why should we hide that? We have nothing to feel guilty about. We intervened to help people, then they started hitting us and we defended ourselves."

"And a man died as a result," said Marat.

"Precisely." Eldar always had to convince everybody that he had done the right thing. "But what man? A man who attacked us as we were trying to protect a girl and her boyfriend from him. I repeat, we were defending ourselves…"

"That's called mutual affray," said Alik. "And you don't get medals for it."

"Nonsense!" Eldar interrupted. "There's a law about necessary measures of self-defense. We were defending ourselves. We have witnesses… the driver. He saw them hitting the young guy."

"But he didn't see who started the fight," said Marat. "We claim that they attacked us. They say the opposite."

"That's why we have to tell the truth, right down to the very last detail," said Eldar. "So there can't be even a shadow of a doubt that our testimony is true."

"You would be right," Marat objected, "if only he hadn't died."

"And what did you say?" I asked Marat. "Did he ask you about Alik?"

"The lieutenant questioned me. I didn't say anything about Alik. I didn't see anything anyway. That guy attacked me when three of them grabbed Lucky. So I had to punch him a couple of times."

"And did you say that?" asked Alik.

"Yes."

"You're all crazy, guys, you're just burying yourselves."

"Don't talk rubbish!" Eldar retorted. "I repeat: we have to tell the truth and nothing but the truth. And we have nothing to be afraid of. Don't you agree?" The question was directed at me.

"I don't know…" I really had only the very vaguest idea of how events would unfold, but one thing was clear: the situation we were in was far more serious than Eldar thought.

"Yes, and there's something else," said Marat. "He asked me if I'd seen that guy lying on the ground. I said I had… And then he asked if Alik was standing nearby."

"And what did you tell him?"

"That everybody was standing nearby, including Alik. I checked the statement before I signed it, and that was exactly what he wrote."

"He seems to be taking a special interest in you," I said to Alik.

"Naturally enough!" he laughed.

*

Of course, it was naïve to expect that a folder as thick as a brick would still be lying untouched in the middle of the street, but when I didn't find it in the car or at home, I could only assume that when I jumped out of the car after Alik, I automatically grabbed the folder and took it with me, and then dropped it in the street. So now the only slim chance of recovering my manuscripts was to go back to the scene of the fight.

By the light of the streetlamp it very quickly became clear that the folder was not lying on the crudely asphalted surface of the street or in the bushes growing along the edge of the pavement.

"They took it, the bastards," Alik said in a disappointed voice as he started rummaging in the sparse bushes again.

Just at that moment a car drove up and two men wearing matching shirts and ties got out of it. They looked just like ordinary civilians.

"What are we looking for?" asked one of them, with a round face, afterwards he turned out to be our investigator. He was walking in front. The second man moved towards Alik.

"All right, get out of there," he said.

Alik didn't answer and carried on rummaging under the bushes.

"Lost something?" the round-faced one asked me.

"Yes."

"I'm talking to you," the second one said to Alik.

"I hear you, I'm not deaf."

The search for the folder in the bushes continued.

"Do you have any proof of identity?" the round-faced one asked me.

"What's the problem?" I asked, taking my passport out of my inside pocket.

"Let me see that, please."

"I.D." the second militiaman said irritably to Alik, who had finally climbed out of the bushes.

"What?" said Alik, pulling a face.

"I'll give you 'what'..." said the militiaman, reaching out and trying to grab Alik by the sleeve of his jacket.

"They're militia," I warned Alik, but I was too late: he threw off the hand that had touched him and stepped forward threateningly. That was enough for a pistol to appear in the second militiaman's hand.

"Hands up!"

"Zeinalov, put away your gun," our investigator who was dealing with me said in a quiet voice; the other man immediately obeyed him. "And you; show him some proof of identity." The last sentence was addressed to Alik.

"Who are you?"

"You'll have to take a ride to the station with us," said the round-faced man, putting my passport in his pocket.

"Give back the passport," said Alik.

"Get in the car. You too…" he said going over to Alik. "And don't do anything stupid."

"I'm not going anywhere with you. Do you have a warrant?"

"Stop it, Alik," I said as sternly as I could.

"You don't know what they're like," he said, still keeping his distance from the militiaman. "You can't trust them. They'll change their tune once they get us in there."

"We could change our tune here," said Zeinalov. "For disobeying an officer …"

"Just try it," laughed Alik.

"Alik, stop it!" I shouted, and something in my voice made him do as I said. I was already standing by the car.

"Get into the front seat, please," the round-faced man told me.

"Get in, get in," said Zeinalov, opening the back door for Alik.

*

The most important thing now is to convince him that our testimony is the truth," Eldar said, still pressuring us. "There are effectively no witnesses. So we have to make him believe completely in everything we say…"

"Quiet," said Alik. "They're coming."

I heard a door open and a sergeant appeared in the yard. He called out two names — mine and Alik's.

"Where are you taking us?" Alik asked as we climbed the stairs to the first floor.

"Police line-up," the sergeant replied reluctantly.

"What line-up?"

"You'll see."

The investigator and Zeinalov were waiting for us in a small room decorated as if for political education group studies from the recent Soviet regime. There were three men in civilian clothes lined up against the wall.

"This way, please," said the investigator, standing us in the line. "Bring in the first one," he told the sergeant.

The sergeant brought in the "erazi", the young guy in the bush jacket who only a few hours early had been beating me so enthusiastically that if it hadn't been for Alik, the militia would have been investigating two killings instead of one.

"Do you recognize any of these men?" the investigator asked him. "Were any of them involved in the fight?"

"Of course." The button eyes stared straight at me. "Those two."

"I see…" The investigator's expression was impervious, giving nothing away apart from his interest in the procedure of identification. "And what did they do?"

"What do you mean?" the "erazi" asked in surprise. "They were hitting us."

"Be more specific."

"We were standing on the corner, talking to a girl we know. Then suddenly a car stopped, and these guys jumped out…"

"How many of them were there?"

"Five… And they just laid into us."

"Be more specific."

"That one…" — the "erazi" pointed at Alik, "hit poor Tamerlane, Khalykov that is … Khalykov fell down and smashed his head against the edge of the pavement. Then he attacked me, and then this one came dashing to help him and butted me in the stomach. I even passed out … When I came round they were long gone, they drove off in their car, and our lads were all battered and bruised. Tamerlane was still alive, but he was holding his head in his hands and being sick."

"Did this man…" — the investigator pointed at me — "… also strike Khalykov?"

"No, not him," said the "erazi", giving me a cunning glance from those button eyes. "That's the one that hit me," he said, looking at Alik again. "He killed Tamerlane, and he tried to kill me too." He squinted at Zeinalov, who was sitting at a desk and writing down everything he said.

"How can you say that?" I exploded. "Neither of us was there when the fight started. Your Tamerlane was killed by someone else, and that was in self-defense, when…"

"Quiet!" the investigator interrupted me sternly. "Don't interfere with our work!"

"Everything he says is lies!"

"Stop talking!"

"Will you please make this man tell the truth! Everything he's telling you is lies! And you know that perfectly well."

"You're the liar," the "erazi" in the bush jacket howled in a surprisingly thin, piercing voice. "I'm telling the truth."

"This is a pointless argument," the investigator said in the same gentle, weary tone of voice. "Try to control yourselves."

"It was someone else who hit him."

"Did you see it?"

"No, but I know for certain. My friends can confirm it."

"We'll clarify that. But for now keep quiet. Sergeant, take him away." The investigator waited until the sergeant and the "erazi" in the bush jacket had left the room, then he walked across to the desk and looked over Zeinalov's shoulder at the statement.

"You shouldn't be saying all this…," Alik told me in a low voice. "Don't get Lucky mixed up in this."

The investigator glanced round and looked hard at Alik.

"Sign the statement."

The three men by the window who had taken part in the lineup came over to the desk. When the statement had been signed, he asked them to go out into the corridor, then he turned to Alik and asked: "Why do you dislike the militia so much?"

"What's there to like you for?"

"You don't think there is any reason?"

"What's it to you what I think?"

"I'm curious."

"Don't lie."

"You've done time, haven't you?"

"Why, does it show?"

"Just answer the questions. What were you in for and how long?"

"Six years."

"Disorderly conduct?"

"That's what they called it."

"And what was it really?"

"Pretty much the same as this time."

"A brawl?"

"I don't remember."

"So you have a history of brawling?"

"Maybe."

The investigator looked at Alik for a while in clear disapproval.

"Take him to the others ..." he told the sergeant. "And you come with me ..." he said to me.

We walked along the same corridor through the entire building and up the stairs to his office.

"Sit down," he said, taking the statement of my testimony out of a drawer. "Do you realize that your testimony contradicts what all the other witnesses say?"

"If you mean those false allegations ..."

"All ten men on the plaintive side claim that the dead man was hit first by Krokin and then he fell and the fight started. Your friend Marat..." — he reached towards a pile of interrogation statements — "saw Krokin close to the body lying on the road."

RUSTAM IBRAGIMBEKOV • SOLAR PLEXUS

"Everybody was close, not just Krokin.

"But ten men testify that Krokin wasn't just standing there, he hit the man who was killed. And, therefore, I'm sorry, but I shall take the liberty of doubting your testimony when you say that Krokin was not involved in the fight from the very beginning. You're trying to help your friend, but…"

"I'm telling the truth."

"But there's no confirmation of that. I think that when Krokin talks, he'll say the same as you; that's natural enough — he'll try to save himself."

"I don't know why these people want to blame everything on Krokin," I said stubbornly, "but, I repeat, he wasn't the one who struck that blow."

"Then who did?"

"Someone else."

"You didn't see it, and according to your own testimony, you couldn't have seen it.

"I was told."

"Perhaps, but since you didn't see it yourself, your claim has no legal force," the investigator said and wiped his forehead wearily. "So you still insist on your testimony?"

"Yes."

"You're an obstinate man… And that's annoying, because your obstinacy is pointless." He stopped speaking and cast a tired glance at his watch. "Haikin told me about you. You know Marik Haikin?"

"Yes."

"He told me about the others too, but he told me most about you…"

I got the feeling that he really wanted me to keep up the conversation and ask him a question. It would have been natural, for example, to ask what Haikin had told him about us, bearing in mind the specific nature of their own relations. But an old belief that you can never expect decent treatment from a servant of the law prevented me from making normal human conversation with this major, or any other member of the government department responsible for maintaining law and order. But he was clearly in the mood to share some of his own intimate thoughts, and without waiting for me to take any part in the conversation, he asked in a soft voice:

"I suppose you've already realized that I'm doing everything in my power to help you and your friends?"

"To be quite honest, that's not exactly impression I'm getting."

He was clearly offended by my answer, or at least he mimicked a hurt expression very skillfully. He said nothing for a moment, tightening his jaws which I could barely make out in his plump cheeks, then said that I would understand later, but in the meantime I had to join my friends again.

He took me to the room where the line-up had taken place. Eldar, Marat and Alik were already there, and Alik winked at me cheerfully when our eyes met.

"Sit down," the investigator said to me, taking a seat at one of the desks. I sat down. Each of us was sitting at a separate table covered with red cloth; to an outsider it would have looked as if we were taking part in some emergency production meeting at a factory.

"It's late," said the investigator, "and we can't put you all up for the night here, so we're going to let you go home until tomorrow. But please do not go out anywhere until morning. I'll be quite frank with you. This is a nasty business that you're involved in. I don't mean just the killing, that's one thing, but there is also a charge of gang affray exacerbated by the fact that by your own confession you were not sober."

"We drank a bottle of champagne between five of us," said Eldar.

"The other side were not sober either, although they deny it, and all in all this is a very ugly business involving drunkenness, brawling and a violent breach of public order, as a result of which a man died. You're educated, cultured people, but…" — he shrugged and spread his hands — "…whatever we might like to do, the law is the same for everyone, and our ability to help you is very limited. If not for this death, it would have been possible to turn a blind eye, as they say, to a few things, but a death requires thorough investigation. And so I'll be quite frank with you: in order to be able to help you at all, I have to have a clear idea of the part of the case that concerns the killing."

"What exactly?" I asked. "What do you mean?"

"You guessed right that this concerns you above all," the investigator replied. "Your attempts to deny that Krokin was involved in the start of the fight have confused the picture. But the testimony of the others won't allow me to set aside the question of your joint responsibility for this Tamerlane Khalykov's death. And so I am obliged to suggest to the public prosecutor that we should arrest all four of you, instead of arresting one and letting the others go free until the trial. I've already warned you, but your friends obviously don't really understand the situation, they're trying to shield each other."

"And what do you suggest?" I asked.

"I suggest that you all should think it over, especially you, and provide truthful testimony. Then three of you will remain free until the trial."

"And Krokin?"

"The public prosecutor decides that question, but I won't pretend — due to the objective circumstances of the case, a favorable decision in Krokin's case is doubtful." The investigator looked at his watch and rose wearily to his feet. "It's time for me to be going."

We went out into the corridor without speaking and turned towards the stairs; I walked beside the investigator.

"In game theory the optimal solution of situations like this is called minimax," he said in a low voice. "If failure is inevitable, you have to act so as to minimalize it as far as possible, reduce its effect …"

"Game theory doesn't deal with people." I said.

"People too. Situations often arise in life when one person has to accept the blow in order to save others. If you're talking about genuine friends, that is. Have you been friends for long?"

"Since we were children," Eldar said proudly.

"I almost forgot," he said, "I saw you on television yesterday..."

Something in his expression made it clear that he didn't agree with the views that we had expressed.

We had been filmed a week earlier at a presentation by the "Bakuite" society in the old Intourist hotel. The huge influx of refugees from the countryside, combined with the departure of significant numbers of born and bred Bakuites, had resulted in a deformation of the cultural life of the city, like a bone in which the level of calcium is suddenly reduced; as a result the philharmonic hall, where touring musicians of the very highest class had always regarded it as an honor to play, had been empty for months. People had stopped going to theatres and cinemas, and in general many things in my native city had changed beyond all recognition.

I don't remember now who it was that first phoned Lucky with the suggestion of organizing a society for the salvation of Baku, I think it was Tofik Mirzoev, who used to be a wonderful clarinetist — an entire generation of Baku girls was in love with him in the fifties and sixties. We had known him since we were children: although he lived in the centre of town, he often used to visit his grandmother, who lived on our street. The presentation by the "Bakuite" society brought together people who didn't see much of each other anymore. The age range was immense — from the seventy-three-year-old classical composer Kuliev to the members of the Quick Wits Club quiz team, who were trying to continue the traditions of Yuly Gusman's famous team of the early sixties. The presence of one of the leaders of the Azerbaijani Popular Front opposition party, who was fighting aggressively for power, gave cause for hope that at least not all of the opposition were as nationalistically inclined as the ones who had burst into the conservatory with the demand to take down all the pictures of "sissies" hanging in the assembly hall (by which they meant Bach, Beethoven and other classical composers). Of course, the eternally young Nargiz Khalilova shone in the company of her younger female friends, who were just as well-groomed, but had never managed to rival her popularity and success with men. Nearby there was a boisterous group of actors from the Russian Drama Theatre, all holding glasses in their hands: Murad Yagizarov, Tanya Gross, Mila Dukhovnaya and their new theatre director, Shurik Sharovsky.

Since Lucky and, indeed, all the rest of us, were regarded as notable characters and active representatives of the traditional Baku way of life and thinking, the TV journalist Tamila Ashumova (daughter of a well-known theatre director and mother of a young film director who was already on the verge of fame) decided to interview us. Eldar said a few words on behalf of all of us, repeating what we had all spoken about many times, that we Bakuites were a special type of people, with our own customs and culture; narrow-minded nationalism had been alien to us since we were children, we had grown up in courtyards where a man's worth was determined by his personal qualities, not by whether he had been born an Azeri, Russian, Jew or Armenian. In a situation where Armenian forces were seizing one Azerbaijani village after another, it required a certain degree of courage to divulge kind feelings for Armenians on television, especially since several hundred thousand new residents of Baku were victims of the Armenians' territorial expansion. And Eldar also said that as a Bakuite he blamed the Armenian nationalists because, in addition to hundreds of thousands of Azeris living in Armenia, they had quite consciously sacrificed the innocent Armenians of Baku, who had been obliged to leave the city, with the result that its complex and intricate ethnic mosaic, created by many years of history, had been destroyed.

Our round-faced investigator was also greatly interested in the subject of Baku. The essential point of what he felt it necessary to tell us was as follows: the Bakuites' feeling of superiority over those who moved to the city from rural areas was not only cheap snobbism, it demonstrated a lack of even the very simplest analysis. Were the Bakuites really responsible for the fact that they had access to more information than other Azerbaijanis? No — it was the result of a specific conjunction of circumstances, a freak of nature: oil had been discovered on the Apsheron Peninsula, so enterprising people from all over the world had flooded into Baku and created the special atmosphere that had shaped several generations of Bakuites. The other, greater part of the Azerbaijani people carried on living their lives, and had become exposed to civilization later and more slowly, but maintained their national customs, traditions and psychology. The investigator himself had grown up in a mountain village, where there were a hundred households for decades and the number didn't change. Some people grew old and died, others went away to Baku, but the overall number of inhabitants remained the same, so that the village neither grew nor shrunk. After school the investigator went to Baku, where he studied and gained qualifications from two institutions, and he was prepared to prove to our entire group that in twenty-eight years of life in Baku he had acquired a level of special knowledge and general culture that was no worse than what we possessed, as native Bakuites. But at least he knew that it was the result of his own efforts, and not a gift from a kind fate that had blessed him with being born in a fortunate place. What had been going on in Baku in recent years was a natural process, Baku and the Bakuites were returning to the bosom of their people, who had been developing for centuries in accordance with the requirements, and abilities, of the national mentality.

When we got outside, we decided we should spend the rest of the night at my place: I lived closer than all the others, and my wife and younger daughter weren't at home that night. Since my father-in-law, a biophysicist and academician, had died, my mother-in-law had been left all alone in a large flat on the Embankment, and even though she was a pure-blooded Azeri, she was still afraid that the flat would be seized by refugees. The old woman's many relatives had tried to impress on her that her fears were groundless, but to no avail: and so one of the children always spent the night with their mother, and that night it was my wife's turn.

We strolled through Baku, enjoying the night. The curfew had recently been cancelled, but we still came across military patrols armed with automatic weapons.

We had two rooms and a glazed balcony, overlooking the street, at our disposal. My older daughter was sleeping in the third room — I adhered to the principle that there should only be one man in the house, and that was why I didn't have any sons. My women loved me, we got on very well, but the day of parting with my older daughter was implacably approaching — she had a fiancé, who was fighting in Karabakh, and the date for the wedding had already been set, in the hope that we would be able to bring him back to Baku for at least a short while. Of course, a way could have been found to keep him in Baku for a longer period than that, but neither he nor his loving fiancée would have done that for anything. The fiancé's parents and I realized that we were making a mistake by indulging the young people's patriotic mood — my daughter's twenty-eight-year-old choice was quite definitely an individual of exceptional abilities. His study of the specific psychological peculiarities of living for an extended period in two simultaneous linguistic environments won him wide renown abroad, but in Baku, after the death of his academic supervisor, there were not many people left who were interested in the problems of bilingualism. As the Azeri proverb says, only the jeweler knows the value of the diamond. Unfortunately, in recent years in Baku the number of jewelers in all areas of human activity had fallen sharply, and mediocrity moved in to fill the gap and make itself at home. And now everything existed and functioned on a different qualitative level, like a hospital in which almost all the doctors had left, and the paramedics and nurses had started treating people.

The way to get my daughter's fiancé back to Baku was widely understood, and everyone around us used it, but the traditions maintained in old Azeri families like those of the bride and bridegroom would not permit the use of bribes.

"What are we going to do?" asked Eldar, as soon as we had stationed ourselves round the table in the large room in which my two grandfathers gazed down at us from the walls: my maternal grandfather was a well known lawyer, and my father's father was a regional municipal council official, with a moustache that drooped down dejectedly on to his chin at both sides.

"To be quite honest, I don't get it at all," said Marat. "Why has everything suddenly been turned against Alik? They could have accused any one of us, and especially Lucky as he struck the first blow."

"Don't get Lucky tangled up in this," said Alik. "Naming him won't make things any better for me."

"Perhaps," said Eldar. "But I wrote in my testimony that he was the first to hit back."

"You shouldn't have, you're only getting everyone in trouble with your truth," said Alik. "What did you mention the champagne for, anyway?"

"Well, I think I did the right thing."

"I don't know," Marat said thoughtfully. "I told the truth: Alik was standing beside the body, just like the rest of us. You wouldn't think there was anything so bad about that, but now my words are being used as circumstantial evidence that the man was killed by a blow struck by Alik."

"Why?"

"Because those 'erazis' are dumping everything on him.

"I don't understand — why have they all got it in for you?" said Eldar, with a glance of sympathy at Alik. "Every one of them. It's not just because you're Russian, is it?"

"What's that got to do with it?" I said. "Who knows why they've all ganged up on him? It could have happened to any one of us."

"I understand that," said Eldar. "But it's just strange."

"It's pure chance," said Marat. "One of them said it was him, and the others backed him up."

"But there has to be some logic, surely?" said Eldar "They don't know any of us … It was Lucky who struck the first blow, and it was Marat who hit them hardest of all…"

"It's a matter of *pure* chance," said Marat, "so there isn't any logic to it at all. The trouble is that we can't say who actually did strike the first blow."

"Why can't we?" Eldar objected. "I said who it was and I don't see how that puts Lucky in any danger. Everybody saw that guy get straight back up and wade into the fight again."

"We saw it," said Marat. "But *they* claim just the opposite, they say he never got up again after the first blow."

"But that's a blatant lie!"

"And isn't it a lie when they say that Alik hit him?" I asked.

"No, it isn't," said Eldar. "In the general ruckus he could quite easily have hit him, and so could any of us."

For some reason we all turned to look at Alik.

"Well, I think I did thump him a couple of times," he said.

"And I hit him too," said Marat.

"And so did Lucky," said Eldar, "but no one can say whose blow actually caused his death."

"And that means there's no point trying to be clever about it," said Alik. "If they all point the finger at me, why get Lucky involved?"

"But they claim that he fell and injured his head after the first blow," I said.

"So what?"

"That's not possible, because you weren't there when the fight began."

"Who cares about that?" Alik laughed.

"I do."

"That's where the problem lies," Marat repeated. "In this false claim that he died after the first blow."

"What difference does it make if it was the first or the last?" said Alik. "If they say it was the first, then it was the first."

"But you couldn't have struck the first blow!" I said.

"So what? They think that I did! What point is there in complicating things?"

"In that case, I could say the same thing," said Marat, getting up: his powerful biceps bulged under the cloth of the shirt that was stretched tautly across his chest. "If we're choosing which of us should take the blame, then why not me? I have the hardest punch."

"In that case, why not Lucky?" asked Eldar. "He threw the first punch."

"Stop it, will you," said Alik, with a wave of his hand. "It's obvious that I ought to take the blame, if that's the way everything's turned out."

"That's still far from certain," said Eldar. "Why not me, for instance?"

"You?"

"Yes, me. Who was it who spotted them and told the driver to stop the car?"

"Oh come on!" Marat objected. "If you think like that, then the driver's to blame for everything: it was him who stopped the car, not you."

"It's impossible to determine which of us is more or less guilty," I said.

"So you think he ought to be allowed to arrest all of us?"

"I don't see any other option."

"But what's the point of that?" asked Alik.

"In some situations you have to act according to your conscience, not just what makes sense," said Marat.

"What's conscience got to do with anything?" exclaimed Eldar. "It's perfectly apparent that every one of us is willing to take the consequences. I never doubted that for a second and I don't doubt it now. But what we have here is a situation from which we have to extricate ourselves with the minimal possible losses. Of course, we can tell this investigator where to stick his proposal and let him obtain permission to arrest all of us. But what do we gain by doing that? I'm just thinking out loud here, of course, we'll take the decision together, as a group; it will be a majority decision."

"It's clear enough," said Alik. "Of course it's better if only one of us goes to jail, and not all of us."

"And who's going to choose that one?" I asked.

"The investigator's already chosen," Alik replied.

"It's a pity that Lucky left," Marat said wistfully. "Maybe he's still in Moscow?"

"When's he coming back?" asked Alik, glancing first at me and then at Eldar.

"In about three days," said Eldar.

I didn't tell them what Lucky had told me the day before as we were on our way to collect Alik: he liked to play up to his image as a lucky, successful winner, which was believed by all his friends and everyone else who ever met him, and he never revealed to anyone the secrets of the reverse side of a life that seemed so untroubled at a superficial glance. So when he told me with a smile that he was flying to Stockholm for a check-up on his right leg and he might be stuck there for a long time, I realized that there was something serious going on.

"Deep-vein phlebitis," he told me with a wink. "It could even mean amputation. But I've already found myself an excellent artificial leg from Nicaragua."

"Why Nicaragua?" I asked in surprise.

"Because they don't make anything else in Nicaragua, but their artificial limbs are the best in the world."

He carried on joking about it, which made it very difficult for me to say anything, so I travelled the rest of the way in silence.

"We need to find that couple who got us into this mess, they'll be able to clear everything up," said Eldar.

"How?"

"Well, they live somewhere in that area…"

"What are we going to do?" asked Marat, as if he were talking to himself.

"We already agreed," Alik declared in a confident voice. "He could quite easily have gone down after I hit him. So let's not create unnecessary problems," he said with the calm confidence of a man who has taken the final decision.

"But even if you do admit to striking the first blow," Eldar objected, "that's still not the end of it. If we're taking a collective decision here, we have to think it all the way through." He looked at me. "You understand that in this situation an awful lot depends on your testimony."

"Yes, I realize that only too well," I said.

"So what do you intend to do?"

"What do you think I ought to do?"

"Well, I don't know," he said uncertainly. "It's just that your testimony contradicts what Alik's going to say…"

"So what are you suggesting?" I asked.

"I'm not suggesting anything," said Eldar. "As I see it, we're trying to make a consensual decision here, and once it's made, I think it's binding for all of us."

"You mean to say that if you three decide I ought to change my testimony, I'll have to accept that?" I wanted to get things clear.

"Of course."

"How uncertain everything is in this life," said Marat. "One single chance movement or careless action and everything's blown to hell, your entire life… Maybe it was something else that killed him, and not a punch at all, but now we'll take the blame in any case."

"That's exactly what we're talking about," said Eldar.

"It's time we got some sleep," I said. "It's three in the morning, The beds are all made up."

"But you still haven't given your answer," said Eldar.

"I still think the same."

"That is?"

"When the fight started, Alik wasn't there. And I can't say anything else."

Alik laughed.

"You're like a broken record stubbornly repeating the same thing; it's time you changed your tune!"

"Is that what you think too?"

"Yes" replied Eldar.

"And you?" I asked Marat.

"I still can't work it all out, my head's spinning. Let's get up early in the morning and think about it."

"You'll have to accept it," said Eldar. "We have a majority."

"Okay, I see. You may even be right, but I'm still going to tell it the way it really happened. I can't explain, but it's not just a matter of Alik. Maybe it's stupid, but I can't sign a statement of something that never happened."

"You have to obey the majority," Eldar repeated.

"I don't have to do anything. I have a conscience, and that's the only thing I have to obey."

"Those are fine words," said Eldar, "but strangely enough, the only thing behind them is egotism, the desire to appear clean in your own eyes."

"That may be the case, but no common interest will force me to do something that I'll feel ashamed of for the rest of my life. Goodnight." As I walked towards the door, I could feel their glances on my back.

"Wait …" said Eldar, getting up and coming across to me. "You really don't get it do you? For twenty years I've been more concerned about our common interests than all the rest of you. And today I'm trying to do everything I possibly can to make sure that three of us — four including Lucky — get out of this mess somehow. It's second nature to me to fight for our common interests above all else!"

"Including your own interests."

"Yes, but if it was necessary, I'd do the same as Alik. When soldiers break out of encirclement, one has to die to allow the others to get away. He does it voluntarily. And there's nothing unjust about it. It's always been that way, and it always will be. You have the right to do whatever you like in everything that concerns only you, but if it's a matter of other people, then our general interests take precedence."

"Is that all?" I asked when he stopped talking. "Have you said everything you wanted to say?"

"Yes."

"No common interest is going to force me to do something that is against my conscience."

I stepped through the doorway and set out across the kitchen towards the balcony overlooking the street, which had been glassed in three years earlier; my folding bed was waiting for me there. I heard footsteps following me in the darkness, but I didn't turn round because I thought it was Eldar. I only realized my mistake when the heavy hand that descended on my shoulder swung me round sharply and I found myself face to face with Marat.

"Why are you insulting us all like this?" His face was distorted by an expression of resentment and the clear determination to get a quick, simple explanation for my behavior.

"I'm not insulting anyone," I said. Only dispassionate, precise words could calm him down now: any attempt to shrug off his question and avoid an answer could end badly for me, he was so angry. "I'm only speaking for myself..."

"Why should we feel ashamed? What have we done that's so bad?"

I tried to free my shoulder, but I couldn't.

"You really don't understand?"

"No."

"You wrote that Alik was standing beside the dead body, didn't you?"

"Yes, he was standing with everybody else."

"At the moment when you wrote your testimony, did you know they thought that Alik was responsible for the man's death?"

He thought about that: the question required deep reflection.

"Wasn't it clear from the investigator's questions what he was after?" I asked.

He let go of my shoulder.

"But so what? I told the truth."

"We're all telling the truth, and carefully selected pieces of that truth are being used to construct a lie that's convenient for everyone. I said that he was the first to jump out of the car, you said he was standing beside the body of the man who was killed. Eldar said something else. And the result is that, technically, every one of us has been truthful, but we've all contributed to burying him."

Marat was shocked by what he heard and it was several seconds before he was able to speak.

"I didn't realize that… I said other things too, in his support…" He broke off and raised his eyes to look at me. "But what about you? Why did you say he was the first to jump out of the car? Didn't you realize how that might be used?"

"Yes."

"Then why did you say it?"

"Why are you now asking me to say that he was involved in the fight from the very beginning?"

"But he's asking you to do it himself!"

"What difference does that make? We're doing everything possible to save our own skins, and it's always easy to find arguments and excuses for that!"

"So what does that make us?" he asked, still trying to grasp this view of our behavior that had suddenly been revealed to him. "Outright bastards?"

"Maybe not bastards, but just ordinary, petty little men," I said. "No better than all the rest…"

"Wait," he said. "That can't be right, we've always been ready to do anything for each other, all our lives!"

"But what's required now is something quite different altogether — we have to share the charges equally. That's much more difficult."

"So you think we should all go to prison?"

If I had said yes, he would certainly have supported my decision, but I avoided giving a direct answer.

"I don't know," I said, "but no one will ever make me say that Alik was involved in the fight from the very beginning."

"Then what about me?" he asked. "What am I supposed to do? I'll do whatever you decide is right. Maybe I should withdraw my testimony?"

"I'm afraid it's too late for that."

"What can we do?" he asked, thumping himself on the forehead in despair.

The slap was so loud that my elder daughter turned over in her sleep on the other side of the wall. I didn't answer his question and simply put a finger to my lips to tell him to be quiet. He nodded dejectedly and went back into the large room. He had been given the divan to sleep on, Eldar and Alik were quartered in the bedroom.

I walked out on to the balcony and unfolded the bed, but before I could lie down Alik appeared.

"Did they send you?" I asked.

"No, I came on my own," he said with a smile. "Thank you."

"Don't talk nonsense."

"That's not what I mean," he said and hesitated as he tried to express something that was obviously very important to him. "You've made your point, I always knew that you were a genuine guy, but you know, if you think about it properly, Eldar is right in his own way …"

"Maybe," I said, realizing that there was no point in arguing with Alik now, because he had clearly come to share the heavy burden oppressing his heart.

"Look, what good will come of it if they decide to arrest you too? You know how difficult it is to get the warrant cancelled afterwards. Even if everything's alright they'll come up with something. It's easy to find some little excuse. Even if it's only that damned champagne. If only we'd done some serious drinking, I wouldn't mind so much, but to claim we were drunk on a single bottle of champagne! And there's no way you can prove a thing." I waited patiently for the end of his tirade, and he realized that he was going on about it for too long. "Well, all right, it's too late to talk about that now. It was something else I wanted to say: basically, I want to ask you to write everything just the way they want. For my sake. So I'll know that at least once I've done something good for all of you. All my life you've done good things for me. Eldar's teaching my Georgy now. But all I ever knew how to do was fight. They won't let me out of their clutches now anyway, no matter what you might write, so thanks for your support but, as they say, the joke's up — understand?"

I hadn't anticipated this turn of events. I was ready to resist pressure from the entire world, and I would have despised myself for giving way to it, but how could I have expected that my willingness to fight to the very end would not be welcome to the very person I was trying to protect?

"What are you saying, Alik!" I exclaimed, almost pleading with him. "They're bound to put you away, don't you understand? They'll put you in prison if I write what you're asking me to. I'm the final witness! As long as my testimony stays as it is, there's always hope, but without it no court can do anything to help you. Surely you understand all that?"

"Yes, I understand all that," he said with a sudden strange note of irritation in his voice. "I already explained to you: I want to help all of you, and as this is the way things have turned out, at least I'll know I'm not in jail for nothing. Can't you see that?"

"Yes," I said in a low voice.

"Tell my son that," he said and fell silent.

I realized I ought to tell him straight away that even though I understood and I sympathized with all his motives, I still had no right to do what they were all urging me to do, following the prompting of the round-faced investigator. That the collective interest, which in our case coincided so conveniently with the optimal game theory solution, did not always conform to the most basic human need to act according to one's conscience. But I didn't tell him that, not even when he got up, thanked me and walked towards the door.

Half an hour later there was another knock at the door of the balcony.

"Who is it?"

"Are you sleeping?" I heard Eldar's voice ask.

"Yes."

"I want to say something to you anyway," he said in a tone of emphatic reproach. "It's your business of course. But I think I ought to add something to what I've already said, and this is it: you're wrong when you think that you care for Alik more than the rest of us."

"I don't think that."

"But that's the way you behave," he went on, "as if you're the only one who has any backbone or courage, and we're all traitors who have no feelings of friendship. Believe me, if necessary I would give my life for any one of you. But this is a quite different situation, the options are cruelly clear: either all of us, or one of us. By chance or otherwise, the choice has fallen on Alik, because of the way things have gone. Any of us could have found ourselves in his place, and any of us would have behaved in the same way as him, I can't imagine anything else happening!"

"But I can," I said from underneath the blanket.

"You mean to say you wouldn't have done what Alik is doing?"

"I mean I want to sleep."

There was a pause, during which I could hear the sound of his breathing very clearly — it was the way people breathe through clenched teeth.

"All right, sleep," he said when he eventually recovered his power of speech, "but I just wanted to say that if it's inevitable that one of us has to suffer and the choice has fallen on Alik, then it's not entirely unjust."

"How do you make that out?" I couldn't resist asking.

"He's always been the most quarrelsome and pugnacious of all of us. You can't deny that. The number of times we've got him out of all sorts of jams..."

"Like when?"

"Plenty of times. Any anyway, in his place any one of us has more to lose than he does."

"What do you mean by that?"

"Well, work. It's much easier to start driving again after a long break."

"How about treating patients?"

"What do you mean by that?"

"According to your logic, the next one after Alik is me, right?"

"Don't be stupid."

"Don't you be stupid," I shouted, amazed at the force of my own anger. "What you say is disgusting!"

After he left I lay there for a long time with my eyes open until I finally sank into a brief sleep that seemed to last only a few minutes.

It had already begun to get light when I woke up, but it was still quiet outside the open window, the daily life of the yard had not started yet. The clock said twenty to six.

I lay there for a few more minutes, then made myself get up and take a wash. Everyone else was still asleep. I glanced into my daughter's room. I could just make out the outline of her slim body under the light blanket and her dark-chestnut hair dangling from the pillow to the floor.

I had to write a few instructions before my friends woke up. I cast a final glance at the bed where my daughter was sleeping together with her favorite soft animal toys and walked back out on to the balcony. When I managed to find a pen that would write (the mysterious disappearance of pens is a constant problem in our house) I wrote a farewell note:

"My darlings, it so happened that last night we were obliged to intervene to protect a young couple who were strangers to us. As a result one of the men who were attacking them died. I think that sooner or later everything will turn out well, but in the meantime there is an investigation being carried out by the Department of the Interior (the Twenty-Six Commissars District, investigator Gamidov.) My dearest ones, do not be sad, you know your father, he would never get involved in a fight for nothing, and the fact that this has happened in the fifty-second year of his life is proof that there's life in the old dog yet and he can still stand up for justice. Take care of each other. Tell Altai to get in touch with either Anar or Yusif Samedoglu, they know me and can help. The most important thing is for the case to be publicised as widely as possible. Kisses to all of you. Dad."

When I re-read the note, I felt like changing a couple of things, but I heard footsteps in the large room — someone was already up, so I went to put the kettle on.

Quite aside from the previous night's events and their possible consequences, the female part of my family had plenty of reasons to feel dissatisfied with me. My wife and I met in the ninth class at school and we married when we had only just graduated from college. Soon afterwards I discovered a desire to write that consumed most of my time and my poor wife was obliged to accept all the burdens of the family — she took on two shifts at the clinic and even saw patients at home; the children hadn't had an easy time of it either, especially recently, during perestroika, and so, although I had never heard a single word of reproach from the members of my family, I carried a feeling of guilt for my own inadequacy as a father down through the years ... It was this guilt and the miniscule fees paid by our publishers that had pushed me into writing for the cinema, where the financial rewards for imaginative writing could be far more substantial. But of the several screenplays that I had written one after another, one — by no means the best — had been filmed in Baku, and another two or three were still making the rounds of the Moscow studios, passed from hand to hand by directors and producers with very positive recommendations. Of course, I could not help feeling flattered by this: it is a nice feeling to know that you can write screenplays set in Russia and no one is disturbed by the fact that they were written by an Azeri who lives in Baku.

And it was quite easy for me to write *Scorpio* — my first "American" screenplay. Until the previous evening I had regarded it as my greatest achievement: life in Baku, the range of my reading, my general learning and education had all helped me to feel and know the world, human beings and human problems so well that a prestigious agency in Los Angeles, thousands of kilometers away from Azerbaijan, had tried to find money and a director to make the film. I regarded this as the result of my constant efforts over the years to combine within myself the national characteristics intrinsic to any normal individual, with a devotion to more general human values and concepts.

As a boy of fifteen I had been astonished to learn that all beauty in the world was subject to a rule that was described by a simple mathematical formula, and that if we admired the perfect proportions of a beautiful woman's body, it was only because the proportions of the parts of that body corresponded to the universal rule of the "golden ratio" — the whole relates to the greater part in the same way as the greater part to the lesser. That was when I came to the conclusion that the lesser part in each one of us is what we absorb as we live and read and develop, and the greater part is what our ancestors and our environment have endowed us with. And ever since then, in my own life and in everything I write I have tried to observe this correlation in my efforts to create a harmonious whole. But as I read the pages of my American screenplay *Scorpio* in the investigator's office, I glimpsed another possible motive behind my efforts to take my creative work beyond national limitations. What if I was merely searching for new markets for my work, searching so intently that the law of exalted harmony that was so dear to me had quite clearly been violated? For many years, while I was writing about my own compatriots, some internal censor held me back, but it stepped aside the moment my characters flew across the ocean and landed in Los Angeles. Did that mean that in my own heart I, who invented and described them, was ready to follow them? Would I, fascinated by the sweet taste of the inner freedom that was suddenly revealed to me and the other opportunities that went with it, follow thousands of Bakuites into emigration? But I had absolutely no desire to leave Baku. Of course, what it had now been transformed into was no longer the city of my childhood and youth, but even after all the blows it had suffered, Baku was still the central bundle of ganglions, the tight plexus of nerves that came together here from every part of Azerbaijan.

At nine in the morning we were in the militia station again. The corridors didn't seem so gloomy and menacing in the morning light. There were two young guys sitting outside the investigator's office.

"Are you waiting to go in?" Eldar asked.

"He's not there," one of the young guys, whose head was completely shaved, grunted in reply

We glanced into the next two rooms, but didn't see any familiar faces.

"What time is Rafik expecting us?" asked Alik, for some reason speaking in a whisper. He was the first to remember the pigs' knuckles that Rafik was supposed to have cooked up for us during the night.

"At ten."

"Maybe we could have one last expedition, as the investigator's not here yet?"

"We haven't got time." I said.

"We could have had a farewell pigs' knuckles party," sighed Alik.

"It's not time for farewells," said Eldar, with a passion reminiscent of his younger days. "We haven't given up the fight for you yet."

"Don't forget about my little Georgy, he's in seventh class now, you know."

"Don't you worry about that."

"Why are you so quiet?" Alik asked me with a smile. "Everything's fine. What else could we have done? We've always beaten up arseholes and we always will." He stuck an envelope into my pocket. "I've written this for Nata to tell her what she has to do. For the future, so she'll know how to behave. You give it to her."

"Okay."

"And in any case, keep an eye on them. You're the one who's in our part of town most often."

"There's no need to be concerned about your family," said Eldar. "We got caught up in a bad business," he went on, talking to all of us. "I don't know how it's going to end, but if Alik goes to prison, we'll make sure that his family wants for nothing."

"Thanks for that," said Alik.

"Surely they're not going to put him away right now?" asked Marat.

"First they'll keep me in a holding cell," Alik explained. "Until the investigation is over. And then they'll send me to the pretrial prison until the trial — I'll let you have the address."

"We can find that out for ourselves," said Eldar.

"Tell Nata not to visit me. I know her, she'll start bringing parcels, knocking on people's doors, groveling."

"Maybe we shouldn't tell her anything just yet?" Marat suggested.

"There's no point in that" said Eldar "She'll find out everything sooner or later."

"Of course," Alik agreed. "We should tell her, but warn her not to visit. I've written everything down for her."

"We'll be coming," said Eldar "in turn. Don't worry about your parcels."

"I'm not worried," said Alik "With friends like you, what do I have to worry about?"

Marat and I glanced at each other, and both turned our eyes away at the same moment. What Alik had said sounded sincere, but it could have been interpreted as a bitter gibe — he clearly felt that in our hearts we had already accepted the investigator's proposal and were prepared to sacrifice him to the so-called common interest in order to escape from the difficult situation.

"I need to buy a cap," Alik announced.

"We can get you one," said Eldar.

"Why don't we go and buy one now?" said Alik, "Whilst we're waiting for the investigator? It'll give me a chance to take one last walk."

"We don't want to cause trouble…" Eldar said doubtfully.

"Things can't get any worse than they are," Alik said with a smile. "And we should have gone for those pigs' knuckles too. There's always time to eat …"

"That's true, we arrived on time, but he's still not here," said Marat. "We have every right."

"Let's go," Eldar said resolutely.

"What you need a cap for?" I asked Alik, as we followed Eldar along the corridor "You never wear one."

"They only take you into pretrial prison with a full set of kit."

As we walked towards the nearest department store, every block that we passed brought back memories of our youth. On the corner of the former Kirov Prospect (originally Large Maritime Street) and the 28th April Street (originally Telephone

Street), I remembered a story that Tofik Mirzoev had told me when the two of us went to the "Circus" restaurant with Borya Gukasov and Rudik Avanesov to celebrate Kyamal Manafla's fiftieth anniversary...

It was the start of the easy-going, sluggish nineteen-eighties. Kyamal had given up playing his clarinet many years earlier and he was running an organization called BOM (the Bureau of Orchestral Musicians). The nickname of Boulder, which he had been given back in the sixties, when he used to dress up in a magnificent white suit to perform Duke Ellington's *Caravan* before the screening at the Nizami cinema, suited him even better on his fiftieth birthday — he had put on about thirty kilograms, bringing his weight up to a hundred and fifty.

The incident Tofik told me about had taken place in the mid-fifties and it had become one of the city's legends. In those days the summer musical theatre (the former music hall) was still open in the Ordubady Park, and there was a *shashlik* restaurant beside it. After he finished his concert before the final showing at the cinema, Kyamal and his friends used to go to this restaurant, where they were joined by his lady love, who was called Rose. By that time Rose, who sold tickets in a summer open film theatre, had already counted the daily return, skimmed off a good chunk of it, and closed the ticket office. Rose was a little bit older than Kyamal, an attractive woman with that sumptuous, sultry kind of beauty on the verge of wilting so typical of southern women when they approach thirty. Rose was madly in love with Kyamal, who had a lisp, so that he pronounced her name with affection as "Wosy". But this spelling can't possibly convey the sound that Kyamal produced when he addressed his beloved. The alphabet simply doesn't have a letter to convey that mingling of "W" and "H".

On that tragic evening Kyamal had already guided his Caravan to its impressive finale and was about to fling the mighty hand grasping his clarinet up above his head in order to hear the rapturous response from his audience, when the feeble-minded Assyrian gardener from the Ordubady Garden came dashing into the foyer of the cinema and shouted: "Rose bye-bye, Rose bye-bye". His howling was drowned out by the sounds of the only big band in Baku and, of course, the poor fellow was thrown back out into the street. But the message had been addressed to Kyamal, and he understood what the weak-minded gardener was trying to tell him. Flinging his clarinet aside, he jumped down from the stage into the hall, dashed through the rows of spectators, who were amazed by their idol's strange behavior, and ran out through the door of the cinema. When he reached the Ordubady Garden, two militiamen were already putting Rose into a black police wagon.

"Kyamal, darling," the poor victim of the law shouted, and those were the last words she uttered before the metal door with the little barred windows was slammed shut in her face.

Kyamal dashed up to the van and wrenched at the door of the metal cell with the violent strength of a madman. The giant looked furious enough to tear it off its hinges. But the vehicle was already picking up speed, and Kyamal did the only thing that he could to demonstrate his love for Rose, who had spent a substantial part of the summer theatre's takings on him — he grabbed hold with both hands of the iron steps under the door, from beneath which he could hear Rose's voice calling to him, and the black wagon dragged him and his magnificent white suit for three blocks, as far as the corner of Kirov Prospect and Telephone Street. And he hung on, sobbing and shouting out just one word, "Wose! Wose! Wose!" in answer to poor Rose's howls of "Kyamal! Kyamal! Kyamal my love!"

The recollection of this story, which had been related to me in detail ten years earlier by three witnesses who had actually watched the drama unfold, distracted me briefly from our own problems. The sound of Eldar's voice brought me back to reality.

"I hoped you've realized by now that we don't have any other way out..."

It wasn't enough for him to make everyone accept the decision imposed on them, he wanted everyone to confirm their wholehearted agreement with him.

As we were crossing the street a car came out from round the corner and separated us: Alik and Eldar ran across the road, but Marat and I were left behind.

"It would have been good if we'd been run over," Marat said quietly. "All of us together, to put an end to everything straight away."

The roadway was empty. Eldar and Alik were waiting for us on the other side, by the entrance to the department store.

"Why are you just standing there?" Eldar shouted.

"If only you knew how I hate him," I blurted out.

"He's not the problem, is he?" Marat asked sadly, and we set off across the street. "We've all been driven into a corner..."

Inside the store we went straight to the outdoor clothing department and from the several caps available Alik selected one made of brown synthetic leather. We all reached into our pockets at the same time, trying to be quicker than the others, and held the money out to Alik. He looked at us with a strange expression, and we put the money away again.

"And before winter sets in you can send me a padded jacket and boots," Alik admonished us cheerfully as he tried on the cap, as if it was a matter of kitting him out for some kind of pleasure outing. "By that time you'll know the address."

The young salesgirl was looking at us strangely, whispering with her dark-skinned friend, who looked a bit older.

"That'll do," Alik said contentedly, looking in the mirror. "Now I'm all ready for the front line."

Eldar looked at me.

"Excuse me, was it you they showed on the television yesterday?" the second salesgirl, the one with dark skin, asked me. "Are you the writer Seidzade?"

"Yes," I said, as usual wincing in embarrassment to hear a stranger call me a writer.

"I've read your stories."

"Have you really?" I exclaimed, putting on an expression of joyful surprise.

"And have you read the novella *A Group Portrait Against the Background of the Sea*," asked Alik.

"No."

"You must read it. It's a great piece of work."

We exchanged glances, and at that moment I saw such genuine pride in me in those blue eyes that had already started to fade, with small brown flecks scattered across their whites, that I felt as if there was no power on earth that could ever make me change my testimony — let them put us all in prison if things were the way the investigator suggested. Alik had only gone to prison that other time because no one else had the courage to teach Eldar's father a lesson. And perhaps that slap delivered in nineteen fifty-two to the face of the most powerful, but not the best, man in our yard had laid the foundations of my ideas about how a man should behave in situations when his dignity was violated.

We walked back to the militia station quickly with Alik leading the way.

"Of course, what we're doing isn't very nice," said Eldar, slowing down to draw level with me. "But the circumstances are beyond our control."

"Shove off," I told him quietly.

"Aren't you ashamed?" he asked, also speaking quietly. "What right have you got to talk to me like that? I've avoided my own father my entire life because of you! Until the very day he died!" Eldar's eyes glared wildly at me, his face suddenly crumpled up like a hurt child's, and the anger I felt for him was replaced by an acute feeling of pity.

Alik and Marat moved on ahead of us without looking back.

"Do you think I'm just trying to take care of myself?" Eldar asked me, almost crying.

I started walking faster. When Alik and Marat did look back, we were already getting close to them. Eldar's footsteps behind me sounded light, almost like a child's. As he got older he had grown terribly thin. I made myself look round at him. When it came down to it, he had done a great deal to keep our friendship intact and, after all, everyone tries to live according to his own ideas about how things ought to be. For the last few years he and Izik, his younger brother, had been trying to get the street on which their father had lived named after him, and they had got a memorial plaque put up on the house. Izik who'd lived with his father and sick mother for most of his life, had recently gone into politics and became a prominent figure in the main opposition party, the Azerbaijani Popular Front. The Popular Front was rising in power, and on the point of making a breakthrough, so Eldar hoped his brother would soon have some influence.

Eldar was not involved in politics and the doctoral dissertation that he had successfully defended so many years ago, with Marat's help, had not made his life any happier. The wife he had inherited from Marat had been involved for a long time with a young rogue and had only settled down recently, as she approached fifty. There was no doubt that the poor guy had made a real mess of his own life.

But even so, I didn't say anything to him. Maybe because I was still uncertain as to whether I could resist his idea of sacrificing Alik for the collective interest.

We approached the door of the investigator's office together. And at almost the same moment he appeared out of the depths of the corridor, moving towards us at a brisk pace.

"I'm sorry I'm late..." He paused to catch his breath and wipe a bead of sweat off his forehead before he opened the door. "Please go in... And you wait here," he said to the young guys who were sitting in the corridor, then walked into his office.

Without inviting us to sit down, he walked over to his desk and took a bundle wrapped in newspaper out of one of the drawers.

"The autopsy has established that the death of this Tamerlane Khalykov was caused by a blow to the back of the head with a blunt metal object. Apparently they had another fight after you left, this time with each other, and someone hit him with a piece of pipe."

"So what now?" asked Marat.

"I'm not going to apologize, because, after all, you did start a fight," the investigator said with cool politeness. "But it has been decided not to take any criminal proceedings against you." He looked at me and a faint, barely visible smile flickered across his face. "Well, and what decision did you come to? Do you still stand by what you said?"

"Yes, he does," Alik answered for me.

"I thought so," said the investigator, turning his glance to Alik. "And you, buddy, don't get into any conflicts with the militia in the future."

"Don't you 'buddy' me!" said Alik. The investigator's eyes turned dark with fury.

"That's quite enough of your cheek!"

"I'm sorry," said Eldar, "but I don't understand why you put so much pressure on us, before you had the results of the autopsy."

"What pressure do you mean?" the investigator asked in surprise. "A routine investigation. You weren't forced to say anything against your will, were you?"

"No."

"The court's medical expert came to work at eight, as he's supposed to, examined the body and gave his expert opinion. We questioned the other side repeatedly and obtained a confession. What is there to be unhappy about?" he asked, looking at me. "But then, if you don't like this version of events, I can offer you a choice of two others. The first is that I suggested the "erazis" should pay me a bribe, but they didn't, and so I decided not to put you in prison. The second is that I knew from the very beginning who hit him, but I didn't let you go straightaway, in order to make you realise a thing or two about yourselves and your 'Baku people'..." He looked at us with a smirk that combined frank contempt with something else that wasn't quite clear, perhaps envy.

"Outrageous!" exclaimed Eldar, barely able to refrain himself from using stronger language. "What right do you have..." He started advancing on the investigator, but Marat and Alik grabbed him from both sides at once...

"Calm down," the investigator said coolly. "You still have to sign the statement." He pushed a pile of sheets of paper covered with writing over to the edge of the desk.

"I looked through the interrogation report and signed it."

"You'll have to come to court when you're summoned."

"What?" asked Alik.

"As witnesses..."

The first feeble but unanimous impulse we all felt when we emerged, exhausted, from the militia station was to go straight home. But in 1992 Baku still retained some of the qualities of the real Baku, and from out of nowhere we were suddenly surrounded by a gang of young men shouting in delight, led by two twenty-year-old giants — Marat's sons. These twins who looked so alike but were so different from each other (one was to become a violinist and the other a microbiologist) had learned that we were in the station two hours earlier, when a militiaman who was a friend of theirs arrived at work. And in the way that things happen in such cases, all their friends and comrades immediately came running, family ties and connections were activated, Marik Haikin had been located and retrieved from his dacha (the militiaman friend said he might be able to influence the round-faced investigator), the names and addresses of the couple on whose behalf we had intervened the day before were established, and they were due to be delivered to the militia station at any moment. The young men preferred not to tell us about a number of informal measures that had also been taken, although these were undoubtedly intended to influence the outcome of the investigation. Against this background, the news that the case was closed sounded rather inappropriate, almost tactless in fact. But even so we were congratulated on a double victory — yesterday's — the young men were in possession of detailed information, including a list of broken noses and dislocated jaws, and today's — our release from the militia station without any bribe being paid was hailed by the young men as a knockout victory over a difficult opponent.

While the torrent of words was still in full flow, I watched Marat's sons admiringly. I didn't remember their grandfather Sultan, I was only three when he left for the front, and the legendary Doctor had been imprisoned before I was even born and then died in the camps, but I had seen the family photographs, and the twins looked just like their forbearers. Of course, there was a bit of their beautiful mother in them as well, perhaps in their remarkable milky-coffee complexions, but in the majestic poise of the head, the line of the shoulders and general bearing they were definitely Agakhanovs.

After we had said goodbye to the young men, Alik dutifully reminded us that as we were leaving Rafik's flat the previous day just before our fateful car trip, he had pointed to a large pot standing on the stove and asked us to be there for boiled pigs' knuckles at ten in the morning.

"How can we eat pig's knuckles after everything that's happened!" said Eldar. "And anyway…"

"We can buy some decent vodka here," said Alik, nodding in the direction of a little shop that had a sign written in English — "SHOP" — with the letters made out of little golden tubes.

"Anyway what?" Marat asked Eldar.

"We'll have to explain everything to him!"

"I'll get the vodka while you carry on talking…" said Alik, heading across to the shop.

"We've got to tell him that she should leave, at least for a while

"Ah, so that's what you're on about…" said Marat, looking at me. "And who's going to tell him that?"

"Everybody!" Eldar said firmly.

"A quartet?"

"Quartet, duet, solo, trio! Any way you like. Surely you realise there are so many refugees in the city now that anything could happen?" He had already forgotten that the idea of the defensive vigils at Rafik's home had been his suggestion, not ours. "We have to have a frank talk with them."

On our way to the trolleybus stop we walked along streets that our feet had trod thousands of times in the long years of our lives in this city, but just as an invisible disease that has no specific symptoms can undermine a healthy organism and alter the features of a man's face, the events of recent years left their morbid mark on the life of Baku. The general atmosphere of unhurried and unconcerned festivity had disappeared from the streets, and for several years now they had been dominated by embittered, scowling faces, agitated movements and hasty footsteps, and bitter sense of a general lack of culture and refinement.

When we arrived, we were greeted with friendly grumbling: it was already eleven, we should have been there ages ago, didn't we know it was unforgivable to be late when a special treat of pigs' knuckles was involved, we could have got off our backsides an hour earlier, it wouldn't have done us any harm, would it?

While Rafik scolded us affectionately and started pouring the thick broth with pieces of knuckles into bowls, we took turns to kiss Aida and then sat down at the table. A pleasant sea breeze was blowing in through the wide open window.

"You all seem a bit out of sorts," said Aida. "Has something happened?"

"Ah, nothing serious," said Alik, taking the first bowl. "This is excellent."

"I didn't sleep all night," said Rafik, filling a second bowl with the steaming amber-gold liquid."

"And how much sleep did I get?" Aida said reproachfully.

"That's right," Rafik agreed, handing me a bowl, which I handed on round the circle to Marat, and he handed it to Eldar. "Neither of us slept. And you know what we were doing? We were talking about you."

"You haven't put enough in," Aida rebuked him when he handed me the third bowl. Rafik glanced at her disapprovingly and picked up the fourth bowl.

"That is, we were talking about us, all of us, and about Baku in general," said Rafik.

At this point Aida interrupted him by rising abruptly to her feet and raising a glass of vodka in her hand.

"If you don't mind," she said, laying her other hand on Rafik's shoulder. "I want to propose a toast…"

Rafik shrugged, gave his place to Aida and took his seat at the table. And why not? The broth been poured into the bowls, the vodka into the glasses and it was the right time for toasts.

"There's something I want to say," Aida began, glancing around our faces, which were all turned towards her. "From the heart… You know how much I love you all, and you know that we didn't decide to come back to Baku because life was bad in Moscow. We had a good life. Everything was fine: work, entertainment, money. But we were homesick. I'm younger than all of you, I never saw the Baku you grew up in, but even in my time there was still a lot left. And while I lived in Moscow for fifteen years, almost every night I dreamed of our yard, the boulevard, the sea, my friends, my parents … I swear to you…"

Rafik nodded to confirm what she had said.

"Every day he used to tell me about you, no day ever passed without that. And yesterday, when you all arrived together, I realised that he's right, you are genuine friends. Let me be honest, for the very first time I believed that genuine friendship really does exist, thank you for that. And I understood why he can't live without you. For that reason I don't regret that we moved here. Come what may Baku is our homeland, no matter what nationality any of us might be. I drink to you, to your hearts, to your nobility, to your friendship."

Aida spoke with the kind of heartfelt feeling that doesn't often appear at the table straight away, with the very first toast. As I listened to her, I felt a warm wave of reciprocal emotion for her and the good things she had said about us, and for my friends with whom, for better and for worse, I had lived with for almost fifty years, and I realised that none of them would ever be able to tell Rafik and Aida the truth — that for their own safety they ought to leave Baku.

Aida's toast had only lasted for two or three minutes, no more than that, but the magic of the words that she pronounced produced its effect — looking round the faces of the people sitting at that table, it was impossible to believe that only an hour earlier the pressure of external circumstances had almost crushed them forever, that their bones had already been cracking and their flesh tearing, and their souls, clutched in the tight grasp of the investigator's fist, had already been bleeding a wretched, colourless liquid that left traces of fresh spots on the dirty floor of the of the district militia office.

As I listened to Aida and watched the radiant faces of my friends, all sorts of different thoughts started running through my head, And one of the thoughts that I glimpsed in that buzzing swarm was this: the entire wide world and the whole of humankind, with its past, present and future, were limited for me to a hundred or so individuals, the few houses in which I had lived and the city streets that I had walked down and was still walking down — all of this was the content of my own little world, my own little mankind, with all the problems that the people in it had had in the past and still had in the present, with their fear and joy, hope and despair. And there was nothing to be afraid of in what the round-faced investigator said about the contingent and impermanent nature of "Bakuism" as a special mode of life and human relations.

Perhaps the destructive force of the blows suffered by Baku and Bakuites in recent years really was fatal, and the predictions that everything that had been accumulated here over the decades would disappear were entirely realistic. But such things had happened before — entire empires, civilisations and peoples had disappeared and were still disappearing under the onslaught of History's blows. And strictly speaking, their appearance had been no less contingent than that of everything else in this world. Our own appearance in the world is a matter of chance, surely? "One wrong move — and you're a father," Alik had warned us when we became college students. But nothing disappears entirely without trace. Even when a mountain disintegrates after towering over the plains for centuries, it doesn't disappear, as it crumbles it covers everything around it with a layer of the rock from which it was made, raising the general level of land around it and enriching it with mountain soils. And the same thing happens with people, everyone leaves his own trace behind when he departs from this life. "It is very important to live your life so that worthy people will come to your funeral," my grandfather used to tell me. And in that sense my life had been a success, the fifty years had not been lived in vain — there at the table, holding glasses that glinted cheerfully in the sunlight coming in through the window, were the people who would carry my coffin. I was certain that for all their shortcomings they were a match for the high standards set by my grandfather, who was wounded in the First World War with the rank of lieutenant, and finished the Second World War with his left leg missing and the rank of colonel. What a joy it was that the ordeal to which we had been subjected the night before had not ended badly. I could not help thanking fate for the fact that my friends were by no means the worst of people and hoping that they felt much the same as they looked at me.

So here's to your good health, my dear friends, and peace to the ashes of those who are no longer with us. The golden ratio of my heart was determined by the life of Baku, and its greater part belongs only to you and no one else.

Dear Reader,

thank you for purchasing this book.

We at Glagoslav Publications are glad to welcome you, and hope that you find our books to be a source of knowledge and inspiration.

We want to show the beauty and depth of the Slavic region to everyone looking to expand their horizon and learn something new about different cultures, different people, and we believe that with this book we have managed to do just that.

Now that you've got to know us, we want to get to know you. We value communication with our readers and want to hear from you! We offer several options:

- Join our Book Club on Goodreads, Library Thing and Shelfari, and receive special offers and information about our giveaways;

- Share your opinion about our books on Amazon, Barnes & Noble, Waterstones and other bookstores;

- Join us on Facebook and Twitter for updates on our publications and news about our authors;

- Visit our site www.glagoslav.com to check out our Catalogue and subscribe to our Newsletter.

Glagoslav Publications is getting ready to release a new collection and planning some interesting surprises — stay with us to find out!

Glagoslav Publications
Office 36, 88-90 Hatton Garden
EC1N 8PN London, UK
Tel: + 44 (0) 20 32 86 99 82
Email: contact@glagoslav.com

Glagoslav Publications Catalogue

- *The Time of Women* by Elena Chizhova
- *Sin* by Zakhar Prilepin
- *Hardly Ever Otherwise* by Maria Matios
- *The Lost Button* by Irene Rozdobudko
- *Khatyn* by Ales Adamovich
- *Christened with Crosses* by Eduard Kochergin
- *The Vital Needs of the Dead* by Igor Sakhnovsky
- *METRO 2033* (Dutch Edition) by Dmitry Glukhovsky
- *A Poet and Bin Laden* by Hamid Ismailov
- *Asystole* by Oleg Pavlov
- *Kobzar* by Taras Shevchenko
- *White Shanghai* by Elvira Baryakina
- *The Stone Bridge* by Alexander Terekhov
- *King Stakh's Wild Hunt* by Uladzimir Karatkevich
- *Depeche Mode* by Serhii Zhadan
- *Saraband Sarah's Band* by Larysa Denysenko
- *Herstories*, An Anthology of New Ukrainian Women Prose Writers
- *Watching The Russians* (Dutch Edition) by Maria Konyukova
- *The Hawks of Peace* by Dmitry Rogozin
- *The Grand Slam and Other Stories* (Dutch Edition) by Leonid Andreev

More coming soon…